LIVING ARRANGEMENTS

A Novel

By

Diann Shope

DEDICATION

This book is dedicated to
Coleman Howland Shope, who hadn't arrived
in time for the dedication of my last book
to "the main guys in my life."

Table of Contents

The Predicament

"Sorry, guys. I got distracted reading the paper and burned the mac and cheese," said Chuck.

"Is *that* what was burning?" said Anne. "I could smell it clear upstairs!"

Patty got up from the kitchen island and headed for the phone. "I'll go order Thai takeout."

"Folks, we've got to get this cook thing settled," said Lionel. "Let's meet after dinner to strategize. Sorry if I sound exasperated—but I am!"

*****

"Maybe no one wants to be around a bunch of old farts," said Chuck. He lounged back in the comfortably worn leather armchair, his long jeans-clad legs stretched out in front of him.

"We're not a bunch of old farts!" Patty said, giving him the teacher's scowl she'd perfected over the years. Frown lines creased her forehead and mouth. "I can't see why it's so hard to find a cook. We offer a decent salary and room and board in a fine old Seattle home, so why can't we find anyone who'll stay?"

Mugs in hand, the residents of the mansion sat around the fireplace in the large and imposing room, its high ceilings lavishly embellished with wood molding; the faintly peach walls glowing in the light of two lamps; Oriental rugs scattered here and there on the polished wood floors.

"I think Chuck has a point," Lionel said. He sipped his coffee. "We all know it's not cool to be old. Who wants to be around old fogies? They just remind you you're going to die one of these days." He got up to poke the fire.

"We're a growth industry," said Anne. "You'd think people would figure it out."

"We don't really know why they left, even though we asked," Lionel said. "They didn't have any specific complaints when they gave notice. Maybe they were embarrassed to say why, so we just have to guess." He sat down again, tugging gently at the crease of his sharply pressed pants. He didn't like baggy knees.

"Whatever," said Patty, waving her hand. "The point is, what are we going to do now? Do we put another ad on Craigslist and wade through all those 'I'll apply for anything' people, or go to an agency, or what?" She passed the Oreos around again and got up to refill coffee cups. "We've got to get this settled so we can move on to the question of our fifth housemate. Our budget has a hole in it until we find that person."

"I'm not worried about the budget yet," said Lionel. "Who we choose is much more important. But I agree we need to get on with finding our cook. Does someone want to volunteer to call a couple of employment agencies?"

"I'll make some calls tomorrow," said Anne. Meanwhile, we need to make up a schedule for who's cooking next week. I have a class Monday night, but I can do Tuesday. Everybody can sign up on the kitchen blackboard."

*****

The next night, everyone was still up when Patty returned from a meeting at the school where she had taught for over twenty years. She was excited to tell them about a prospective cook she'd learned about from one of the board members, and she filled them in as they sat around the kitchen island. The pale-yellow paint and the recessed lighting made the kitchen luminous; it had come to be a second living room, even though it was set up to be a caterer's dream. "So it's this Russian couple. She's a nurse, and he's a chef and had his own restaurant in Moscow. They wanted to sell the restaurant and start over in the US, and they got lucky in the green card lottery. What do you think? We could invite them to see the place and meet us, tell them what we're looking for, and see what works out."

"Sounds like a possibility," said Chuck. "I wonder how good their English is."

"It doesn't have to be perfect," said Anne. "I rather like broken English and accents. They're so much more interesting than boring old American. OK with me, Patty," she said, scooting back her stool. "I'm bushed. See you all tomorrow."

"Fine with me too," said Lionel. "I like the idea that she's a nurse. You never know what's going to happen," he said, tracing a pattern in the granite countertop with his fingertip.

"Well, thank goodness we're all pretty healthy," said Patty. "Though with most of us in our seventies, we've got to be realistic about what's coming down the pike." She took a cookie out of the cookie jar. "Anyone else want one?"

Mother and Daughter

Anne was reading in the library Friday evening when she heard the doorbell ring. Opening the door, she found her daughter, Giselle, standing under the porch light on the blustery February night. "Oh, hi, honey—what a nice surprise! Come in. Want some coffee or tea?"

"A glass of wine would be nice—if you have any."

"Sure, come on in. Red or white?"

"White, please." Giselle followed her mother into the kitchen. Sitting down at the island, she said, "You can probably guess why I'm here, Mom."

"Since it's been about three or four months since we talked, I'm guessing you're here for a visit and you're going to fill me in on what's up with you and Margot." Anne had a hopeful look on her face as she took a bottle of white wine from the refrigerator and half filled two glasses.

"Margot's doing fine in school, but she's a pain in the butt otherwise."

"Sounds perfectly normal—she's a teenager. You were a pain in the butt when you were that age too." Anne smiled at her daughter.

"Gee, thanks for the compliment, Mom. You're always so positive."

Anne tried to keep her voice level, but her smile was a little forced. "I didn't mean that in a bad way, and you know it. You just choose to interpret anything I say in the most negative way possible. When are you going to get over your teenage rebellion?"

"I'm not rebelling. I'm just acting like anyone would act who had such lousy parenting. But I didn't come here to get in a fight. Can we just skip that for once?"

"Fine with me," answered Anne, sighing. "Why does it always have to go this way? It seems like we can't be together for two minutes without being at each other's throats. This isn't the kind of relationship I want to have with you, Giselle. Can't we find a way to get along better?"

"Our relationship is what it is. It's been this way for years. I don't have the energy—or time—to navel-gaze about why you and I don't get along." Giselle took a sip of wine.

"OK, got it," said Anne, her arms crossed over her chest. "Let me guess: you need money again."

"Yes, I do. You know how hard it is to support a teenager as a single parent—after all, you did it yourself. Margot wants to go to a music camp this summer, and I can't afford it. I can barely pay the rent, and I've almost maxed out my credit cards."

"Giselle, we've been through this a million times. I live on a fixed income. I can't subsidize your lifestyle and bail you out of bad decisions. I've done that more times than I care to admit, but you never seem to learn."

"It's not about learning, Mother Dear. It's about how expensive it is to live these days. I don't live a posh lifestyle. You know that!"

"No, it's not posh, but you don't live within your means. You spend money you don't have. Your apartment is full of stuff you don't need—no one needs. And then you don't have money to pay for Margot's music camp."

"I didn't come here to have you criticize how I spend my money," Giselle said, her voice rising. "I was hoping you'd want to do something for your granddaughter."

"You were hoping I'd provide something that you didn't want to sacrifice for," Anne snapped. "Why doesn't Margot get a job if she wants to go to summer camp? Lots of kids have jobs. Besides the money, they get a taste of the real world."

"Don't think I haven't suggested it, but she just ignores me." Giselle stood and picked up her handbag. "Forget it. I'll just tell her that her grandmother doesn't care if she goes to music camp or not," she said. "I knew this would be a waste of time, but I figured I'd undergo the humiliation for Margot's sake."

"Spare me the guilt trip, Giselle. If you were really humiliated, you'd get your financial act together. But it's easier to blame me for all your problems than to take responsibility for your own life. I made my share of parenting mistakes, which I regret very much, but you're a grown-up now. At some point you have to play the hand you've been dealt and stop complaining about the cards."

"Thank you for that wonderful bit of parental wisdom, Mother. I'll show myself out."

Anne sat down at the island, chin on her hands. She heard the front door slam. It had been this way for years, she reflected, since Giselle was a teen. As a child, she had a sunny disposition, loved being with Anne at ballet class and rehearsals, loved being read to before bed. Raising her had been a struggle, even though Giselle's father had paid child support. He'd visited a few times, but he was more interested in his career than his child. It seemed to Anne that Giselle had never really moved on from being a rebellious teen; she was still stuck there, preoccupied with herself and what she wanted. Unlike Giselle's father, Margot's father was a nice guy who had wanted to marry and help raise his child, but Giselle had spurned him, preferring to go it alone.

As Anne sat there, slumped, thinking glumly about her daughter, Patty came into the kitchen. "Want some ice cream?" she asked, removing a carton from the freezer.

"No, thanks. I'll just finish my wine."

Patty knelt to pick up the lid she'd dropped on the floor. "Oof, it's getting harder and harder to pick things up. Sometimes I wonder if I'm going to be able to get up again!"

Anne didn't respond.

"You look a little dejected, Anne. Something bothering you?" asked Patty, getting out the chocolate sauce.

"Giselle was just here."

"Oh, I see," said Patty, who knew how strained Anne and Giselle's relationship was.

"It was the same old thing: requests for money, recriminations, the whole sorry tale. I just don't know what to do differently to break this cycle! I hardly know my granddaughter, because my relationship with Giselle is so bad."

Patty sat down beside Anne at the island. "Wish I had some good advice for you. It seems like you and Giselle are stuck."

"Yes, that pretty well sums it up. I want to get unstuck, but I don't know how, and she seems OK with the way things are—or at least she doesn't seem to have any motivation to try to improve them." Anne looked off blankly, trying to fathom where things had gone so wrong. "But you know, I'm tired of feeling guilty! I go round and round trying to figure out what to do, and I never get anywhere. When is this going to end?" She drained her glass, put it in the dishwasher, and slammed the door shut.

The Cook

Mikhail Azarov had agreed that he and his wife, Karina, would arrive between three and four on Sunday afternoon. Alighting from the bus, they walked through the fine old neighborhood of big trees and houses in one of Seattle's upscale residential communities.

"God's mother!" said Mikhail. "These people must be rich as Abramovich! Georgi told me they were old people looking for hired help." They walked past large well-maintained homes and stopped before a three-story mansion on a double lot, surrounded by lawn and shrubs. The late-winter flowering plums and crocuses were just coming out, adding pink-and-yellow cheer to the drippy gray afternoon.

Yes, this was the right address. They rang the bell and waited before a paneled oak door with beveled glass windows. It was opened by a plump, smiling woman with curly gray-blond hair.

"You must be Mikhail and Karina. I'm Patty Carson. Come in, come on in! Let me introduce you to my housemates." They followed her into the spacious living room with a grand piano in the corner. The three other people, who were sitting, stood to meet them. Patty said, "This is Lionel Blackburn, this is Anne Aikens, and this is Chuck Ganatt."

After the coats were hung up and the formalities completed, they all sat down. "Would you like tea or coffee?" asked Patty.

"Tea, please," Mikhail said.

"Same for me," said Karina.

"Great," Patty said. "Why don't we tell you a bit about ourselves. Lionel, will you start?"

"Sure," said Lionel as Anne poured tea and passed the cream and sugar. He was a trim man of medium height, with a full head of brown hair, graying around the edges, and lively brown eyes. "I'm seventy years old, and I was a professor of mathematics at the University of Washington for about forty years. I also play the piano with some amateur groups and give a few lessons."

He looked over at Anne, a slender, erect woman with collar-length straight gray hair. She smiled back affectionately.

"I'm also seventy," Anne said, "and I was a professional ballet dancer when I was young. When I got too old to dance, I went to work for the ballet company in their school, and then in their office. I'm retired now, but I teach movement to children at the community center a few blocks from here, and I volunteer at a preschool." Anne looked down at her hands. "I have a daughter and granddaughter here in Seattle, but I don't see them very often." She smiled at Lionel again. "Lionel and I met years ago. He used to accompany me when I'd do little ballet demonstrations in local schools. That was before he was a full-time professor."

She stopped and looked at the man sitting next to her. "Your turn, Chuck."

While he was listening to each story, Mikhail couldn't help wondering how such different people could decide to live together. How did they know who was messy and who was neat? Did they care? How did they decide how much to spend on food? Who got the nicest room?

"I'm the house artist," drawled Chuck, a tall, rangy man with a gray ponytail and vivid-blue eyes. My studio's out in the garage. I've done a lot of things in my life, because you can't hardly make a living as an artist." He shifted in his chair and uncrossed his long legs. "I got in trouble in high school and ended up in a juvenile detention facility. I was real lucky, because when I was there they were running an art program, and that's where I learned about painting. That was it—I knew that's what I wanted to do. Later, I was in the Navy, then I worked as a mechanic, a bartender, you name it. Anything to keep buying paint and canvas. Anyway, I met Patty's husband, because he owned an art supply store, and I worked for him and we got to be friends. She introduced me to Lionel and Anne." Chuck rubbed his chin. "What else? Oh, guess I could add I've never been married. No kids," he said, with a glance toward Anne.

"Chuck's seventy-two—he forgot to tell you," said Patty. "I'm sixty-nine, and you already know from your cousin that I'm a retired grade-school teacher. I was looking for an accompanist for the movement teacher at my school, and Lionel showed up. He was retired by then, and looking for things to do. We've been friends ever since. My husband died five years ago, but I have a son and two daughters all living in the Seattle area. They're all married, and I have five grandchildren."

"Now that we've introduced ourselves," Lionel continued, "we thought we'd tell you about our situation, and what we're looking for—it's a somewhat unusual arrangement. And then maybe you can tell us about yourselves, and we'll have a tour of the house. Just stop me anytime you have questions."

Mikhail and Karina nodded.

Lionel centered his cup on its coaster. "I don't have any family, and I didn't want to live in a retirement home, so I came up with the idea of finding some housemates for a long-term living arrangement. It took about a year for us to find each other, and about two years ago we chose this house. I paid for it and for the remodeling with some money I inherited, but we all participated in making the decisions." He pulled his left shirt sleeve down a quarter inch under his sweater to match his right sleeve "We each contribute a monthly amount to pay expenses, like food, utilities, taxes, maintenance, staff, and so on. None of us like to cook, though some of us can do it better than others." He glanced at Chuck, who sank a bit lower in his chair.

"We want someone who will cook dinners for us every night," Lionel continued, "have food available for us to make our own breakfasts and lunches, and do the shopping. We don't have any special dietary needs now, but we may in the future. As much as possible, we like fresh, local, organic food, lots of taste but not too rich. We do the dishes. One or two nights a week, you wouldn't have to be here, if the meal were prepared in advance. That would give you some time off. We think this is about twenty hours of work a week, and we're offering twenty-five dollars per hour, which works out to about two thousand dollars per month. Then, of course, the apartment comes with the job—no rent for that. Do you have any questions so far?"

"About the cost of the food?" asked Mikhail.

"Oh," replied Patty, "You'd have a separate budget for that.

"Yes," said Anne. "And we'll increase it when we get our fifth housemate. We hope to do that in the next few months."

"Now, would you like to tell us a bit about yourselves?" asked Lionel with an encouraging smile. He seemed to sense that they were nervous.

Karina looked at Mikhail, who began. "Our families are from Ukraine, but we lived in Moscow all the time. My father worked in factory. I attended school for cooks and then joined army. I worked very hard and made special dishes for my commanding officer. He offered to buy restaurant for me after army—was good man. My business was success, but when the Soviet Union broke apart, the criminals took over. If I didn't pay them money, they would . . . break my restaurant or burn it. They threatened Karina. So we decided to leave, and I sold restaurant." Mikhail had been wringing his hands as he talked, looking mostly at the coffee table, occasionally glancing at his wife and the others. He gestured that Karina should continue.

His wife was fair with thick dark-blond hair, which she wore in a plait down her back. "I am nurse. I worked twenty years in hospital in Moscow. I want to learn about new kinds of health care, but is very hard in Russia. We would like to start restaurant in Seattle, but Mikhail's cousin Georgi tells us it would be very expensive. He says we should wait, save more money, learn how things work in America. So we are looking for jobs and place to live. We cannot stay with Georgi's family much longer—is burden for them."

"You're very brave!" said Patty. "You're like the first Americans—just pull up and leave and go somewhere where things can be better. Good for you! OK, now let me show you the house. Then we'll come back and talk more with the others about what comes next."

They went through the living room to the library, a wood-paneled room filled with overflowing bookcases and artwork; a desk in the corner held a PC and a printer, and comfortably worn chairs and lamps were scattered around the room. Then they passed through to the breakfast room, which had seating for four. Adjacent to that was the kitchen. Mikhail breathed a sigh of admiration. There was a commercial gas range, a gigantic refrigerator, lots of cupboards and counter space, and a large built-in chopping block. "*Bozhe moi*, to cook in such a kitchen. Is a dream!"

"We never had any complaints about the facilities from our previous cooks—we're not sure why they left. We all love to eat, and don't like to cook, so you wouldn't have anyone spoiling your broth," Patty said. "I'm going to let you poke around the kitchen for a while. Feel free to open all the cupboards and drawers. Nothing's secret. I'll be back in about fifteen minutes, and we can finish our tour."

Mikhail and Karina went through the drawers and cupboards methodically. "Dull knives—good I have my own!" he said. "Good pots, except sauté pan. Plenty of silverware and dishes. Look at graters—all different sizes. Wonderful! Pepper grinder, sea-salt grinder, nutmeg grinder." He continued to inspect the drawers under the countertops, delighted with the contents.

"Mikhail, what are all these things?" asked Karina. She had pulled out drawers in the island.

He found a coffeemaker, a coffee grinder, a waffle iron, a regular blender, an immersion blender, a food processor, a sandwich grill, a yogurt maker, an electric can opener, an electric knife sharpener, regular and handheld mixers, and some items he couldn't identify. There was a toaster and another coffeepot on the counter.

"I could be most happy here," Mikhail said, smiling at his wife.

When Patty returned, they continued through a formal dining room, with more art and a table that could seat twelve, overhung by a chandelier made up of ten lights, each topped with a little linen lamp shade. Then they went back to the foyer and up the elegant curving staircase. "There are five bedrooms on this floor, and three bathrooms, including a big guest bathroom with laundry facilities. Oh, I forgot to show you the powder room on the main floor. You can see that on the way back."

They continued up another flight of stairs. "And this is the cook's apartment. There's a sitting room, bathroom, and bedroom. This floor has a view of the Cascades." She led them to the east-facing windows, where there was just enough light to appreciate what would be a spectacular view of Lake Washington and the mountains on a clear day. Streetlights and porch lights were appearing as day changed into night.

On the way back to the living room, Patty pointed out a small elevator that had been added at the back of the house. "For when we're old and decrepit," she joked.

After they were seated, Lionel continued with the description of their experiment. "What we want to do is grow old as a family. An 'intentional family,' if you will," he said. "We don't like the American model for getting old—end up alone, or in a facility being cared for by strangers, or be a burden on your family. We have an agreement that we're not going to complain about being old. We try to do things that will help us age gracefully and be helpful to others. And we want to enjoy the life we have left as much as possible. That's where your help would come in."

"One more thing," said Chuck. "This may not appeal to you, but we're looking for someone who really wants to be here. We don't want somebody who's just looking for a job, who'll move on in a few months or a year. We know it's not a lot of money, but you'd have time for other work, if you could figure out the right thing."

"So. Next steps." Lionel smiled. "Since you don't have any business references, we'd like to give you a little test. Here's a hundred dollars to prepare a meal for six, and we'd like you to give us menus for a week of dinners." He handed Mikhail five twenty-dollar bills. "Would it work for you to cook for us this Wednesday evening?"

"Yes, our pleasure to cook for you Wednesday," said Mikhail. Dinner ready at six o'clock." He stood up. "We thank you for the tea. Thank you very much," he said with a slight bow.

"Yes, thank you very much," said Karina. The others rose and shook hands as Patty brought their coats, then they went out into the chilly night and walked back toward the bus stop in a daze.

The couple had agreed to speak only in English to each other in private—except for Saturdays. It was a struggle, but their fluency was improving rapidly. "I worked eighty hours in week for that much money, when business was very best!" said Mikhail.

"Such an apartment in Moscow would cost two or three times more than ours did," said Karina. "Oh, how I would love to live in such a beautiful place!"

On the bus ride, they discussed their expenses, how much they could save, and what options there were for other work, especially for Karina. For the time being, that was an unknown. "I feel these are good people, very good people," she said. "We must be sure that we could stay with them a long time, as they want. Are we willing? What would prevent us?"

"If they have not told truth, it would be OK to leave. Or if they were unpleasant to us. If they act different in future from how they are today, it would be OK to leave. But what if we have chance to make more money and can't do it and still work there?"

"How much more money do we need? All you want is to cook, and as long as we have good home and food and friends, what do we want more money for?"

"Our health. Georgi says doctors are very expensive here. And when we are old—who will take care of us? We need to save money for our future. And I still want to own restaurant."

They rode in silence, thinking over all these points. Karina took her husband's hand. "We cannot know everything now," she said. "But for as long as we can see into future, this . . . opportunity looks very good to me. I have good feeling about it."

He smiled his covert smile, to hide his bad teeth. "I agree. We should take this opportunity." His smile faded. "If our dinner is success."

*****

The housemates were meanwhile discussing their recent visitors. "I think this looks very promising," said Patty, clearly proud that she had found the couple.

"We'll leave you to your meditation now," Anne said as she and Chuck left for the kitchen. "I'll make sure

Chuck doesn't incinerate his version three mac and cheese."

Lionel and Patty settled into the sofa. Patty put a soft mohair shawl around her shoulders, Lionel spread out a fringed tartan blanket for their knees, and they lapsed into silence. They had been meditating for years, Patty with a group loosely associated with a church, and Lionel in a Buddhist group. When they moved into the house, they had begun meditating together, and now it was a daily occurrence every afternoon at five.

The grandfather clock struck a melodious ending chime at six.

"Well, my meditation wasn't very calm tonight," said Patty. "Lots of thoughts. I caught myself looking for some emotion that could be causing all that, but I didn't come up with anything. Maybe an insight will come later." She sighed. "It's so easy to slip into analyzing, thinking about why I'm thinking, and getting judgmental about having thoughts instead of accepting them. I just keep going back to the mantra, or following my breath, and reminding myself thoughts are OK—just don't get hooked on them."

"Maybe it's some concern about new housemates. Did you feel some anxiety when the last cook came?"

"'Anxiety' is probably too strong a word. Perhaps . . . discomfort. Yes, I think that's it. Getting used to new people just kind of soaks up energy, and then if it doesn't work out, it's awkward and all that. Maybe I'm just a little worried about these two, and whether it's going to be a good fit, et cetera." Patty folded up the shawl and draped it across the back of the sofa. "I sure hope Mikhail and Karina work out," she said. "I'll go set the table."

The Beginning

The interview with the Azarovs and the conversation afterward lingered in Patty's mind. As she got ready for bed, she marveled again, as she had many times, at how this intentional family had come to be.

About three years ago, Lionel had been sitting in the quiet corner of a neighborhood coffee shop, his latte in front of him, when she came in. She waved from the counter and placed her order, then walked back to join him. "How nice of you to invite me for coffee, Lionel. It's been too long—six months or so, is it?" The latte machine hissed in the background and the baristas chatted with each other as Patty put her coat and bag on the adjacent chair and sat down.

Her latte arrived, and they caught up on each other's lives and people they both knew.

Then Lionel said, "You don't have to rush off, do you, Patty? I have kind of a big topic I'd like to discuss with you."

She smiled. "Oh, good—you always have interesting things to talk about, Lionel. I have plenty of time."

"I want to talk to you about getting old."

Her eyebrows rose, and she settled back in her chair to listen.

"I've been thinking about how I want to spend the last part of my life, and I've been trying to focus on what really matters. What do I have in my life that I value and want to keep, and what don't I have that I want to add?

If I can." He shifted in his chair. "I've figured out that music and staying connected with young people are what I want to keep. And I'm lonely, so I want to add relationships. I want people around me whom I really care about and who care about me." He picked up a pen and doodled on a small notebook lying on the table.

"Mmm. You've clearly been giving this a lot of thought." She sipped her coffee and looked up at him, surprised at his candor. "I'm curious. Was it hard for you to sort all this out? Did it take a long time? And do you feel any awkwardness talking about it?"

"No, once I got to the question—What do I want now?—the answers came pretty quickly. And because there's so much less time available, there's more pressure to get on with it, you know? And that pushes aside the concerns about what people will think of me when I say these things. I don't have time for all that. I just don't care as much what people think as I used to. Anyway, I'd like to hear what you think about getting older."

She leaned her elbows on the table and thought for a moment. "I've heard so many people my age say that they look in the mirror and wonder who that person is. I've had that experience too. It seems to me that in the course of just one year, I looked old. The age spots, the wrinkly skin—you know, the changes that're common to everyone. But it seemed like it happened in a short amount of time. Maybe it really was gradual and I just noticed it all of a sudden." She dabbed at a spill on the table with her napkin. "Anyway, it seemed like . . . like I had come to look old. But I didn't *feel* that much different. Of course, I noticed that I had less energy—I didn't bound up steps like I used to, and there were these little aches and pains. But basically, I felt like the same person I'd been in my thirties, forties, fifties."

Looking out the window, she said, "Not that I didn't change. I did. I grew up, I learned some lessons in life, I've outgrown some immature ways of being. But I've felt like the same person, just getting rid of old baggage—Goodness! I'm just babbling on. I didn't know I had so much to say about getting older. I guess I haven't been aware of how much I've been thinking about it. You probably don't want to hear all this!"

"No, I really do. There aren't many people who are really willing to talk about this subject—and who've really thought about it. I'm interested in whatever you've been thinking, Patty. Please go on." He gestured encouragingly.

"Well, I've been thinking about us retirement-age folks. We've done our careers. People keep working, and that's fine, but most of us have achieved what we're going to achieve career-wise, and we're ready to back off or give it up entirely or move into something different." Patty stared at a painting hanging on the wall beside them, but she wasn't really seeing it as she spoke. "And your family responsibilities are much less—kids grown and so on. The family stuff shifts from focusing on kids to taking care of elderly relatives and friends. Death is just so much closer, so much more real, and that forces us—unless we're too afraid—to think about getting ready. What haven't I done that I need to do and want to do? What's on my bucket list? If I knew I'd die tomorrow or next week, what would be the most important things to do? Those questions come up at various times in our lives, but I think most people are too scared or too busy to really think about them." She paused as her gaze traveled around the room and back to Lionel's face. Anyway, back to your process. How are you going to find the people you want to be with?"

"By having conversations like this," Lionel said. "Whenever I find people who might be likely prospects, I try to find a way to sound them out. Of course, I'm starting with people I already know. I've explored this topic with about half a dozen people over the past couple of years. And when I find someone who's interested, I'm sure that person will know other people who might fit."

"What happens when you find these people? You just try to spend more time together?"

"I'm hoping that we'll move in together."

Patty's eyes widened. "Wow, that's pretty gutsy! How would that work?"

"I don't know how it would work. I think that would be up to the group. So once a group comes together, three or four or five of us, we can talk about the practicalities: where would we live, how much would it cost, what issues would we face, what kind of problems we anticipate—all that. We'd need to work it out together. And from what I've read about intentional communities, there's a lot to work out!" He laughed. "I don't want to underestimate the interpersonal challenges."

"How many prospects do you have, Lionel?" She leaned forward, elbows on the table. "And am I one of them?"

"Yes, you're one of them, if you're interested. I have one other interested person—her name is Anne Aikens. What I'd like to propose is that you think about all this, and if you want to consider it further, have dinner with Anne and me next week. Meanwhile, if there's someone you think might be a good addition to the group, let me know."

And that was the beginning.

Jeremy's Problem

On Monday afternoon, Lionel answered the doorbell at four o'clock, and there was Jeremy, right on time for his weekly piano lesson. The tall, thin teenager smiled shyly, removed his music from his backpack, and dropped the bag by the door. He followed Lionel into the living room, seating himself at the piano. "How's it going, Jeremy?"

"OK, Mr. B. I worked hard on the Mozart, and I think it's coming along. Shall I play it for you?"

"I look forward to it; begin when you're ready." He settled back in his chair to listen to his favorite and most talented student.

Jeremy had come to him two years earlier, referred by a mutual acquaintance. The eldest of six children in a strict Christian fundamentalist family, he coped with adolescence and his family situation by losing himself in music. His father wouldn't pay for music lessons after Jeremy turned fourteen, saying it was time for Jeremy to become a man and earn his own money. The boy had taken on a paper route and mowed lawns to earn enough to continue his lessons, but the work had cut into his homework and practicing time, so Lionel told him he would no longer accept payment, saying it was a privilege to teach such a talented student. Jeremy's skills had progressed rapidly. But today he was playing badly.

At the end of the lesson, they would usually chat for a few minutes, as they did now. "How's school, Jeremy?"

"It's OK. Grades are good, and playing in the orchestra is way cool. But I'm pretty busy trying to keep up."

"I assume you're going to enter the competitions again this year? You did so well last time. The Mozart would be good. And the Chopin—you have a real insight for Chopin."

"Thank you. Yeah, I plan to enter. It makes me nervous, but I know it's good for me."

"You need to be preparing for college applications, you know. You have a lot of talent and you work hard. I'm sure you'd have a chance for a scholarship to a good school."

"Yeah, well, I'd really like to go to college, but my parents won't pay for it if I study music. My dad says there's no way to make a living in music, so it would be a waste of money."

"Well, if that were true, there wouldn't be a Seattle Symphony, or an opera, or concert series all over the place, or a recording industry. Sure, most people aren't going to make a *lot* of money as musicians, but lots of people make a living performing or teaching, or both. If you were to get a scholarship to a college that had a good music program and also offered a teaching credential, I'll bet your parents would reconsider. But whatever they say, it's important to do what you love and what you're good at."

"Yes, sir, I'll remember that," Jeremy said, fidgeting with the sheet music on the piano.

"You seem distracted today. You made more mistakes than you usually do, and you seem . . . not quite here. Is something bothering you?"

Jeremy folded and unfolded the corner of a piece of music. "Mmm, uh, well, it's kind of embarrassing. This girl asked me to go to a dance, and I had to say no, 'cause in my church we don't dance. I felt like a weirdo. She looked at me like I was crazy. But it's not just the dancing. I don't know anything about girls—how to talk to them, what they like, you know. And I don't know how to figure it out. I can't talk about it with my parents. I'd just get a lecture about abstinence, and sex is for when you're married, and stuff like that. I haven't got many friends, and the ones I do have don't know any more than I do— they just pretend they do."

He had continued to mutilate the music as he talked, and then just stared at the ceiling when he stopped talking. There was a silence while they both thought about the situation.

"I know it's hard for young people to talk with older people about topics like this," Lionel said. "Sex seems to be such an embarrassing topic, even though it permeates our culture: advertising, entertainment, politics. I think it's especially hard for young people because it's an unknown." Lionel shifted in his chair and then went on, with a glance at Jeremy to gauge how he was reacting. "At the same time, it's an important part of life: biologically, socially, psychologically. So it's important and it's unknown, and that makes people anxious. Then there're all the taboos that we pile on top of it, which just makes it worse."

"Yeah, everybody wants to be cool—and hot, at the same time. How weird is that?"

"Language is strange, isn't it?" said Lionel, smiling. "But the important thing is that you get it, you seem to understand that all your peers are in the same boat, you're not the only one who feels awkward and wonders how to act, how to be attractive to the opposite sex, whether what you feel is normal or not."

"If you just watch and listen, it's pretty easy to see how scared everybody is. Maybe not scared. More like uncomfortable or something."

"I think scared is a pretty accurate assessment. And it's not just teens. Most of us adults are walking around scared all the time too, but our fears are so deeply buried and covered up that most people can't see them or admit them." Lionel straightened the book on the table beside him to align with the edge of the table.

Jeremy turned on the piano bench to face him. "What are they scared about?"

"The same thing teens are scared about. Am I acceptable? What should I do with my life? Am I doing the right thing? Am I lovable? I think it all gets down to the same basic thing: people are scared that they won't have love, that they'll be alone. And they're afraid of death—though I don't think teens worry about that so much, because it seems so far away." Lionel picked an imaginary piece of lint off his slacks and then looked up at his student. "I'm sorry if this came across as a lecture or something, Jeremy. That's the *last* thing I'd want. I enjoy talking with you, and I sure don't want to overstep my bounds. It was good of you to humor me."

"Well, thanks for the lesson, Mr. B, and for listening to me." Jeremy rose and gathered up his music, and they walked to the front door, where he stuffed the music back into his bag. "You're easy to talk to," he said, glancing at Lionel. "And you didn't overstep your bounds. See you next week."

Lionel watched him lope down the sidewalk, his shoulders slightly slumped, his red hair glinting in the last rays of late afternoon sunshine. *My surrogate grandson,* Lionel thought. *I hope I don't blow it. What a gift that he'll even talk to me at all.*

Lionel spent a half hour looking through the crowded bookshelves in the mansion's library. He selected a few books, which he stacked on an end table, then went to the kitchen, put on a denim apron to protect his slacks and sweater, and began dinner. It was his night to cook.

"Which of your three fabulous dishes are we having tonight?" asked Chuck, coming in from his studio. He washed his hands in the kitchen sink.

"At least I've got three—you've only got one," said Lionel, trying not to smile in triumph.

"Well, my mac and cheese has variations, you know. Sometimes I put in olives, sometimes mushrooms," Chuck said, taking a beer out of the fridge and sitting down at the island.

"Pizza tonight," said Lionel, removing two prepared crusts, sliced mozzarella, bell peppers, and pepperoni from the fridge, and marinara sauce and a can of olives from a cupboard. He poured himself a glass of red wine from a bottle sitting on the counter.

"We done good on this room, didn't we?" Lionel's housemate said, looking around appreciatively at the recessed lighting, the cork floor, the light-colored granite countertops and the warm wood cupboards. "I like being in here."

"Yes, I agree. We did a good job. There're enough windows, and that shade of yellow you chose is just perfect. I hate dark rooms," Lionel said, slicing the peppers and olives.

Patty came into the kitchen, dropped her purse on the little desk beside the doorway to the dining room, and pulled off her gloves and coat, throwing them on the desk too. "I'll set the table. Are we eating at the usual time?"

"Six it is, the usual time." Lionel got out two pizza pans and began assembling his creations. First a layer of cheese, then red sauce, then the olives, pepperoni, and pepper slices.

Patty got herself a glass of wine and sat down beside Chuck. "I just love watching someone else cook, don't you? All those years of cooking meals for a family, trying to fix things that would please everyone and be healthy—gracious, I'm glad that's over!"

"I hope they appreciated you, Patty. I bet they did. I never had anyone doing that for me," said Chuck. "We had to scrabble as best we could. Sometimes I had a can of tuna for breakfast. And I ate a hell of a lot of peanut butter," he said, rubbing his eyes.

Just as the pizza was coming out of the oven, Anne came in. When she glanced at the desk, Patty jumped up and said, "I'll just put these things away and be back to set the table."

When she returned, Anne had set out the napkins, silverware, and plates around the big island. "You didn't have to do that, Anne," she said. "I was planning to do it."

"No problem, Patty. I'm just helping out. What kind of salad dressing do people want?"

"Let's just put it all out and people can choose," said Lionel. Anne put six bottles of salad dressing in the middle of the island while Lionel served the pizza. "Blessings on the meal, everyone."

"And blessings on the cook," said Patty, smiling at him, among appreciative murmurs from the others.

"OK," said Lionel, between bites, "the topic for tonight's dinner conversation is, what books do you give a teenager who knows nothing about sex? I've got a couple of ideas, but I'm interested in your suggestions."

"How about *Lady Chatterley's Lover*," suggested Chuck.

A choking sound came from Patty. "It's a good one to put on a list, but that's not where I'd start," she said. "How old a teenager, and boy or girl?"

"A sixteen-year-old-boy from a religious family where dancing is not allowed and sex is not discussed."

"Shit," said Chuck under his breath, shaking his head. "Poor kid."

Anne said, "I assume he's OK with your getting books for him, Lionel? Sounds like a covert operation to me."

"I didn't tell him I was going to do this, but he was pretty forthcoming about his ignorance and how uncomfortable he is around girls, all the normal stuff. I picked out some things from the library shelves. I don't know whose they are. Doesn't matter anyway, but take a look and see if you have any other suggestions. There's one on tantric sex—with drawings—that should be of interest," he said, grinning. "Every position known to man. And woman, I hasten to add."

"Well, I think he's a pretty unusual boy," Patty said. "Most kids wouldn't be caught dead talking to an adult about sex."

They were silent for a bit as they ate their pizza.

"Hmm," Patty said. "I was just thinking it might be good to go through the teen section of the library and find a couple of novels, the kind that girls read. That would give him an idea of how girls think. I'll volunteer to do that. Also, I was remembering a book I read about the differences between the male and female brain, and how our physiology and biology affect our behavior. That would be a really good one, because he'd know that a lot of what's going on in his body is normal, that he's not a pervert or something. She got up to serve seconds. "Anyone want another slice?"

The Test

Mikhail had spent hours at his cousin's dining room table while everyone was off to work and school, planning a week's menus and what he would prepare for the Wednesday night dinner. "Look at this one, Karina. I think it is better."

"Mikhail, you drive me crazy! I cannot count how many menus you've made. We discuss them again and again. They are all very good. You did what they asked, so make list and get everything at store tomorrow."

"I will go today and get supplies and make it for Georgi's family tonight. Then I will be sure I have everything, and I can see if they like it. We can shop again tomorrow." His brow was furrowed with worry.

*****

They arrived at the mansion about three o'clock Wednesday afternoon, laden with four bags of groceries and a backpack containing Mikhail's knives, two aprons, and a stockpot. Lionel led them to the kitchen. "Please use anything we have that you need—food, or utensils or whatever. I'll be in the library if you have any questions. Everyone will be here about six."

Karina smiled shyly; she began unpacking their groceries, and Mikhail got out his knives and the stockpot.

Thirty minutes later, Karina had found the cloth napkins, placemats, and a fine old soup tureen; she set the table in the dining room. By five forty-five, the smells of baking pastry and soup with caraway wafted through the house. The borscht was finished and simmering, the piroshki waited in the oven, and arugula salad with pears, pecans, and goat cheese graced the salad plates.

Chuck stuck his head in the kitchen. "I won't come in and bother you, but I wanted to say it sure smells good in here! The others will be here pretty soon."

Anne came into the kitchen next. "May we help you serve? Is there anything we can do?"

"No, please be seated, and we will serve," said Mikhail, mopping his brow with a handkerchief.

Anne left and then came back in. "But there are only four places set. We expected you to eat with us. We don't want you to feel relegated to the kitchen!"

"Oh, no, cook does not eat with guests. We will eat later. Please sit down, and we will serve."

The dinner got rave reviews as Mikhail hovered between kitchen and dining room.

Anne: "This is the best borscht I ever ate! What are the seasonings, Mikhail?"

Patty: "This piroshki crust is so *flaky*. I can never make flaky crust. Mmm, it just melts in my mouth."

Chuck: "I don't think I ever had goat cheese. It's pretty good stuff."

Lionel: "These baked apples are just wonderful. There's some spice in the sauce that I can't identify, but I can tell there's some lemon rind in the whipped cream."

They had their coffee and tea in the living room with Mikhail and Karina, and discussed the suggested menus that Mikhail had prepared. Everyone agreed they looked very healthy and appetizing.

Mikhail handed Lionel an envelope. "We spent thirty dollars for dinner. Here is rest of money."

The housemates looked at one another. Lionel's reserved smile had broadened to his eyes. "I think I can speak for the others, Mikhail and Karina. This was a very fine dinner, we like your proposed menus, and we hope that you will take our offer and help us out with our cooking."

Karina looked at Mikhail and nodded, and Mikhail said, "We accept your offer. We will be very pleased to help you with cooking."

"Oh, wonderful!" Patty clapped her hands. "Now we need to talk about some details. We really do want you to eat with us. But we'll let you make the decision of when that will be. In time, we hope that you'll feel a part of our family. And we want to do the dishes. It's important to us to participate in the running of the house. That's part of the deal, so you have to let us do that. This isn't a matter of the cook and the guests—it's not like your restaurant in Moscow."

Anne took the couple up to their new apartment, so they could confirm what was included and what they would need to provide themselves. It was arranged that they would move in on Friday.

Frictions

The Friday morning newspaper covered half of the breakfast room table, topped with Patty's coffee mug and a plate of half-eaten toast. Anne was sitting down with her smoothie at the other end of the table when Lionel came in with his microwaved oatmeal. Patty apologized for taking up all the space and folded up the newspaper.

"Maybe you could read the paper at the island, Patty," Anne said. "There's lots more room."

"I'm sorry I'm infringing on your space," Patty said. "I really like to eat in here with everyone else. I don't want to be banished to outer darkness."

"Don't get all uptight," Anne replied. "The breakfast room isn't my personal space, and I'm not trying to banish you. I just thought you'd have more room at the island, since you like to read the paper while you have breakfast."

"I know you think I'm messy and clutter the place up. I can't even put my purse on the kitchen desk without you rolling your eyes."

"Come on, Patty," Anne said. "You're projecting your stuff onto me. No, I don't like clutter, but I can put up with a certain amount. Did you hear me complaining?"

"You don't have to do it out loud. I can tell." She walked into the kitchen and put her dishes in the dishwasher. Then she put the lunch she'd made the night before into a paper bag and crammed that into her big satchel of things she'd take with her to her day of teaching. She was a substitute for three local independent schools and worked two or three days a week.

As she waited under her umbrella for the bus, Patty thought about the exchange she'd had with Anne. *I like orderly surroundings as much as she does, so why don't I have them? Why do I have so much clutter in my room, and why do I drop things anywhere and then have to go find them and put them away, instead of putting them where they belong in the first place?*

She boarded the bus, swiped her commuter pass through the card reader, and sat down to watch the traffic splashing puddles onto the sidewalks and unwary pedestrians. Memories arose of her mother coming into her bedroom and chiding her for the mess. "You'll grow up to be a slob—you're already a slob!" *What a terrible thing to say to a child!* Her mother had been big on "shoulds" and "oughts,'" and not much on praise.

Patty mused on these thoughts and absently watched the brightly colored umbrellas bobbing down the street as she was carried to her workplace.

*****

Later in the morning, Lionel walked into the laundry room to get his clothes out of the dryer, only to find them wadded up in an overflowing plastic basket. He hated wrinkled clothes. He took the basket to his room, dumped out the clothes, and carefully hung and folded them, smoothing out the wrinkles as best he could. Some items would now need to be ironed. He seethed.

At lunch, everyone but Patty and Karina was in the kitchen. "I'm *really* annoyed that someone took my clothes out of the dryer and threw them in a laundry basket. Now they have to be ironed!"

"Well, that would have been me, Lionel," said Chuck. "I needed clean jeans for a meeting with a potential client at one o'clock, so I put them in the washer about seven and checked back on the dryer three times during the morning, and you didn't come back to take out your stuff, so *I* did. I didn't know it was yours. I don't like the idea of pawing through other people's clothes trying to figure out whose they are."

"I'm sorry I didn't come back for them sooner—my apologies. But couldn't you have just sort of shaken them out and laid them across the basket to minimize the wrinkles?"

"Look, man, I just took the clothes out of the dryer like I do my own. I don't care about wrinkles. If it's such a big deal, don't leave your stuff in the dryer for hours!" Chuck slammed together the halves of the sandwich he was making, slapped it on a plate, and walked into the breakfast room to eat.

"We have global warming and famine in Africa, and you're getting all huffy about wrinkles?" said Anne.

Lionel frowned. Then he smiled ruefully. "You're right. This is ridiculous. I'm sorry, Chuck!" he called. "It's old baggage. I've mentally sorted through this thing about wrinkles before—where it comes from and so on. But then I forget and lapse back into my 'thing' about wrinkles. I'll try to do better about remembering to take my clothes out of the washer and dryer."

"We've all forgotten our laundry at one time or another," said Anne. "And it's probably going to happen more often as we get more forgetful. How about if I make up some little name cards for each of us, and we can put them on top of the washer or dryer so we'll know whose stuff it is. Then if that person forgets, we'll know who to remind."

"Sure, let's try that," said Lionel. "But really we—I— just have to be more responsible about not forgetting." On his way to the library, he patted Chuck on the shoulder and murmured another apology.

*****

Patty and her housemates gathered after dinner Sunday for their weekly musicale. "Concert" seemed too formal a word for it, especially since they sometimes ended up singing, but they all wanted music in their lives and Lionel loved having someone to play for. This evening, he played Rachmaninoff and Tchaikovsky in honor of Karina and Mikhail, who had spent most of the day settling into their third-floor apartment. They all sat around the living room with their coffee, enjoying the music.

Patty noticed, not for the first time, Anne and Chuck's easy closeness. They sat thigh to thigh, his arm along the sofa top behind Anne's shoulders. Was it impossible for her to find someone at her age? It had been possible for them, so why couldn't it be for her? She was happy for them, glad they had found each other at this stage in their lives. But she was still envious.

Ever since Lionel had contacted her about joining the group, she had thought about him as a potential partner. Not often. She just occasionally tried on the idea and wondered if it might work. It wasn't just a matter of proximity; he was still a good-looking man and he was a really nice guy—considerate, thoughtful, upbeat. But she didn't see any signs that he might be looking for someone.

As she listened to the music, Patty thought back to the night she had brought Chuck to dinner as a prospective member of their group. She had always thought of him as a pretty laid-back guy, but on their way to the restaurant he'd seemed a little stiff. Anne and Lionel had already arrived and were sitting in the middle of a semicircular booth. Patty made the introductions and then took the seat next to Lionel, leaving Chuck to slip in beside Anne. There was some chitchat about the weather and the traffic and the menu until the drinks arrived.

After they'd ordered their food, Chuck said, "So, Lionel, tell me about what got you going on this group-living thing. Patty said it was your idea to start with."

"Yes, well, I had this idea that maybe I could find a congenial group of people to live with, rather than ending up alone in some . . . 'home' or . . . facility. I thought if we pooled our resources we could come up with something better than going it alone." Lionel took a sip of wine. "And that's just the location side, the place. I also wanted to be with people I care about and who care about me. I don't have any family, just some distant cousins I never knew. So I thought it would be good if I could find some people with shared interests and compatible personalities to live with. An 'intentional family,' if you will."

"Don't you think it would be difficult to live with a bunch of strangers," Chuck said, "at our age?"

"Sure, I think it will be hard work. It's kind of scary, actually—at least to me. But what's the alternative? Living alone until I'm senile and getting plunked into a nursing home by some social worker? A lot of people don't have any choice, but a lot do, and they just slide along the path of least resistance until it's too late and they're in some situation they really don't like. I'm trying to be proactive. But I don't assume it'll be easy."

Anne fiddled with her reading glasses as she said, "We've all roomed with someone, family or not, at some time in our lives. We can remember the annoyances of having to listen to someone's favorite music that you hate, or finding their dishes left on the countertop, or the dessert you were saving eaten by someone else. We could all come up with long lists of things we don't like about living with other people. But, as Lionel said, what's the alternative?"

"When we've talked with people about this idea," Patty said, "most of them freak out about what they might not like: What if I had to listen to Fox News, or what if I got overruled and they painted the kitchen pink? They think more about what they might not like in a situation they find hard to imagine than they do about a much more likely situation—living with their kids or in a retirement home."

There was a pause in the conversation as Chuck took in what Patty had said. He took a drink of his beer and said "Yeah, well, the devil you know is not as scary as the devil you don't know, isn't that what they say? So, are you the Fox News crowd or the NPR crowd?"

The other three laughed and looked at each other, waiting to see who would answer. Lionel said, "I don't watch much TV, but when I do, it's usually PBS."

"Me too," said Anne.

"Me three," said Patty, and they all laughed again. "And I love NPR. OK, have we typecast ourselves? Have you fit us into a stereotype?"

"Yup, got it," said Chuck, "a bunch of free-thinking liberal aging hippies. I'd fit right in."

More laughter, and then their dinner arrived and conversation slowed. "Looks like you're not a salad kind of gal," said Chuck, looking at Anne's towering burger and stack of fries.

"No, I've always had the appetite of a horse, and a high metabolism or something. Anyway, I've always been able to eat a lot and not gain weight. Of course, it helped that I was a dancer for many years. Must have burned off thousands of calories a day." She dipped a fry in ketchup and looked over at him. "How do you stay so trim? Hate to cook?"

"Naw, I don't hate it. I just never had the occasion to learn how," he said. "But I usually get involved in what I'm working on and forget to eat."

As they ate and chatted, Patty was aware of how close Chuck was sitting to Anne. He wasn't maintaining a polite distance. True, the booth was snug, or maybe he was oblivious, but Patty sensed it was something else.

"Patty said you're a painter," Anne said. "What do you paint? Or maybe I should ask *how* do you paint—oils, acrylics, watercolors?"

"Mostly figurative work, various media," he said. "I like to experiment around. Right now I'm doing mostly oils. As a matter of fact, I just had an idea for a new painting."

"Oh," said Anne, eyebrows raised. "Tell me about it."

"I'd like to paint your hands."

She put down her fork and took a drink of her wine. Then she looked at him with a slight smile on her face. "Oh, you would, would you? That sounds very interesting."

Their attention was diverted when Lionel said, "Well, Chuck, are you open to continuing these explorations with us? We're not asking for a commitment or anything—it's too early for that. But is this something that interests you?" He smiled. "If not, no problem. We've had lots of people say this idea wasn't for them. And we're still friends."

"Yeah, sure, I'd like to continue the . . . exploration," said Chuck, with a quick glance at Anne. I've got lots of questions about how things would work: you know, expenses, where we'd live, that sort of thing. But count me in for this phase." He leaned forward, forearms on the table, and said, "This is the most interesting thing to come into my life in a long time."

Patty had picked him up, and as she drove him back to his apartment she said, "Well, what did you think? You seemed a little uptight on the way to dinner."

"Patty, you know I haven't got any degrees. How do you think I felt, going to lunch with a math professor, a ballerina, and someone with a master's in education? Yeah, I was a little uptight, but they seem like real nice folks. I'm looking forward to getting to know them."

Patty's reverie about the group's formative days was interrupted when suddenly Lionel stopped playing in midphrase. He looked confused. "Goodness—it's just gone out of my mind. This hasn't happened to me since I was twenty!" He sat quietly, looking at his hands. Then he began to play again and continued to the end of the piece. "Well, at least it finally came back. Sorry, my friends. I hope this was just a one-time thing."

"It doesn't matter, Lionel," said Patty. "You could have stopped several times, and we still would have enjoyed it. You're entitled to forget now and then when you're seventy. Don't worry about it. Could we sing something? How about 'You Are My Sunshine'? And 'Tell Me Why.' That's a good one for bedtime."

"Let's sing something different," said Chuck. "You always suggest the same thing. How about 'Yellow Submarine' or 'When I'm Sixty-Four'? Somethin' a little more lively."

Patty examined her fingernails, her lips pursed.

"You OK with that, Patty?" Chuck asked. He must have noted her expression.

"Sure, no big deal. I just like to sing the ones that remind me of getting tucked into bed when I was little."

Lionel had been rummaging through a stack of music on the piano. "Here's a book of Beatles music. We can sing both Chuck's and Patty's requests—we don't have to choose. Come stand around me so you can see the words." Then he launched into "When I'm Sixty-Four."

*****

In their apartment later, Mikhail and Karina traded impressions of their new life, as they had the previous two evenings. "It doesn't seem real," said Karina. "Beautiful house and city. Stores are filled with everything I could want—things I didn't know about and no one even needs. Is clean, no one is threatening us. Our employers want us to eat dinner with them, and they play beautiful music for us. Is a dream!"

"To have kitchen with everything chef could want is . . . *beyond* my dreams," said Mikhail. "I could not imagine something like this. What does it mean, Karina? Why are we here?"

"In Russia, we were more lucky than many people," Karina said. "I had good job, and you had successful business. But was such struggle. For so many years, everything was struggle. Now we don't have to struggle so hard, so we can think about how to help in the world. God does not want us to be selfish and think only of ourselves."

Mikhail wandered around the apartment, running his fingers across the desk, plumping the cushions on the sofa, straightening an icon on the wall. He looked out the window at the lights twinkling in the distance. "We must take very good care of our new family. That is one reason we are here. It is very easy now, but as they grow older it won't be so easy. We must look for ways to help them."

"One day they will need nurse. I have talked to Patty about working as nurse. I would need to go through American training programs to do same work I did in Russia. It would be very expensive—and difficult, because my English is still not so good. But I could start with less training and begin as low-level nurse. She will show me how to find out about training programs on the internet. Perhaps I could use some money from sale of restaurant to pay for my training. Then I could get work as nurse. I am excited to think about these possibilities!" She got up from the sofa and went to stand beside him at the window. "We are very blessed, Mikhail. Come to bed now, husband."

*****

Anne's bedroom door was ajar when she heard a light knock. Propped up against her pillows, book in hand, she looked up to see Chuck, leaning against the doorjamb, in the old thermal underwear he wore for pajamas. "You up for some company tonight?"

She took off her glasses and patted the bed beside her. "Sure, but I warn you I'm too tired for any hanky-panky tonight."

"Hanky-panky. Man, I haven't heard that for a while!" he said, shutting the door and crossing the room to her bed. She pulled back the covers, and he got in next to her. "Really, I'm too tired too. At least I think I'm too tired." He grinned at her and pulled the blanket up to his chin.

She smiled at his gambit but put her glasses back on. "What's making *you* tired?" she asked. "Did the kids give you a hard time this week?" She always liked to hear about Chuck's job volunteering at the county juvenile detention facility.

"No, the kids were fine. There's one kid, about sixteen, who reminds me a lot of me at that age. He's really got talent, and if he can just get his act together, he could go places. The other guys, there's a range of interest. They're so bored they'll do just about anything, but some are more into it than others." Chuck rubbed his eyes. "I think I'm tired because of eye strain. But I've got good lighting in the studio, so I'm not sure what's going on."

"Maybe you should have your eyes checked. When was the last time you did that?"

"God, I don't know. Years ago."

"Chuck! At our age you're supposed to go every year or two!" she said, frowning at him. "Promise me you'll make an appointment tomorrow."

"Yes, ma'am. Whatever you say. I definitely want to stay on your good side. Otherwise, I might not get to sleep with you."

She looked at him over the top of her reading glasses. "On another topic, do you think Patty's been a little . . . testy or something lately?"

"Hmm," he said, staring at the ceiling. "Yeah, I think you're right. She's usually so upbeat. Any idea what's bothering her?"

"No idea. But I think I'll ask her if this goes on much longer. I can put up with it—it's not that big a deal. It's just that we agreed we'd talk to each other when something's wrong, rather than pretending everything's OK. I don't want to pry if she doesn't want to talk, but I feel like I should at least ask." She put her glasses on the bedside table and turned off the light. "Time to go to sleep." She turned on her side, her back to him.

He turned so they lay spoon-fashion.

"Oh," she sighed, "I like the feel of your lanky body down the length of mine. It's so . . . solid . . . and warm."

"Well, I sure like the feel of your body," he said, running his hand down her flank. "Lean, but nice round places too. Jesus, women's bodies are wonderful . . . G'night. Annie," he said sleepily.

"Good night, old man."

A Visitor

Patty heard the doorbell chime and hurried to the front door to welcome Susannah, a friend from her meditation group. "Come in! I'm so glad we finally got our schedules matched."

"It took a while, didn't it? How can we be so busy when we're retired?" asked the attractive silver-haired woman, stepping inside and unwinding her scarf.

Patty hung up her friend's coat and led her into the foyer. "Shall we have tea first and then the tour, or tour first?"

"Oh, let's have tea and chat a bit first. I want to hear more than the bits I've heard before and after meditation. This living arrangement and this house are such big changes in your life—I want to hear all about it. I can tell already it's a wonderful house! How do you like the neighborhood?"

"We love it here. Our neighbors are really great. We were amused to find out that they refer to us as 'the mansioners.' I'm not sure why, since most of them live in houses just as big—I guess it's just shorthand for 'those crazy old folks who moved in together.' Anyway, they're lovely people."

They settled in the living room in front of a coffee table holding an ornate silver tea service, a little vase of flowers, a plate of tiny tarts, and a half dozen of the assorted English teacups Patty's mother had passed on to her. "Oh, how lovely!" said Susannah. "A proper tea party."

"Yes, I thought I'd drag all this stuff out. Might as well use it while we can. I don't know what's going to happen to it when I'm gone—none of my kids want any of it. But I love using it. Sit down while I fill up the teapot." Patty left the room and returned shortly to set a full teapot on the big silver platter.

"Remember when we were talking at a meditation retreat a long time ago about who you really are?" said Patty. "Someone was saying that your stuff—the physical things you get attached to—is just a reflection of who you think you are. Even photographs. They're just a picture of who you thought you were at a given moment." She poured the steaming liquid through a strainer into two flowered bone-china cups and handed one to Susannah. "I wonder what it says about me that I wanted to keep these teacups. That'll be a good dinner topic with my housemates."

"Yes, I remember that conversation," said Susannah, "and it really helped me when I moved into my condo. I had to get rid of a lot of things. There just wasn't room. That was part of the reason I wanted to move: it forced me to deal with all the stuff and think about why it'd been valuable to me. Was it keeping me stuck in some old version of myself that I didn't want to be anymore? When Will moved in, he didn't have a lot of stuff, except books. Those books are an ongoing issue," she said, smiling and setting her cup on its saucer. "He appreciates a tidy house, but somehow everything seems to be covered with books. Oh well. He's worth it. If it's OK for me to ask, do you and your housemates have issues that you have to work out?"

"Sure, it's fine to ask, but, honestly, there aren't many. It's more a matter of, at least for me, my own insecurities and how they get . . . activated or something, by certain situations. Like just the other day, I was all uptight because *I* thought Anne thought I was messy. But I was just projecting my own attitudes about myself—it wasn't Anne at all. I'm the worst when it comes to leaving things around, but they're tolerant." Patty poured more tea into Susannah's cup, then leaned back against the cushions.

"We talked a lot about potential problems before we all made our decision to do this," Patty said. "Of course you can never anticipate everything. But we're all grown-ups and we try really hard to be considerate of each other. If something's bothering us, we try to ask whether it's our own attitude or if it really is someone else's behavior that's the problem. That's been very good practice in not being judgmental, and letting go of attitudes that get in the way."

Susannah took a napkin and put a tart on her plate. "There's always a trade-off, isn't there? Having everything just the way you want it and being lonely, or compromising on the details of daily life and not being lonely." She paused, teacup in hand. "Oh, that didn't come out the way I meant. I don't mean to say that everyone who lives alone is lonely—I don't think that. But it was *my* experience. I appreciated having everything just the way I wanted it: my kind of music, no one else's undeleted emails in my inbox, and so on. But I don't mind those things anymore. I'm so happy to be with Will—and all his books!" She laughed.

"Well," said Patty, selecting a tart. "It was kind of scary for all of us before we made this decision—moving in with a bunch of strangers, at our age, for heaven's sake. We had to commit, or it wouldn't work. But it's so clear now to all of us how much it means to have each other and this gorgeous house. We're so grateful to each other and to . . . I guess . . . the universe. I know some people wonder how we could do it at our age, but it's a nonissue for us now."

"Hello," said Lionel as he walked into the room smiling. "You must be Susannah. Patty told me you were coming, and I've been looking forward to meeting you— a fellow meditator. I'm Lionel." He shook Susannah's hand and sat down while Patty poured him some tea.

"I've been looking forward to meeting all the housemates," she said. "How fortuitous that two meditators ended up in the same household. I'd think the odds of that happening were pretty unlikely. When did you get started meditating, Lionel?"

"Oh, ages ago, in the seventies. The Transcendental Meditation movement was really big then, and I tried that, but eventually I got to Buddhism, and that seemed a good fit for me."

"So we've both been meditating about the same amount of time. We could talk about that for a long time, but I really want to ask: Do you two think that you and your housemates are unusual, that maybe you have something that most people our age don't have?" Susannah said. "I mean, how many people in their seventies would try communal living?"

Patty and Lionel looked at each other, then Patty answered. "We've talked about that quite a bit," she said. "I think there are levels of communal living. A retirement home is communal living in some ways, a group family home is more so, and I guess what we're doing is at the far end of the continuum. In other places, most of the decisions are already made: when the meals are served, what's served, whether or not there are outings and where to, what the furniture looks like in the common rooms, and so on." She stopped for a sip of tea. "You just go with the place that's closest to what you like and can afford. But here, we make all the decisions together, especially who we're going to live with. So I guess we're different in that it wasn't so clear what we were getting into, like it would have been if we decided to live in a retirement home. And that takes a certain amount of courage and willingness to change."

They heard voices in the kitchen. "Oh, Chuck and Anne are back," Patty said. "I invited them to join us if they got back in time." The other two housemates came into the living room, shedding shopping bags and coats.

Patty did the introductions and began pouring more tea.

"Oh boy, Mikhail's tarts!" said Chuck, dropping onto the sofa and helping himself. "I'm starved. Shopping does that to me."

"Before you two came in," Susannah said to Chuck and Anne, "Patty and Lionel were filling me in on how you all decided to embark on this grand experiment. I was asking if you're unusual, because you all decided to live together in your later years. Do you think you are?"

"Hmm," said Anne, settling back in her chair with her tea. "I guess I'd say yes, given the reaction I get from most people when I tell them about our . . . arrangement. But I'm not sure I could say in what way we're unusual."

"Hell, I've always been weird, so I don't think much about how I'm different from other folks," said Chuck, adding another tart to his plate.

"Didn't you have some reservations when Patty invited you to explore living with us?" asked Anne. "I remember that first dinner, you didn't just say, 'Sign me up!' You had a lot of questions."

"Yeah, but I was ready to sign up. I just didn't say so right away," he said, giving her a sideways look. "All those questions were just about details—how's it gonna work and that sort of thing. I never had any doubt about doing it. I was just hoping you guys would decide I'd fit in."

"It was touch-and-go whether I'd vote for you," said Anne. "The deciding factor was that I figured you'd be good at picking out the paint colors for our house."

Following that good-natured jibe, Patty invited Susannah to follow her for the house tour, leaving the rest of the housemates to polish off the tea and tarts.

The Art Walk

"Hey," said Chuck at the dinner table that night. "It's First Thursday tomorrow night. Anybody want to go gallery hopping with me?"

They all wanted to go. Karina and Mikhail had never been to Seattle's historic district, and the others hadn't been there in recent years.

Right after dinner the next night, they got on the bus toward downtown and Elliott Bay. As they rode, Patty explained to Karina and Mikhail that part of the waterfront had been filled in and built up over the years. She encouraged them to take the tour of old buildings that still exist underground, below the present-day streets. "I've got a book about Seattle's history. I'll find it in our library, if you're interested."

The bus let them off three blocks from Pioneer Square. They admired the low-rise brick buildings, the hand-carved totem pole, and the historic glass pergola as they strolled toward Occidental Park.

"This was all forest once upon a time," Patty told Karina and Mikhail, gesturing at the densely developed hill to the east. "The loggers cut the trees and skidded them down these hills to the water so they could be taken to lumber mills. That's where the term 'skid road' comes from. But it also means a place where people go who are down on their luck. I'm not sure how that transition came about."

"If we get separated, let's meet at First and Madison at nine o'clock," Chuck said. "And if you get tired of this weird contemporary art, or walking around, or it starts raining, just duck into a tavern—there're lots around here," he said, gesturing to the surrounding area. They trooped into the first gallery, hung mostly with huge abstract paintings, and paused before one of them.

"Chuck, how do you know if this is 'good' art or not?" Lionel asked. "It's not representational, so you don't even know what it's supposed to be."

"It doesn't matter what it's supposed to be," said Chuck. "What do you feel when you look at it?" They all stood looking at the gigantic canvas.

"Well, I like the big splotches of really strong colors," said Anne. "It feels generous, or maybe even extravagant, those big swatches of color. It feels like the artist wasn't inhibited, like she was saying to herself—or himself—'I don't care how much this canvas costs, or that it's too big to hang in most people's homes and I don't know who will want it. I just want to put these colors on this white space.'"

"I find it intimidating," said Lionel, his arms across his chest. "I get what you mean, Anne—I feel that sense of extravagance—but at the same time, it makes me feel like there're no limits, no boundaries. It's kind of overpowering."

"Well, isn't it good to break out of boundaries? Not to be limited? I like that feeling," said Patty as they moved to the next painting and stopped in front of it. "Women wore girdles when I was young, and, boy, was I glad when that went out of style. That was a limitation I could do without!"

"Maybe these should be called the 'Anti-Girdle Series,'" Chuck said. "What do you feel when you look at these paintings, Karina?"

Karina searched for words as they gazed at the painting hanging before them. "I think, confused . . . or not good enough. Is difficult to find right words. I think about all I don't know about painting and art. I have never been to art gallery. I have been to museums, but very few, and I didn't know what I saw. I feel I should know more. So this painting reminds me of what I don't know, and I feel . . ." She stopped.

"Inadequate?" filled in Patty.

"Yes—that is the word. Thank you, Patty."

"Well, I think you just need to go to art galleries more often," said Chuck. "I'm pretty sure the artist who painted this wasn't intending to make people feel inadequate, but what you said brings up the most important thing about art, Karina. And that's how it makes you feel. It could feel really different to each person, depending on what each one brings to the artwork. So don't worry about whether you understand whatever the artist meant. Maybe she didn't mean anything consciously. Maybe she wasn't trying to express a thought or a concept. But she probably had a feeling about what she was doing. Maybe you have a different feeling, and that's OK too."

They moved slowly around the gallery, stopping at each painting to consult their feelings and compare notes. "This is hard work for me," said Lionel, squinting at the little signs beside each artwork. "I can barely read the signs, and they don't help me understand anyway." He turned to Mikhail, who was standing beside him, hands clasped behind his back. "I'm trying to get a feeling other than intimidation, and I'm not getting anything. And that makes me feel . . . stuck or something."

"Is that not worthy?" asked Mikhail. "'Worthy,' is that right word? You learn something about yourself when you look at these paintings. That is good, yes?"

"I think 'worthwhile' is the word you're looking for," replied Lionel. "And, yes, you're right—it's worthwhile to learn you have some emotional limitations. It's kind of depressing, but if you don't learn these things about yourself, you never know what you're missing. You never know that life could be different than it is."

Chuck was behind them listening to this exchange. "A lot of people feel stuck by modern art, Lionel. Partly, it's because most people aren't trained artists. You know how you enjoy something more when you know something about it, like music?" Lionel nodded. "Well, it's the same with painting. If you've studied composition, for example, you can look at a painting and see whether the artist knew what she was doing or not. Or if you've ever tried to get a certain color with oil paint, you know how difficult that can be and you appreciate how an artist did that. But now that so much artwork is nonrepresentational, it's hard for ordinary people to know what to think."

They wandered in and out of galleries with the other art walkers, enjoying the overheard conversations and the variety of dress: black clothing with piercings and tattoos, orange and blue hair, low boots and tall high-heeled boots, leggings topped by leather skirts, extravagantly wrapped scarves, all interspersed with chinos, jeans, and REI flannel shirts.

One couple stood in front of a landscape of Mount Rainier and the surrounding foothills, rather ordinary except for a six-inch gash in the middle. "I think it would be really nice over the fireplace," the man said. "The trees are the same color as the green in the sofa."

"Yeah, and I like that gash," the woman said. "It takes guts to buy a three-thousand-dollar painting with a gash in it."

In front of a line of round brown ceramic pieces, a twentysomething guy said, "Oh, and here we have the turds—the art turds."

"No, dude, those aren't art turds. It says right here they're 'islands of desolation, an archipelago of despair.' Can't you tell the difference between turds and islands?"

Anne and Chuck had lost the rest of the group, but at eight forty-five, they meandered down First Avenue, looking in the windows of Oriental rug stores and rock shops, avoiding the puddles that reflected the old-fashioned streetlights. When they reached the bus stop, the others were there waiting for them.

"Chuck, Lionel and I were wondering why you don't show your paintings in a gallery," Patty said. "I've heard you say you'd like to sell more of your work."

"Good question," Anne said. "I can't believe we've never talked about this before."

The bus arrived, almost empty. They arranged themselves in the back, facing each other, and continued their conversation.

"So how *do* you sell your work, Chuck?" asked Lionel.

"I don't sell much, but over the years I've built up a small clientele. They maybe want something new or need a gift. Their friends admire a piece and get referred to me. It's not much, but it brings in a little."

"Do you have a website?" said Patty. "Does that work for artists?"

"Naw, I don't know how to do that, and I couldn't afford to pay someone to make one for me. I guess it could work, but how would you get people to know about it? Same problem as getting them to see your work when you don't have a gallery."

"Well, it wouldn't hurt to look into it," said Anne. "Why don't we ask around, find out what's involved, how expensive it would be? If it would help you sell your work, maybe the sales would cover the cost of having the website built."

Chuck examined his hands. "Well, it wouldn't hurt to ask, I guess. Besides the money, I need more space. I've got so much work stacked up in the studio, and I'd really like to get rid of it. If a website would help with that, that would be a good deal."

"How about a gallery?" said Lionel. "Wouldn't that be even better?"

"See, the thing about art these days is that there're trends—stuff is 'in' or not 'in.' A note of tension had crept into Chuck's voice. "I don't do the 'in' stuff, so I'm not going to be represented by a gallery." He could feel his gut tighten at the thought of hawking his work to gallery owners.

"But how do you know unless you ask?" said Patty.

"I just know."

There was silence for a few blocks.

The bus stopped in front of a coffee shop. The driver got up and called back to them, "Be right back, folks. I've got a latte waiting for me, and I'm ahead of schedule." And he dashed off.

"Bet he doesn't do this during the day," said Patty. "Just for fun, I'm timing him."

He was back in ninety seconds. "Thanks for your patience, folks," he said, saluting them with his cup.

"I feel a project coming on," Patty said, choosing to ignore Chuck's discomfort. "I think we should help Chuck sell his work. Would you mind, Chuck? We could run some ideas by you and see what you thought and then decide if it might be worthwhile. Nobody has to participate. Only if you want to." She looked at her housemates hopefully.

"Well, I appreciate your enthusiasm, Patty," Chuck said, trying to be positive. "I've pretty much run out of that when it comes to promotion—I just want to do the art. But I'm open to ideas."

He wasn't really open to ideas; he resisted all things associated with marketing, even though he'd been increasingly worried about his lack of sales. He was barely able to make his share of the monthly household payments.

The Diagnosis

As Chuck walked home from his early afternoon eye appointment the following week, he was shocked out of noticing the big old trees, the design their bare branches made against the sky, the birds, the things he usually noticed when walking. The optometrist had done many tests in his two hours at the doctor's office, and Chuck was dismayed at the diagnosis. Macular degeneration—he was going blind. He couldn't think of a worse fate for a painter.

Instead of going into the house for his usual afternoon cup of coffee, he climbed the stairs to his studio, converted from servants' quarters over the garage into a spacious, well-lit room. He sat down in the worn and sagging overstuffed chair beside his scruffy little table and looked around a studio most painters would die for: an eighteen-square-foot space, warm in the winter and cool in the summer, with a lavatory and lots of windows. His supplies were neatly stowed along one wall, and rows of finished canvases were stacked against another. The one constant in his life was painting, and he'd managed to do it for over fifty years. What would he do with himself now? How would he contribute his share of their monthly costs? Maybe they could rent the studio to bring in some income.

At a quarter to six, the intercom buzzed in the now-dark room. "I'm sure you're lost in a painting," came Anne's voice. "But it's time for dinner."

He went into the house and washed his hands in the kitchen sink, then trudged into the dining room, sat down, and spread his napkin across his knees. "Well, I finally made it to the eye doctor, and the news wasn't good. I'm going blind," he said, plunging his fork into his baked squash.

Shocked silence descended.

"My God!" said Patty. "How sure are they?"

"Pretty sure," Chuck replied.

"Can you give us any more information?" Anne said. "What causes it . . . is it progressive . . . if it can be treated. They must have told you more than just you're going blind." Her voice was level and calm.

"They told me it's called 'macular degeneration.' It's pretty hereditary, and about thirty percent of people over seventy-five have it. It shows up in different ways, like your vision gets blurred or distorted, you have trouble telling the difference between colors, you can't read. After that, I didn't take in much more."

Conversation ceased while they absorbed this information.

"How can we help, Chuck?" Lionel asked.

Chuck put his fork down and wiped his mouth on his napkin. "This food is really good, Mikhail. I don't know, Lionel. I guess I'm kinda dazed. I don't know what the implications are, other than I'm not going to be able to do the only thing I've ever wanted to do." He paused, alternately twisting and smoothing his napkin. "I feel like I did when I was sentenced to jail as a kid—scared and frantic. What would it be like? What would become of me?"

"I'm going to Google it and see what I can find out," said Anne. "I'll start right after dinner. I want you to make another appointment, Chuck, and I'll go with you and ask questions. I'm sure there are things that can be done to slow it down or compensate or something. We just have to find out what they are."

"I appreciate the offer of help. But I don't know what I need right now, and I feel like I just want to be alone and think about it for a while."

There was an awkward silence until Patty said, "Please pass the salad," and stilted conversation resumed.

*****

At bedtime, Anne stood outside Chuck's bedroom door, thinking about her life in ballet. A dancer knows when she starts ballet that her career will be short, if she's even good enough to have a career. All that effort, so much work and sacrifice, and it's all over in a few years. She knew all that, but it was still a shock when that time had come: It was over. She couldn't keep up with the younger dancers any longer. She knew what it felt like to lose the most important thing in your life.

She knocked gently. "Come in," came the faint reply.

"Why are you sitting in the dark?" she asked, crossing the room in just the light from the hallway. She turned on the bedside lamp and found Chuck slumped in his chair.

"Thought I might as well get used to it, see what it feels like," he said, turning a glass of whiskey round and round on his knee

She sat on the bed, looking at her hands clasped in her lap. *What's the right thing to say?* she wondered. There were so many unknowns to his situation: how bad it was, what could be done to ameliorate the symptoms, what unexpected good things might come from it. He would grieve the loss of his sight, rightly so, and they had to let him. But when was the time to help him see that it might not be as bad as he thought, that maybe there were things he could do that would help, that it could be worse?

She knelt beside his chair and took his hand in hers, laying it next to her cheek. "I'm not going to try to cheer you up. But I'm available to talk—all of us are—when you're ready. And if you don't want to be alone at night, just let me know." She left the room and quietly closed the door.

*****

At dinner two days later, Anne related what she'd learned at her and Chuck's visit with the doctor earlier that day. After recounting facts about the diagnosis and treatment, Anne stopped and looked at Chuck. "I'm just charging ahead. Is that OK?"

"Yeah, it's fine. I'm avoiding talking about it, but I know I should understand all this sh— stuff," he said, not looking up from his plate.

So she went on, describing the symptoms and adding, "Chuck has early-phase degeneration in the right eye—he doesn't notice any problem with that eye yet—and intermediate degeneration in the left eye. That's the one that has blurriness. As the degeneration continues, he may have difficulty recognizing faces, and he may need more light for reading or whatever he's doing."

"Is there any treatment, or way to slow the degeneration?" asked Patty.

"Yes, his doctor gave us a list of recommendations. I'll put it on the island, so the rest of you can look at it too. Chuck hadn't read it when we went to see the doctor, so

I read it to him and had a few choice words about his head-in-the-sand attitude. The main recommendation is to have regular eye exams, because things can change quite suddenly. He needs to take this special vitamin formula, eat right, and avoid too much direct sunlight. Oh, and he should wear sunglasses and a wide-brimmed hat to protect his eyes from UV light."

"Gonna look like a goddamned movie star," Chuck mumbled as he buttered his bread.

"I just remembered I have a friend who has macular degeneration," said Patty. "He's about your age, Chuck—and it went away about a month after he started taking the vitamins. I don't want to minimize this," she went on. "Naturally, you're anxious about it, but it sounds like it could be a lot worse than it is. You could have many years of pretty good eyesight ahead of you. Good enough to continue painting for a long time."

"Or," he said, "it could get really bad in a couple of months, and I wouldn't be able to paint at all. That's a real possibility too." He glared at her.

"Well, you can focus on the positive or the negative," said Lionel. "And I'll bet what you chose will affect the outcome."

"Sorry, guys," said Chuck, getting up and picking up his dishes. "I know you mean well, but you're not the one facing blindness. I'm not feeling very philosophical right now. I'm mad as hell!" He took his dishes to the kitchen, and they heard them clattering into the dishwasher.

They sat mulling over Chuck's situation and his reaction to it as Karina brought in apple crisp.

Anne said, "Of course he's angry and upset. We just have to let him be that way for a while. If he gets stuck in it, then we can try to help him get some balance back."

"Well," said Lionel, "this is exactly the kind of thing we knew could happen eventually to any of us: serious physical issues. And it's part of why we wanted to live together, and not face these things alone. So here it is, and we have to figure out how to deal with it, for ourselves and for each other."

An hour later, Anne went into the kitchen, where Mikhail was preparing his shopping list for the next day and contentedly rearranging things in his new work area. She noticed that he liked to touch the cooking utensils and look through the cupboards, as if he still couldn't believe his good fortune.

"I've been researching macular degeneration, what's happening to Chuck's eyes," she said. "I don't think I'll ever get used to the internet, how much information there is and how easy it is to get! Anyway, I've found out that diet can help. So I've printed out some articles about nutrition for you. Maybe you could incorporate some of this into your menu planning and cooking." She slid a few sheets of printed materials across the island to him.

"Yes, I will read carefully and make all the changes I can. I'm glad to know there is a way we can help. Is very sad, this news."

"It is, but it may not be as bad as he thinks it is. And life is about change, so we need to help each other when difficulties come along. Good night, Mikhail."

Karina's New Job

In the middle of March, Karina answered an ad she found on Craigslist. A nurse was wanted for an elderly man who was at home, bed-bound. As requested, she emailed her credentials, and a reply came back right away. A Mrs. Augsburgh asked if Karina could come for an interview the next day. The address was near a bus route, and Lionel told her that the address was in a very nice neighborhood called Washington Park.

Karina arrived a little early and walked around the neighborhood of big old houses with huge lawns and lush gardens. Precisely at three thirty, she rang the doorbell. A minute later, no one had answered, so she rang again. She began to wonder if she'd mistaken the time and was debating what to do when the door opened.

"Hello. You must be Karina. I'm Mrs. Augsburgh. Please come in. I'm sorry to keep you waiting—I was on a phone call that I couldn't end when you rang the bell." She had the phone in her hand. "Let's go in the kitchen, where we can chat. I'll make some tea."

She led the way through an enormous dining room with ornate furniture and heavy swagged draperies, then through a butler's pantry and into the kitchen, where she motioned to Karina to sit down in the breakfast nook. Karina didn't know whether to take off her coat or not.

Mrs. Augsburgh kept up a steady flow of conversation. "I'm glad you could come so quickly for an interview. We need someone who can start right away. We have four nurses, three on an eight-hour shift, and one on the weekend. But one of them quit suddenly—very inconvenient. I certainly won't give him a good reference!"

As she talked, she turned on an electric teakettle and got cups out of the cupboard. "My father—actually, he's my father-in-law—anyway, he's been bedridden for several months now, since he had a stroke. We don't want to put him in a convalescent home. He's not going to convalesce, after all, and those places are so dreadful. So we've arranged full-time care for him here." She placed a cup of hot water in front of Karina and offered a box of Lipton tea bags. "So, tell me about your background. From your résumé, I'd say you're overqualified for this job."

"I was educated at best nursing school in Russia—at that time, the Soviet Union—and I worked in emergency room for twenty years at two hospitals in Moscow, one where the diplomats and high-level government officials go. My husband and I have been in US for few months, and I am still learning about requirements for nursing here. Probably I will not go to school for three years to get degree I already have, even though US degree would allow me to work as RN here. I may change my mind, but I am preparing to be certified as nurse's aide. You could say I'm overqualified, but I would say that I like taking care of people." She smiled at Mrs. Augsburgh, who returned a perfunctory smile.

"Well, we certainly couldn't pay you as an RN, since you aren't one—at least as far as the US is concerned. We're offering the rate for a nurse's aide. You would be working eight a.m. to four p.m., Monday through Friday. Two weeks of unpaid vacation a year, illness to be covered by arrangement with the other nurses. There's really not very much work. Just making sure that he doesn't get bedsores, feeding him, watching for another stroke. He hasn't improved much since the stroke last November, and I don't expect him to. I'll take you up to meet him and the evening nurse, Amparo. I think I just heard her come in." They retraced their steps to the foyer and proceeded up a grand staircase lined with a worn Oriental rug and down a dark hall to a large bedroom, whose door was open.

"Hello, Amparo. This is Mrs. Azerpov . . ."

"Azarov, said Karina, smiling.

"Oh, sorry, Mrs. Az-a-rov. She's from Russia and hasn't been here very long. She's interested in taking Lewis's place." Amparo smiled at Karina and said with a heavy Filipino accent, "Welcome to Seattle, Mrs. Azarov. I, too, am new to this country."

"Come meet Father." She crossed the room and stopped beside a huge four-poster bed containing a wisp of a man. "Father, wake up, I want you to meet Mrs. Azerpov. She'll be taking Lewis's place."

Karina was startled at how fast things were moving. Mrs. Augsburgh talked as though an offer had been made and accepted.

Mr. Augsburgh opened his watery blue eyes and turned his head toward them, regarding Karina. "Hello, my dear. I'm very pleased to meet you. I will miss Lewis, but I'm sure you're a very nice person. I try not to be too much trouble."

Amparo looked at him fondly and said, "You are no trouble at all, Mr. Augsburgh. No trouble at all."

"Well," Mrs. Augsburgh said, "let's go downstairs and finish our business, shall we, Karina?" She led the way back to the foyer. They stood in front of the door, Karina still in her coat. "Do you have any questions for me?" the woman said. "If not, you may start tomorrow. I'm favorably impressed with you, and I think you'll do fine."

"I would like time to think about your offer, Mrs. Augsburgh. This is first position I have applied for, and I don't know what questions I have. I would like to go home and think about it and call you tomorrow. Would that be all right?"

"Certainly. Just don't take too long. Good jobs are hard to find, and I can't wait forever. Thank you very much for coming this afternoon." She opened the front door, and Karina stepped out. She turned to thank Mrs. Augsburgh, but the door was already closed.

On the bus ride home, Karina tried to make a mental list of the pros and cons of the offered position. She didn't like Mrs. Augsburgh, but perhaps there was something in her life that made her—what was the English word?—unsympathetic. Or maybe she was just one of those rich people who thought their money entitled them to treat other people badly. That house looked like something out of *Downton Abby*, which she and Mikhail loved to watch. But why did Lewis leave suddenly? She wished she could talk to Amparo before making her decision.

She gave her impressions to everyone at dinner.

"Well, what are the positive aspects of this, Karina?" asked Patty. "From what I've heard, I wouldn't touch it with a ten-foot pole. I don't think this is a good prospect for you. I'm sorry not to be more encouraging, but I think you could do much better."

"Well, I liked Mr. Augsburgh. Maybe I did not have enough time with him to decide whether to take the job, but I go on intuition. I'm not very . . . rational."

Mikhail was nodding vigorously, his mouth full of salad. Karina laughed at her husband and went on. "I liked Amparo. Seems like nice person, fond of Mr. Augsburgh. Would be much easier than working in emergency room. I do not have much to do here, and I would be earning some money for classes, or for starting business, if Mikhail wants to do that. So those are the positive reasons."

She could tell that the others were doubtful. But after sleeping on it, she called Mrs. Augsburgh and accepted the position.

*****

Karina soon discovered that her job was not demanding at all. In fact, it verged on boring. So she took advantage of a lot of spare time by taking nursing courses online, using a laptop she and Mikhail had decided to purchase. The Augsburgh house had Wi-Fi, so Karina spent several hours of her shift immersed in the requirements for a certificate as a nursing assistant. She already knew a lot of the course content, but some was newer information, and English was a second language, so it was challenging enough.

She also enjoyed talking with Mr. A. His lucidity varied, but when his mind was clear, she would read to him. "Shall I read newspaper to you, Mr. A?" she asked him one day after he'd finished his breakfast.

"Oh, no, my dear. Thank you, but it's too depressing."

"One of my housemates told me about electronic newsletter that only has good news. I receive that every day. Shall I read the topics to you, and see if anything sounds interesting?"

"Well, I'm willing to try. It's very kind of you, Karina."

She got her laptop and settled in the chair next to his bed. "Here are topics for today: one about youngest female Olympic boxer. They are making movie about her, and people are contributing online to help them make movie. There is article about how Americans think in different ways about the environment. They want some places to be untouched, wild and natural, but they know these places have forests and minerals the world needs. Then there is article about"—she read from the screen—"'using computers to map the genome of a virus'—I don't know what that means—and how that helps scientists understand basic things about biology."

"Let's try the one about the environment, if you don't mind," he said, smiling at her.

Gradually, she learned to read a few paragraphs and then stop and ask him a question, to assess his interest and see if he was following. Sometimes she'd suggest another topic. He was too polite to say he wasn't interested. Perusing the shelves of her house's library, she discovered a collection of short stories by Russian authors, which she brought along with her one day.

"I used to read fiction, in college," he said wistfully. "I enjoyed it immensely, but then I thought I shouldn't waste my time. I should study things that would help me in my career."

"Are you sorry you stopped?"

He smoothed the binding on his blanket and looked out the window. "Oh, yes, that was one of many regrets. What did all those months and years of business get me? Money, but that's about all. I didn't pay enough attention to my wife, and now she's gone. I didn't pay enough attention to my son, and it seems to me he's going right down the path I followed."

"Do you talk with him about your regrets?" Karina asked, aware that she might be overstepping her bounds.

"No . . . no, I haven't. I don't know why, really. Perhaps I don't want him to know I feel I wasted my life, that I neglected my family."

"But he would want to know your feelings. If he didn't feel neglected, he would want to tell you. If he did feel neglected, you would feel better if you told him your regrets. Is that not true? I think he would want to know how you feel about your life, where you are proud, what you regret. It's important for children to hear these things from their parents. At least, that is what I think. We have no children, so I cannot speak from experience, except what my mother told me on her deathbed. She said, 'Be loving.' I don't always know how to do that, but I try, every day." Karina felt she might have become too personal "I think I have tired you, Mr. A. I will let you rest now and I will do my homework."

Sex Education

Patty had no substitute-teaching jobs for a couple of days. One morning, she went to the neighborhood library and looked through the teen section, selecting a couple of novels she thought might give a young man an idea of how teenage girls think. She took them into their home library, where Lionel was sitting beside a stack of books about sex and relationships.

"My God!" he said. "What I would have given for this much information when I was Jeremy's age,"

"Yes, me too," Patty said. "Don't you think if they read some of this, kids would be more comfortable with the opposite sex, have fewer hang-ups than we had?" She dropped down into a chair opposite him.

"I think it would help a lot. But you know how it is. The first time you do something—anything—you don't know how to do it, and you worry about whether you're doing it right. When you're a teenager, it's so important to fit in, not to look stupid or whatever."

"Not just when you're a teenager. Most of us spend our whole lives trying to keep up appearances. It's nice to get older and realize that doesn't matter so much."

"If it doesn't matter so much, why are you fussing about Anne thinking you're messy, Patty? What's all that about?"

Patty twisted the afghan fringe around her fingers. "Oh, that's just old stuff. I've been thinking about that, trying to figure out where it comes from. One thing that occurred to me is that sometimes Anne reminds me of my mother. Maybe it's the way she wears her hair. I'm not sure what it is, but occasionally when I'm around Anne, memories of my mom come to me. She was always after me about something, so all those feelings come up, even when Anne isn't being critical at all. I think she's right— I *am* projecting my stuff onto her. Good lord, sixty-nine years old and I'm still dealing with my mother! Does this ever end?"

Lionel laughed. "No, I think we work on ourselves right up until the day we die. Isn't that what it's all about, getting rid of the stuff that keeps us from really enjoying life, from relating to people in a loving, helpful way?" Lionel closed the book he'd been reading and put it on top of the stack for Jeremy. "I look at these books, and I think about all I didn't know about sex and relationships, not just as a young man, but as an adult. All I missed because I was ignorant, or misinformed, or scared, or inhibited. It's sad. And it's too late now. Guess I just have to wait till the next incarnation," he said with a rueful smile.

"What happened to your marriage, Lionel? Do you mind my asking?"

"No, I don't mind. I was very straight-laced, even prissy, you might say, as a young man. I fell in love with Greta because she was everything I wasn't— spontaneous, uninhibited, open to anything. I thought she'd loosen me up. But it turned out she was a little too loose. She got bored with me and had an affair with one of my colleagues. We divorced after five years, and I just retreated into my shell. In my fifties, there was a woman, a possibility . . . but I didn't have the courage to pursue it, made all kinds of excuses about why it wouldn't work."

"You said you think it's too late. Too late for what?"

He looked surprised. "Too late for a sex life, of course. I'm seventy, after all."

"Well, maybe," she said, "but if you had it to do over again, would you do things differently?"

"Of course I would! I've chastised myself for years for being too fearful, for missing out on relationships *and* sex, on such an important part of life."

"Well, at our age, we probably wouldn't have the kind of sex that twentysomethings would have, but I'm not ready to give up the idea totally. You said yourself it's important to let go of what keeps you from enjoying life fully, so maybe you should rethink this part of your life." She stood and straightened the afghan on the back of her chair. "Anyway, I hope Jeremy will get something out of all this. I look forward to hearing about his reaction. Time to finish my laundry."

*****

Lionel stayed in the library, enjoying the early spring sun pouring through the windows, and mulled over their conversation. So Patty was still interested in sex. That gave him more to think about. He moved to the computer, Googled "sex over 60"—and lost track of time. An hour or so later, he went back to the stack of books he'd set aside for Jeremy and began reading with a new perspective.

Finally, tired of sitting, he put on his coat and went out to walk around the neighborhood and ruminate more. So here it was—an opportunity to do what he said he wanted to do: give up the old limiting ways and live more fully. Did he have the guts? It was a lot easier to just pretend that part of life was over. But if he could gather up his courage, how would he start? What should he do first? It had been so long, he didn't even remember what turned him on. Well, some of those books had suggestions for people with sexual hang-ups. He'd go look at what was recommended.

Is that what I have: sexual hang-ups? Yes, afraid so, he admitted to himself. *But I don't have to be ashamed; I just have to figure out how to get rid of them. Which is probably not so easy to do.*

*****

Patty put her laundry in the dryer, then made a cup of coffee and sat down in the breakfast room. Lionel's remark about it being "too late" confirmed her surmise that for him, sex was no longer a part of life. She rarely saw him give that automatic glance of appreciation or sizing up or whatever it was that men involuntarily seemed to do when a woman walked by. He never said anything the least bit suggestive. Until this thing with Jeremy, she couldn't even remember his using the word "sexy."

What causes people to give up on sex, to lose interest? she wondered. Maybe they'd never had good sex, so there was no incentive to keep trying, or they got tired of it after years of disappointment. Maybe there was a self-imposed lack of opportunity, or a doubting of one's attractiveness. Maybe it was just a lack of hormones.

But *she* was still interested, sometimes more than interested. Sometimes her body hummed with desire. She wanted to be wanted—it was such a turn-on to be desired. She longed to touch, to please, to be wrapped in the arms of a man who didn't want to let her go.

Could it be like that for her and Lionel? She found him attractive and she was very fond of him. Why couldn't he feel the same way about her?

She remembered the night she and Lionel and Anne had dinner with Chuck as a prospective housemate. There was an immediate click or attraction or something between Chuck and Anne—Patty could see it. Chuck didn't leer, didn't make inappropriate remarks, but it was clear as she got to know him that he really liked women. The man/woman thing wasn't over for him! But for Lionel, it seemed that sex didn't matter anymore, that there was no more vive la différence.

*****

That afternoon, when Jeremy had finished his piano lesson, Lionel cleared his throat and said, "Jeremy, remember a couple of weeks ago we were talking about dating and sex, and your discomfort about . . . not knowing as much as you'd like to know? Well, I've gathered some books for you to look at—only if you're interested, of course. I don't want to assume anything, or embarrass you, but I thought it might be easier for you to read here than at the library, or at home."

"Uh, well, I appreciate the thought, Mr. B." Jeremy had turned bright red. "Um, I don't know what to say."

"Tell you what. I'll just leave them over there on that table in the library and you can either come early or stay after your lesson and read. If you want to take any of them with you, feel free. You might want to read the library books first, since they'll have to be returned. But keep the others as long as you like. I'm not expecting you to read them, and I won't be hurt or upset if you don't want to. I hope I'm not being presumptuous in doing this. I just thought the information might be useful to you." Lionel got up. "OK, we're finished for today. I'll see you next week." He left the room, so Jeremy could stay or go, as he wished.

*****

Jeremy went into the library and sat down by the stack of books Lionel had pointed out to him. He took them off the pile one by one and skimmed through them, amazed at the variety of information now available to him—privately, with no one to tell him he was a sinner or a pervert, or to rib him about what he didn't know. He was soon lost in the *Kama Sutra.*

Twenty minutes later, he realized he had missed his bus. That was a good excuse for why he'd be late getting home. He could tell his parents that he was working on a special piece for the upcoming competition—which was true—and Mr. Blackburn wanted to spend more time with him. They wouldn't mind, as long as he got his homework and his share of the housework done.

*****

"Jeremy, you're playing exceptionally well today," Lionel said at the following week's lesson. "You almost always play well, but you seem inspired today."

Jeremy blushed. "Thanks, Mr. B. Maybe it's because I feel happy or something. I read some stuff from the books you got me, and I'll read some more today. It's like I'm out of prison . . . or at least I'm not stuck anymore . . . I don't know how to explain it. Anyhow, I feel more . . .

free. I guess that's what it is. And it makes me feel good. You know—everything looks positive."

Lionel smiled. "I'm very glad to hear that, Jeremy. Stay as long as you like. Or come earlier if that works out better. Now, let's hear your competition pieces."

That evening, Jeremy took home one of the teen novels Patty had brought home from the library. It was about a girl who thought she was plain and had only one friend, and who had a crush on the captain of the basketball team. After he did his homework, he got in bed with his novel and a flashlight, so he wouldn't disturb his brother, sleeping beside him. About midnight, his mother quietly opened the door. "I saw the light under the door," she whispered. "What are you reading so late?"

"Oh, nothing, just a novel."

"A novel at midnight on a school night? What's it about?"

"It's about this girl who has a crush on a guy. I'll turn out the light now. I didn't know it was so late." He put the book on the floor and turned out the light.

She sat down on his bed. "That seems like a strange book for a boy to be reading. Why did you choose that?"

"Oh, I thought it would give me some idea of how girls think. You know—what they like and don't like." He plumped his pillow and pulled up the covers.

"Well, you don't need to read novels to know what girls like. They like honest, clean, smart, hardworking boys. Boys who will respect them and be considerate. Lots of girls would like you, Jeremy. You don't have to worry about that. Now, go to sleep. You've got a full day tomorrow." She patted his shoulder and closed the door quietly behind her.

Jeremy thought about what his mother had said. The qualities she'd mentioned that girls would like were ones boys would like in girls too. So was that all there was to it, just be a nice person and the opposite sex would like you? What about manliness, and bravery, and protection and strength? He dropped off to sleep, still pondering these questions

Mikhail's Prospects

Carrying the bags of groceries he'd just bought for that night's dinner, Mikhail stopped at a little storefront catering business, contemplating the HELP WANTED sign on the window. He went in.

"Hello. May I help you?" A smiling middle-aged woman came from the back of the establishment, wiping her hands on her apron.

"I saw 'Help Wanted' sign. What kind of help?"

"We're looking for serving people for large events. Might you be interested?"

"Yes, I look for part-time work. Please to tell me the duties and the pay."

"You have a lovely accent—I'm guessing Russian?"

"Yes, we have been here six months. I have green card. Now I am cook for some old people. Is very nice job, but I have time for more."

"Well, we've been in business for twenty years, so we have an established clientele. We do weddings, receptions of all kinds, business lunches and dinners. Parties of up to a hundred people. We've recently lost two of our servers, so we need to replace them. Everyone gets paid for a four-hour shift, even if it's less than that. Then it's hourly after that. It's usually at least four hours by the time we load the truck, get to the site, unload, and then serve and bring everything back. We pay fifteen dollars per hour for people starting out. Plus, everyone gets a share of the tips. The number of hours per week fluctuates, depending on how many clients we have.

We're busier on weekends and around the holidays, of course." She motioned for Mikhail to sit down at a little bistro table near the door, and sat down across from him. "Could you tell me about your background? Do you have experience?"

"Yes, I worked in hotel kitchen, went to cooking school, owned restaurant in Moscow for many years. My job is twenty hours each week, very easy, pleasant—I like it very much. Very good people. But does not fill my time. So I look for another part-time job."

"It sounds to me like you're overqualified for what we'd want you to do. But you're willing to work at a lower level, in exchange for having a flexible schedule. Is that right?"

"Yes, just right. My employers have told me I can take other work as long as it doesn't . . . He searched for the word.

"Interfere?" she said.

"Yes, thank you."

"My name is Marie Carlisle." She extended her hand. "If you could drop off your résumé and a copy of your green card, I'll talk with my partner and we'll give you a call. And your name is . . . ?"

"Mikhail Azarov." He shook her hand. "I am very pleased to meet you. Will bring the documents soon. Thank you very much."

Mikhail and Karina had a lot to discuss after dinner that evening. He was very excited about his job prospect, thinking about where it could lead him. "If I do well, I will make more money. And I will learn how catering business works in this country. Then maybe I can start my own catering company, instead of restaurant. It would be small, what I could do in our kitchen here. What do you think?"

"Was a very good idea to talk with Ms. Carlisle, Mikhail. If these are good people, you will learn much. Maybe you will want to stay with them, become one of their chefs. Or maybe you will want to start your own business. There will be time to explore different possibilities."

"I will take my papers tomorrow. Maybe I will hear from her soon. I will tell our housemates at dinner tomorrow."

*****

The next day, Mikhail stopped at the caterer's. "Good morning, Ms. Carlisle. Here are papers."

Marie Carlisle smiled at him. "I think you're really interested in this job—that's good for us! Can you sit down and have a cup of coffee while I look these over?" She gestured to the chair he'd sat in the day before. "I'll be right back."

She returned carrying a little tray with two mugs, two spoons, a sugar bowl, and a cream pitcher. "Please help yourself, Mikhail." He stirred two spoons of sugar into his coffee and took in the little office and what he could see of the work space behind.

"Well," she said, "everything seems to be in order, and you have lots of experience, so I'm sure you'll do fine. When can you start, Mikhail?"

"This evening I will tell my employers about my plan, and make sure there is no problem. How often will you need me? Is possible I could work at certain times regularly? Or is each week different?"

"We're approaching the busy season—especially graduation parties and weddings, so we'll usually have something every Friday and Saturday night, and then the occasional weekday luncheon or cocktail party. We'll probably need you more for the evening events—they're usually bigger and we need more staff. Would it be a problem for you to work regularly on Friday and Saturday nights?"

"I think it will not be problem. I do not have to be present every night, as long as dinner is prepared. My wife can finish up if I am not there."

"Well then," said Marie, "welcome to Carlisle Catering! If you can be here Saturday at four thirty, we'll get you started. White shirt, black pants, dark shoes." She stood and offered her hand. "I look forward to working with you."

"Thank you very much, Ms. Carlisle. I will work hard and do good job for you."

Mikhail walked home, proud and elated that he now had two jobs in his adopted country. He found it difficult to believe how much life had changed in the past twelve months.

The Hospital

Early Sunday morning, Anne was awoken by a buzzing sound. She sat up, trying to figure out what the noise was. OK, it was her cell phone, but where was it? She rarely got calls. She turned on the light and looked for the big bag that she carried her life in, hoping to find the phone there. Yes, she could hear it. She dumped the contents on the bed, picked up the phone, and answered, "Hello?"

"Gramma, it's me, Margot."

"Margot! What time is it?"

"It's about two, I think. I don't know what to do. I just got home and there were like three messages on the machine, telling me to call Harborview Medical Center. I called, and they said Mom was in a car accident. She went out with some friends for dinner. They want someone to come down there. What should I do, Gramma?"

"Oh, sweetheart, let me think. Um . . . Tell me the number they wanted you to call. I'll call and see what else I can find out, and I'll call you back. Now don't worry. Everything will be OK. We'll be together soon—you won't be alone. Wait, I just need to get some paper . . . OK, now I'm ready." She scribbled down the number and told her granddaughter, "I'll call you back in a few minutes."

The news was not good. Giselle was in the operating room with multiple serious injuries, and Anne was advised to get there as soon as possible. She crossed the hall to Chuck's room, knocked quietly, and went in. She knelt by his bed and touched his shoulder. "Chuck, wake up," she said in a low voice. "Chuck, I need you to help me." She shook his arm.

"What? Anne, what's wrong?" He sat up, rubbing his eyes.

"Giselle's in the hospital, a bad accident. They want someone to come right away. Margot's home alone, and she sounds really scared. Would you come to the hospital with me? I think I can drive OK. But I don't know how to get Margot. They live way out in the North End, and it would take too long to go get her and then come back to the hospital."

He was up, pulling on his paint-splattered chinos and a sweatshirt. "Let's see . . . We don't know if she has an Uber account, so I'll call a cab while you get dressed, Annie. I'll give them a credit card number so they'll pick her up. Can you get me the address?" he asked, as he fumbled under the bed for some shoes.

She was back in a moment with her address book and her credit card. "I'll be ready in a minute."

She hurried to her room and called her granddaughter. "Sweetie, we're sending a cab to pick you up and bring you to the hospital. It'll be all paid for. Stay inside and watch out the window and go out when you see it arrive. Chuck and I will be waiting for you at the hospital. OK? Can you do that?"

"Yeah, I can do that. I'm scared, Gramma."

"I know you are, Margot. I'm scared too. But let's try to be positive."

Anne left a note on the kitchen island, then they got in the van that the mansioners shared, backed carefully into the alley, and drove to the hospital, ten minutes away.

They found their way to the ER's reception area, where a social worker was paged to come and assist them.

"Would you stay near the door and wait for Margot?" Anne asked Chuck. "I think her hair is purple now. You remember her, don't you?"

"Yeah, I know I'll recognize her. We'll come find you." He gave Anne a hug and attempted a reassuring smile.

*****

Chuck leaned against a wall outside the automatic doors in the unseasonably warm early morning, thinking how good a cigarette would be right now. Even though he'd given up smoking decades ago, he never stopped wanting to smoke. He still missed that little kick that came each time he lit up. His thoughts careened around in his head: *What would it be like to lose a daughter? What would it be like to* have *a daughter, or a son?* Did he regret not having kids of his own? He and Annie had been close for only a year or so, and she hadn't been through anything like this in that time. How would she take it if Giselle died? Well, he'd soon find out. And how would she react when he died, or how would he feel if she went first?

A taxi pulled up, and Margot got out. The harsh mercury vapor-streetlight turned the purple streak in her long dark hair iridescent and reflected off the multiple studs in her ears.

"Margot? I'm Chuck Ganatt, one of your grandmother's housemates. I think we've met a couple of times. Anne's inside, trying to find out what's going on."

"Yeah, I remember you. Thanks for waiting for me." Her voice shook. "I'd like to go find her now and see how my mom is."

*****

Anne was still standing by the receptionist's desk. Harborview was the county hospital and the trauma center for the region. Even at three a.m., many people filled the chairs. Some sat on the floor, others in wheelchairs. Anne turned when she heard the doors open, and extended her arms toward Margot, who rushed into them.

"What's happening, Gramma? How is she?"

"I don't know, sweetheart, but apparently it's very serious. She's still in the operating room."

The receptionist stood and said, "Ma'am, if you folks could just take a seat, someone will be up shortly to brief you."

They looked for three empty seats together but could find only two, with one opposite. Anne and Margot sat down next to a young couple with a crying baby, and Chuck sat next to a man of indeterminate age in dirty clothing, who had a bandaged hand and looked like he'd been in a fight.

They had been there about five minutes when a middle-aged woman, dressed in a navy pantsuit and wearing an ID tag around her neck, appeared before them. "Hello. I'm Sonia Olson. I'm the social worker on duty." She looked down at the clipboard she was carrying. "You must be Margot?" She looked at Margot questioningly, and when Margot nodded, she looked at Anne and said, "So you must be Anne. I'm very sorry to be meeting you under such serious conditions, Margot and Anne."

Anne introduced Chuck, and Sonia said, "I'm going to take you to a more private space, where you can talk with the doctor." She shepherded them through a maze of halls into a small but pleasant room, with artwork on the walls and comfortable chairs, and invited them to sit down.

They had been there just a moment when a tall woman with dark hair, dressed in scrubs, entered the room. "Hello. I'm Dr. Ellis."

Sonia introduced the three of them. "Please sit down, everyone." Dr. Ellis gestured toward the chairs. "I'm afraid I have very bad news for you," she said, looking first at Margot, then at Anne. "Giselle was injured very badly in this car accident. We lost her in the OR—we tried everything, but we couldn't save her."

Margot gasped and groped for Anne's hand. Anne could hardly believe what she'd heard. She stared at the surgeon and then slumped back in her chair.

"I know this is a terrible shock," Dr. Ellis said. "Basically, her head injuries were devastating, and she also had severe damage to her internal organs. We did everything modern medical treatment could do, but it wasn't enough, I'm afraid. I'm so very sorry." Dr. Ellis paused, looking from Margot to Anne. "I don't know if more information will help you or not, but I'm ready to answer questions if you want details. It's our experience that a lot of detail at a time like this is hard to absorb."

There was a long silence.

"Can . . . can we . . . see her?" asked Anne.

"Yes, you can see her. Sonia will take you to where she is. But before you go, you might want to think about how you'd like to remember her. She was pretty banged up by the impact of the accident, and you may be shocked when you see her. On the other hand, seeing her may make her death seem more real, not like she just disappeared one night. Sonia will answer your questions about what happens next and will also help you with the paperwork. You'll need to sign papers as next of kin." She shook hands with all of them. "Again, I'm so sorry to be bringing you this sad news."

After the doctor left the room, Sonia said, "I'll take you to Giselle now, if you'd like to see her."

Anne looked at her granddaughter. "I'm going to go, Margot, but if you don't want to, it's OK."

"No, I want to go too, Gramma."

The two of them followed Sonia, their arms around each other's waists. Chuck was close behind.

When they arrived outside the door, Sonia said, "I know Dr. Ellis told you this, but I just want you to be prepared. She was in a bad accident. There are chairs on either side of the bed. You might want to sit down until you get used to things a little bit."

Margot almost collapsed when she saw her mother. She sank into one of the chairs and slumped forward, her eyes locked on her mother's face, as if searching for some good sign.

Anne sat down on the other chair and looked at her daughter's swollen, bruised visage, the bandages visible below her hospital gown. She was so pale and so still. Mother and daughter took Giselle's cool hands in theirs as they tried to fathom what they were seeing. Anne's only child was gone. Margot's mother was gone. Sonia came in with another chair, for Chuck, and then left them, stunned and bewildered.

"Gramma, tell me this is just a dream," Margot pleaded, her voice shaking again. "I'm going to wake up in a while, and it'll all be over, right? Tell me this is just a dream!"

"I'm hoping the same thing, Margot, but I'm afraid it's not a dream."

The three sat there in silence, Margot and Anne still holding Giselle's hands, still trying to grasp the reality of the situation.

Sometime later, there was a gentle knock at the door; Sonia had returned. "Margot, Anne, I can only imagine how difficult this is for you to take in—no warning like you'd have with an illness. Things are likely to be very surreal for you for the next few days or weeks. We have some materials that I'd like to go over with you before you leave. I think you'll find them helpful." She stopped to see if they were taking in what she was saying.

They didn't say anything, so she went on. "I'll be waiting just over there at the nurses' station. When you're ready to leave, come find me."

It was unclear to Anne how long they sat with Giselle. She didn't want to leave—it seemed so final. But at last, they left her room and sat down in another room with Sonia. She provided them with coffee and showed them what was in the packet. It included information on where the body would go next; how to plan a funeral or memorial service; grief counseling; legal matters that needed attending to. Anne was overwhelmed.

Sonia wrote out the first steps, to help them get started. "Can you get home OK?" she asked. "Should I call a cab for you?"

"Our car's in the garage, and we don't live far away," Anne answered. "We'll take Margot home with us—we have a guest room where she can stay."

"You're welcome to stay here as long as you like. Is there anything else I can help you with?"

In response she got blank looks, and then Anne shook her head .

"I'm so sorry for your loss, Anne, Margot, Chuck. Here's my card. Please call me if there's anything else I can help you with." Sonia shook hands with all three of them and left the room.

"How come I'm not crying, Gramma?" Margot said. "How come you're not crying?"

Anne took one of Margot's shaking hands in hers and held it tightly. "We're in shock, sweetheart. The tears will come later, I'm sure." She took a few more sips of coffee, then said, "OK, I think I can go now, if you're ready, Margot."

Margot nodded.

"I think I'm OK to drive. Chuck, just tell me if I'm losing it, and we'll pull over and get a cab."

*****

"Would you like anything to eat?" Anne asked her granddaughter when they'd made it home safely.

Margot shook her head.

"OK, I'll take you to your room. But you can come to the kitchen anytime and get whatever you want." She led the way up the stairs to the guest bedroom. "You know where my room is, the next door down. Come get me if you need anything. Shall I stay and tuck you in, like I used to when you were little?"

"Yeah, I'd like that, Gramma. Uh, do you have a T-shirt or something I could sleep in?"

"Sure, I'll go get something. There's a new toothbrush and towels and everything in the bathroom." Anne left and returned shortly with one of her nightgowns and a T-shirt. "Take your pick, sweetheart. I hope you can sleep."

Margot kicked off her shoes, stripped off her Nirvana T-shirt and tight black jeans, and got in bed wearing Anne's nightgown. Anne sat down on the bed, smoothed Margot's hair back from her face, and kissed her forehead. "I don't mean to treat you like a little girl, Margot. I know you're a young woman now. I just kind of revert to how I used to take care of you, since I've seen you so little these past few years. Try to get some sleep. We've got a lot to figure out in the next few days."

"Gramma, why did this happen?" Margot's voice trembled. "Was it because Mom and I were always arguing? Is that why she went out with her friends—to get away from me?"

"Margot, this accident had nothing to do with you—don't even think that! All teens disagree with their parents. It's natural, and there's absolutely no connection between your mom's death and your relationship with her. It was an accident. So don't put a guilt trip on yourself, sweetheart. The loss is hard enough." She smoothed Margot's hair again and gave her another kiss.

Chuck was sitting on Anne's bed, waiting for her. He stood when she came in and took her in his arms. "What do you need, Annie? Shall I make you some tea? Do you want to be alone, or would you like me to stay?" He held her close and ran his fingers through her disheveled gray hair.

"I don't know what I need, Chuck. Would you just sit beside me on the bed for a little while?"

She lay down, and he covered her with an afghan and sat down beside her, propped on a pillow. Anne stared at the ceiling for several minutes and then asked, "When does it get real? Right now it seems like a bad dream, but I know I'm not going to wake up from this. It's only going to get worse. My biggest worry is how it will affect Margot. I know she and Giselle loved each other, but they didn't get along. Maybe it was just the adolescent-rebellion thing—God knows I had plenty of that with Giselle!" She paused, hands over her eyes. "I guess I'll just have to watch and see how she reacts, and try to help. I don't know her very well, because Giselle didn't bring her around very much. I volunteered to babysit when she was little and stay with her when she was older so Giselle could have some time off from the single-parenting job, but she rarely took me up on it. Did she hate me so much? What kind of a parent was I that my daughter kept my grandchild away from me?" Tears streaked her cheeks.

"Annie, Annie," Chuck said softly, taking her hand and squeezing it gently. "I really doubt you were a bad parent. You know Giselle had a chip on her shoulder, and you did your best to get around that, you tried to have a positive relationship with her. You'll probably never know why she didn't respond. Maybe she would have in time. But you have to go on from here. Don't get stuck feeling guilty about something you probably couldn't have changed. Focus on Margot and trying to help her."

Anne continued to stare at the ceiling, her hand limp in his. Then she turned to him and said, "You're such a good friend—more than a good friend, but a friend too. Thanks for going with me and for your good advice. I'll try to follow it. Now go to bed. I'll be all right." She kissed his hand and feebly attempted a smile.

It was already getting light, and she couldn't sleep. Thoughts, memories, and questions rioted through her head, interspersed with the muffled deep bong of the grandfather clock in the front hall: the half hour, the hour, another half hour . . . She needed to call Margot's school and tell them she'd be out for a while. She'd need clothes. Where was Anne's copy of Giselle's will? Who was legally responsible for Margot now? Should they have some kind of service? What kind? Giselle had been a firm atheist, but what about Margot? What would be meaningful for her? Do I have enough money to take care of her? Would she want to live here? Could she live here?

Long Lost

When Lionel heard the doorbell Monday afternoon, he realized that in his preoccupation with the accident, he'd forgotten to call Jeremy and cancel their lesson. He invited Jeremy to sit in a chair rather than at the piano bench. "I'm afraid I'm not able to pay attention to your lesson today, Jeremy. I'm sorry I forgot to call you. You know Anne, one of our housemates?"

Jeremy nodded.

"Well, her daughter was killed in a car accident Saturday night, and Anne's granddaughter, Margot, is staying with us while we try to straighten everything out. Her father's apparently not in the picture. So I'm kind of preoccupied." Lionel rubbed his forehead. "But you can stay and practice, if you like. You've come all this way, and I'd hate for it to be for nothing. It would probably be good for me just to listen for a while. Take off my teacher's hat. But if you don't want to, if you'd rather go work on homework or something, please feel free—"

"Oh, no, if it would make you feel better to hear something, I'd be glad to play," he said, moving to the piano, his face full of concern. "Anything in particular?"

"No, whatever occurs to you would be fine."

Jeremy thought for a few moments, hands on his thighs, then began a Chopin piece.

Oh, this child, this young man, thought Lionel. *How did he know what to play? How did he discern the sadness and yet the peacefulness of this nocturne?* Lionel rested his head against the back of the chair, eyes closed.

He opened his eyes at the last note and saw Margot in the library, peeking around the corner, tears running down her face. She disappeared as soon as she saw he had noticed her. Jeremy, his back to the library, played for another fifteen minutes.

Lionel got out his handkerchief and dabbed his eyes. "Thank you, Jeremy. That was just what I needed. Very healing."

Jeremy nodded. "Sure, I'm glad you liked it. If there's anything else I can do, Mr. B, just let me know."

"Thanks. I'll do that. Now just make yourself at home—stay or leave, whatever you like. I'm assuming we'll have our regular lesson next week. I think I'm going up to have a nap."

*****

Jeremy played on for another half hour: songs he'd learned when he first started taking lessons, hymns, favorite classical pieces. Then it was time to go home.

"You play really well."

Startled, he turned around to find a girl about his age slumped against the wall, her crossed arms clutching her midsection. Her hair was caught up in a messy ponytail, and her pale, pretty face was sad

"Oh, uh, thanks." He stood up. "I'm Jeremy Freeman, one of Mr. B's students."

"I'm Margot."

"Oh, uh, Mr. B told me about your mom. I'm really sorry." He looked down at the floor. "I know that's kind of a lame thing to say, but . . . I don't know what else to say. Sorry." Then he looked at her and said, "I know it doesn't make up for losing your mom, but you're lucky you have some really nice people to live with, or take care of you or whatever." He slipped on his jacket and picked up his backpack. "Well, it's time for me to catch my bus. Bye."

She gave a little wave, and he left.

*****

That evening, Margot was in the living room with her grandmother and the other housemates to discuss a memorial service for Giselle. Just as they were about to begin, the doorbell rang.

"I'll get it," said Margot.

She opened the door, and there stood a well-dressed middle-aged man, with dark hair and dark eyes.

"God, you look just like her!" he said. "Margot?"

She nodded.

"Margot, I'm your father."

Margot gasped, then stared, then slammed the door in his face.

*****

Anne saw Margot run through the hall and up the stairs. "What on earth?" she said.

She went to the door and opening it found a man she had always liked but hadn't seen for fifteen years. "Mark! Come in, come in." She gave him a big hug. "I'm so glad to see you again!"

"Well, I'm not sure Margot's glad to see me! But it's wonderful to see you too, Anne. You look great."

"Thank you, Mark. My ego could use a little boost right now. Come in. Let me introduce you." She led him into the living room.

"Everyone, this is Margot's father, Mark Nevins. Mark, these are my housemates." Anne introduced everyone, and Mikhail went to get another coffee cup. "Well! I don't know where to start," said Anne, sinking into her chair.

"Then let me start, Anne. An old friend of Giselle's and mine called me. Giselle must have told her where you lived, because she knew. I'm sorry to drop in like a bombshell. I thought about various options: call, write, email. But I knew I wanted to come in person sooner or later, so I decided to just come and try to make the best of it. I expect it'll take a while for Margot to get used to the idea of having a father around—after she didn't have one for so long." He looked down at his hands. "But I'm really hoping she'll be willing to give me a chance. The only plan I had, Anne, was to come talk to you and get your advice." There were worry lines on his forehead, and his shoulders were hunched, as if he were expecting an attack.

"Well, let's try to sort out what we need to do right away, and then go from there," Anne said. "We were just sitting down to plan a memorial service for Giselle. Do you have any thoughts about that, Mark?"

"I'd like to be there, if that's OK with Margot and everyone. But other than that, I don't feel it's my place to be involved in this conversation. I loved Giselle. I was ready to marry her when we found out she was pregnant, but she turned me down . . ." He sat up taller. "Sorry, this isn't the time to go into all that. It's just that I've been rehashing a lot of old stuff since I got the news, and . . ."

He paused. "Anyway, if you'll just let me know when and where the service will be, I'll be there. Here's my card. You can reach me by email or my cell. I'm staying at a B-and-B over on Broadway. I'll just leave now and let you folks get on with your planning. But I hope to spend more time with you after the service. I've got a lot of catching up to do, and I want to be involved in Margot's future, in whatever way I can."

Anne walked with him to the door.

"Anne, I'm really sorry about Giselle. I know this is a huge loss and shock for you and Margot."

She gave him another hug, and he left.

Anne climbed slowly up the stairs. She knocked on Margot's door and went in to sit beside her, where she was slumped on the bed. "He's gone, Margot. He didn't want to intrude on our discussion tonight, but he wants to come to the memorial service." She waited to see if Margot had anything to say and then went on. "You're getting hit with a huge amount of emotional stuff. It's got to be very difficult, I know. But we'll support you, we'll help you get through it. It's hard for me too."

"Parents are really undependable, you know?" said Margot, frowning. "My mom goes off for dinner with friends and never comes back. My father never bothered to be a father and then he shows up out of the blue! What kind of parents are those?" Margot twisted a strand of hair round and round her finger.

Anne put her hand over Margot's. "Sweetie, those are legitimate questions, but I don't know how to answer. And I think it might be a while before you get some answers that make sense to you. But meanwhile, we have to go on, difficult as that may be. I'm going back to talk with the others about the memorial service for your mother. I'd like you to join us, but if you don't want to, we'll just go ahead." She squeezed Margot's hand and went back downstairs.

"I don't know what she'll do," Anne said to the group who looked up expectantly from their seats in the living room. She sighed. "Let's just go ahead. Giselle did make a will, and she gave me a copy. I have power of attorney, and I'm to be Margot's legal guardian. I don't know what would happen if Mark challenged that, but let's not worry about that now. Giselle wanted to be cremated and to have her ashes scattered somewhere on Puget Sound. Other than that, she didn't leave any instructions."

"What would be most helpful for you, Anne?" Lionel asked. "It seems to me that memorial services are more for the living than the dead. As long as you don't do something you know Giselle wouldn't have liked, I think you should do whatever's meaningful to you and Margot."

Anne leaned back against the sofa cushions. "There should be a time for people to say what they'd like to say about Giselle, the things they'll especially remember about her. And I'd like music. Will you play, Lionel?"

He nodded, "Of course I'll play Anne. I'm happy to."

"And will you do the food, Mikhail?"

"Yes, yes, I am already having ideas. Happy to do the food, Anne."

Margot sidled into the room, eyes downcast. Anne patted the seat beside her. "Here's a seat, sweetheart." She summarized what they'd talked about so far.

"I want to know if Mom will be there," Margot said.

There was a long pause and then Patty said, gently, "What do you think, Margot? Do you think she'll be there, one way or another—her soul or her spirit or something like that?"

"Yeah, I do." Margot glanced up at the group and then resumed looking at her hands, folded in her lap. "I just wondered what the rest of you think."

There was another long pause. "Well, *I* think she'll be there too, Margot," said Patty. "It's not like she disappeared completely just because her heart stopped beating. She's in another world now, or another reality, but it takes a while to leave this one, even without a body. So I think it's very possible you'll feel her presence from time to time. At least, that's what I believe."

No one said anything for a while, and then Chuck said, "I'm not very good with the words, Margot, but I believe what Patty just said. People don't just disappear. They continue, or go on, or however you want to say it, but in a different way."

Lionel leaned forward, arms resting on his legs. "We Buddhists—and a lot of other people—believe in reincarnation, that the soul comes back for repeated earth lives, and gets a chance to . . . um . . . try again, do better the next time around. Something like that."

"Well, it sounds like we all think she'll be there," said Margot. "So I'd like it to be something she'd like. A nice place, flowers, music. And a time when we can tell her . . . what we didn't say . . . before."

They decided to hold the service Saturday afternoon.

Worries

Karina was beginning to get the feeling that Mrs. Augsburgh didn't really want her father-in-law to get better. Karina had suggested a different diet—more vegetable soups and easily digested foods—and volunteered to cook them, but Mrs. A had demurred. Karina had also asked to be present at the doctor's next visit; she had a number of questions for him. But Mrs. A always scheduled his visits after Karina's shift was over. Then there was the matter of Mr. Augsburgh's variable level of alertness. On the days the doctor was coming, he was more present, a bit livelier. But on the other days, he was groggy or asleep. Karina began counting the pills that could account for the grogginess. Sure enough, on the day before and the day of the biweekly doctor's visits, only one pill was given. On the other days, he was given two.

Karina and Amparo always chatted for a few minutes as one nurse was leaving and the other beginning her shift. As she was putting on her sweater Tuesday afternoon, Karina said, "Amparo, do you always give Mr. Augsburgh the same dosage of this prescription?" She held up the bottle. "One a day?"

"Oh, yes, that is what Dr. Benson prescribed."

"Well, it's very strange. I've noticed that more than one pill per day is missing from the bottle. How do you think that could happen?" Karina handed her the bottle.

Amparo looked baffled. "I don't know . . . I am very careful with the medications. I write down everything I give him."

"Does Mrs. A come into his room when you're not there, Amparo? I think she is giving him more than doctor prescribed."

Amparo gasped. "Oh, no, Karina. She would not do something like that!"

"Well, how else to explain the missing pills? Do you know if she comes in when you are not there?" Karina asked again.

"Yes, sometimes I am fixing something in the kitchen, or calling home. There have been times when I come in and she's visiting him."

"He would not know she was giving him extra dosage. He cannot count how many pills he has had and when. And besides, he trusts her."

"Karina, what are you suggesting? This is very bad!"

"Let's try something, Amparo. Stop giving him this medication, except on the day before and the same day Dr. Benson comes. If she is giving him a dosage, then he will get right amount. She will never think to count pills, and probably will not notice number isn't going down as fast as it was. Then we can see how Mr. A responds. This isn't critical drug. It is just to help him sleep, so worst that could happen is he does not sleep as well. But I think we will find he is less groggy and more alert, and still sleeps well. Does she know that you keep record of when you give him medications?"

"No, it is something I do for myself. I keep it in my purse."

"Well, continue to record. And we will start recording how he responds, see if he is more alert."

"Karina, this causes me much worry. I cannot afford to lose this job, and if I am accused of not following the doctor's prescription, I would never get a nurse's job again!" Amparo was wringing her hands, her forehead creased with worry.

"Yes, it could be a risk. I understand, Amparo. Maybe there is another way. Let me think tonight, and we will talk again tomorrow. Would you count the pills to verify that more are disappearing than should be?"

"Yes, I can do that after Mr. and Mrs. A go to bed. They are very regular, always in bed by eleven o'clock."

That evening as dusk fell, Mikhail and Karina sat on the sofa in their apartment. He settled back, his head on the sofa and took her hand. "So much good luck is coming our way! I have worked for Ms. Carlisle two weeks now. She likes me, and I see how the business works, how improvements could be made. I am thinking I could start my own business one day. I am excited thinking about it and tell myself to go slow. There is no rush." He smiled at his wife. "How was your day?"

"Yes, we have good luck, and I am very happy that you like both your jobs." She squeezed his hand, but her face wore a tight expression. "I have problem, Mikhail." She snuggled closer to him, still holding his hand. "You know I do not like Mrs. Augsburgh." She looked up at him, and he nodded, his face taking on a look of concern. "I think that she"—Karina chose her words carefully— "does not want her father-in-law to get well. She keeps me from talking to the doctor and won't listen to my suggestions. Now I have discovered that she gives him more drugs than doctor prescribed. I am almost certain she is doing that, and I'm trying to know how to be sure."

"What will you do if you find it is true?"

"I don't know yet. I want to hear your thoughts. The nurse who comes after me, Amparo, she was shocked when I told her. She doesn't want Mr. A to get wrong dosage, but she is afraid to lose her job. So I try to prove what I think without involving her. What do you think?"

The frown on Mikhail's forehead deepened. "If you are right, you should not work for this woman. You must quit."

"But I can't just leave Mr. A. What will happen to him?"

Where's Home?

Anne was at Giselle's apartment with Margot and Mark to see what needed to be done there. They started by cleaning out the refrigerator, then moved on to making piles of things to take back to their house and piles to go to Goodwill or Value Village. "Margot, why don't you go through all your things and pick out what you want to have with you for the next few months, what you'd like to store—like winter clothes—and what you're ready to part with," said Anne. "That's a place to start. And then after that, take a look at your mother's personal things—clothes and so on—and decide what you'd like to keep for yourself." Margot disappeared into her room.

Chuck stood, hands on hips, surveying a room in which every surface was covered with things. "What are we going to do with all this shit?" he said quietly. "Half of this stuff we already have, and the other half no one needs!"

"Yes, I know," said Anne, rubbing her forehead. "We had many conversations about Giselle's spending habits. I've been reading a book about how the brain works, how we make choices, and I'd say the part of Giselle's brain that responded to instant gratification was stronger than the part that weighed the consequences of spending more money than she had." Looking around, Anne said, "This is a legacy I'd rather not be dealing with, but I suppose we have to. Before we leave, don't let me forget to look for Giselle's paperwork: bills, bank statements, credit card records, stuff like that."

Anne's cell phone range, and she dug it out of her bag. "Mark, how are you?" Pause. "We're hanging in there, still kind of dazed. At the moment, we're at Giselle's apartment, Chuck and Margot and I, trying to sort through a mountain of stuff." Pause. "Well, sure, it would really help if you could shuttle bags of stuff to Value Village for us. We'll be here at least until lunchtime." She gave him the address.

Margot came into the living room with some commando boots, a big container of bubble bath, and an armload of clothing. "I can get rid of this stuff, Gramma. I don't know why I got this bubble bath. I hate the smell."

Anne's heart sank. "Is that all you can part with, sweetie? Everything in your room is something you want to put in your room at our house?"

"Yeah, Mom got me a lot of cool stuff, and I want to keep it." She went into her mother's room.

Anne looked at Chuck, who shrugged his shoulders. "Maybe she'll change her mind when she can't get out of bed because there's no room. I'd say you'd better put this discussion on the back burner for a while, Annie."

Anne sighed, then went back to work on the kitchen cupboards. She found a stash of grocery bags and began filling them with perishables.

Thirty minutes later, there was a knock at the door. Chuck opened it to find Mark holding a large bag from Top Pot Doughnuts, a big carton of cardboard boxes beside him on the sidewalk. "Good morning. I figured you might need some boxes, so I stopped by U-Haul and picked some up."

"Good thinking—we hadn't gotten that far. Come on in, Mark. We've just about finished with the first pass through the kitchen, and we're trying to get up the energy to start on the rest of the place."

Anne came to the door. "Oh, what a dear you are!" Let's sit down for a moment. She took the doughnuts from him, and he dragged in the carton of boxes.

"Where's Margot?"

"She's in her mother's room, choosing what she wants to keep." Anne nodded toward the door.

*****

Mark stood in the doorway. Margot was in front of her mother's dresser, holding something and crying. "Hello, Margot," he said softly. "Is there some way I can help?"

She shook her head.

"Would you like a doughnut?"

She shook her head again. "I gave her this necklace when I was ten," she said. "I took a class at a bead store and made it for her." She wiped her eyes on her arm. "What're you doing here?"

"I volunteered to help with whatever needs doing. Anne said she could use someone to take stuff away, once you've sorted through it, so I brought some boxes. I wish I could take away the hurt, Margot, the sadness. But I can't, much as I'd like to."

"Well, don't think you're just going to come in here and, like, take her place after all these years!"

"I don't think that. I know I can't replace your mother," he said. "But I can step up to my responsibilities as a father. I should have found a way to do that sooner." He put his hands in his pockets and then took them out again. "We can talk about all that later. I'm not making excuses for myself. It's just not exactly a straightforward situation."

She wouldn't look at him, just wiped her eyes again.

"Are you sure I can't get you a doughnut?"

She shook her head, and he went back out to sit down with Chuck and Anne at the kitchen table.

"Man, I haven't had a nice greasy, sugary doughnut for ages—what a treat!' said Chuck, wiping the sugar from his fingers and reaching for his coffee. Thanks, Mark! They don't buy junk food at our house."

"I don't buy it very often either, but once in a while it's just the thing, isn't it?" he said, taking a jelly-filled doughnut out of the box.

Anne was eating her doughnut with a preoccupied look on her face. "Giselle told me a few months ago that she was thinking of moving. She was kind of vague about why, and I didn't ask. But I remember that she said the lease was up on September first. So what are we going to do with this place for the next few months? I imagine it would be costly to try to break the lease."

"Maybe there's some provision in the lease about death," Mark said. He sat there for a second. "But here's another idea. Why don't I live here, at least until the lease runs out?"

"But why would you do that?" Anne asked, startled.

"Well, I can live anywhere. I work from home mostly. I'm an independent contractor. Like I told you the other night, I've been thinking about how to make contact with Margot, and nothing's keeping me in Palo Alto. This might be just the thing. I won't have to go looking for an apartment, it's already furnished, and it would help out you and Margot."

"What exactly do you do, Mark?" asked Chuck.

"I write software applications. That's how I met Giselle. We were both in the same program in college. Anyway, I've got very salable skills, and companies like to hire contractors—so they don't have to pay benefits and it's not hard to lay them off. I don't have any trouble finding work. I've got a good strong résumé and references. And I can live pretty much anywhere. So this could work out really well. You wouldn't have to make decisions about all this stuff right away. We could move it out over time. I'm sure that would be less stressful for Margot. For both of you."

"But what about your home in Palo Alto? Don't you have things to pack and move . . . and all that?"

"Yeah, there're some things I'd want to ship up here, but not much. I'm not really into having a lot of stuff anymore. I can fly down there and have everything wrapped up in a week."

Anne was rubbing her forehead again. "That sounds like it could be a good situation for everyone—almost too good to be true! But are you sure, Mark?"

"I'll think about it some more, but I'm pretty sure. I'd already made up my mind to move back to Seattle. Margot's my biggest priority now, and I have to have a place to live, so this looks like a good option. If we could just clear out one bedroom, and the personal things you and Margot know you want to keep, I could deal with the rest of it."

"Let's see what Margot thinks," Anne said.

*****

Anne sat down on the bed next to her granddaughter. Margot was looking into space, with Giselle's jewelry box

111

in her lap. "Margot," Anne said, "it's possible we don't have to make all these decisions about what to take and what to keep as soon as we thought." She explained what Mark had proposed. "I'd like you to come out and join us, so we can get your input. Another thing we need to talk about very soon is school."

"OK." She got up and followed Anne to the kitchen table, choosing the seat across from Mark. He pushed the doughnut box toward her, and she absently chose one filled with jelly.

"So, Margot," Anne said, "have you given any thought to school and whether you want to stay where you are or move?" She took a sip of her now-lukewarm coffee.

"Um . . . a little. I have a couple of good friends at my high school, but not a lot. We're not in the popular crowd," she said, tossing her hair. "It's kind of scary to think of starting in a new school. But it's also like having another chance to be somebody else. No one will know me or have any opinions about me, so I can be whoever I want." She took a bite of doughnut. "Also, at Shorewood, everyone knows my mom died and I'll feel like people are staring at me all the time."

"So, there are pros and cons to both staying and moving?" Mark asked. She nodded, not looking at him. "What about the schools themselves? What do you like about Shorewood, and what's good about the other possibilities? You could go to Holy Names. It's right in Anne's neighborhood. Or Garfield is close by. But I haven't lived here for quite a while. What are those schools like now?"

"Garfield's got a great music program," Anne said. "I don't know much about Holy Names, but I don't think we could afford a private school anyway."

"Well, let's not rule it out," Mark said. I think I could make it happen, if Margot thought she'd be happy there."

"You'd pay for me to go to a snooty private school?" She looked at him, wide-eyed.

"Well, not a snooty one," he said. "But the private part isn't an issue."

"We're in the Garfield attendance area," said Anne, assuming that Margot would be living with her, "so if you want to go there, it's just a matter of signing up. But there're only about four weeks of school left. Does it even make sense to transfer to a new school at this time of the year? If you want to stay at Shorewood and finish the year there, we'll just figure out a way to get you back and forth to school."

"Or she could stay here with me," said Mark, "and get to school the way she has been. But you don't have to decide right this minute, Margot. It's a lot to think about, so why don't you sleep on it."

Margot looked from Mark to Anne, bewildered. "Yeah, it's a lot to think about. I definitely don't want to decide right now."

The Memorial Service

The rest of Anne's week was filled with arrangements for Giselle's memorial service. Since the weather forecast was propitious, and she didn't expect a large crowd, the housemates had decided to have the ceremony outside in their yard. Patty brought her considerable organizational skills to bear, and everyone was happy to take orders. Anne was in charge of notifying people, and she and Margot wrote the obituary. Mikhail was in charge of food. And Patty managed the rest: ordering folding chairs, dishes and glassware, napkins, and a small sound system.

Friday, the flowers started arriving. Karina was in charge of placing them throughout the house and attaching the cards to the arrangements. By noon on Saturday, a profusion of flowers filled the downstairs, and Karina was trying to group the overflow on a table in front of the chairs Chuck was setting up on the lawn. They expected from thirty to fifty people.

Anne bustled out, dropping another arrangement on Karina's table, then stopped in front of Chuck, hands on her hips. "Where're your hat and sunglasses? You know you're not supposed to go out in the sun without them. Honest to God, Chuck!"

"Why in hell are you so mad at *me* for going blind? Jesus, Anne! Why don't you just calm down."

She suddenly felt deflated, as if she were getting smaller and smaller as she stood there. "Sorry ... I'm sorry, Chuck. I'm overwrought and taking it out on you. It's because I'm scared. Now that Giselle's gone, who'll take care of me if you can't, or Patty or Lionel?" she said. She was suddenly furious again. "It's happening, Chuck, what we've known for fifty or sixty years was going to happen. We're getting old—frail and sick are coming soon. Now it's really here, in our faces. I'm not mad at you. I'm just scared." She turned and ran into the house.

At two p.m., the chairs were full and two dozen or more people stood behind them. Margot stood at the microphone. "Hi. I'm Margot, Giselle's daughter. Gramma said I could go first because I'm nervous. I can't talk, but I wanted to play a song for my mom, one that she really liked." Margot sat down, arranged herself and her cello and began Schubert's "Ave Maria."

People dabbed at their eyes, discretely blew their noses, studied their surroundings—did what people do on emotional occasions when it isn't quite clear what behavior is appropriate or how much they should reveal about what they really feel. When Margot finished, Anne rose to stand in front of the group.

"I'm Anne, Giselle's mother. A dancer, not a word person, but I'll do my best. Perhaps some of you have seen the ballet *Giselle*. It's sad, the heroine dies. But she was beautiful, she loved and protected her prince, she didn't succumb to hate and vengeance after a betrayal. It was for these traits that I named my daughter Giselle.

"I've had so many memories these last few days: Giselle's first steps, her first words, watching her imitate the dancers when I'd take her to class or rehearsals. She grew up to be a very strong person and she gave me a lovely granddaughter." Anne wiped tears away with her hand and took a deep breath. "I can't believe she's gone . . ." Here she broke down completely.

Chuck was immediately at her side, handing her a handkerchief and putting his arm around her waist. He nodded to Lionel, sitting in the front row, who rose to continue.

"Anne and Margot invite anyone to speak who would like to. They'd like very much to hear your remembrances of Giselle. After everyone's spoken, we hope you'll all come into the house for refreshments."

A tall man with thinning hair and stooped shoulders stood up. "I'm . . . was . . . Giselle's boss. This is a sad occasion, but it's also a time to remember what was special about the person who's . . . no longer with us. I worked with Giselle, off and on, for over ten years. She was very smart, an excellent programmer, and a very hard worker. Her team could always depend on her to go the extra mile or do whatever it took to get the job done. That's not easy to do when you're also a single parent. Margot, if you apply yourself to your music like your mother applied herself to her work, we'll see you at Carnegie Hall."

He was followed by tributes from other coworkers and friends, and fifteen minutes later it was over. People moved toward the house, chatting quietly.

*****

Mark watched his daughter from a distance. He didn't want to intrude, but he wanted to be ready to support her if he could find a way. She had a plate of food and seemed to be responding well to the awkward condolences that were coming her way. Lionel was playing the piano, and Patty, Karina, and Mikhail were circulating with trays of petit fours and canapés.

In the kitchen, he found Anne with Chuck's arms around her. "How can I talk to people? How can I eat, when my daughter's dead? Our last words were harsh, and the words before that. No matter how hard I tried, they were always harsh."

"Annie, darlin'," Chuck said into her hair. "You've got to pull yourself together for Margot. I'm not telling you not to grieve, just not now. Can you do that?" He stroked her back.

"OK . . . yes . . . I'll try." She touched his cheek, then wiped her eyes and took a deep breath.

Mark slipped out without their seeing him and went to find Margot. She was sitting in an armchair beside Lionel's piano bench, a plate of food untouched on her lap. He sat down beside her. "Hi. How're you doing?"

She looked at him blankly. "I don't know. I feel kind of numb. And dumb. I don't know what to say to all these people."

"They know that, Margot. We're all searching for the right thing to say, and there isn't one. We're all just doing our best. So don't worry about it. Your music was very moving—a lot of people were crying. I'm sure your mom would have been very proud, and she would have enjoyed it a lot."

Margot just sat there, gazing off into space. Then she looked down at her plate and said, "Thanks. Want some food?"

"Don't you want it?"

"No, I'm not hungry. I'm sure it's good though. Mikhail's cooking is really great." She handed Mark her plate.

An hour later, all the guests were gone and the house was littered with plates, half-empty cups, crumpled napkins, and half-filled serving platters. Mark collapsed in the living room with Margot and the housemates.

"I'll just rest for a little bit," said Patty, "and then start in on the cleanup."

"Let's all rest," said Lionel. "Then we can all help."

"It was a very nice . . . affair," said Mark. "Giselle would have loved all the flowers. I remember I brought her flowers the first time we went out. That was a smart move on my part, even though I didn't know how much she loved flowers." He smiled at the recollection.

"What was she like when you met her?" asked Margot.

"Oh, very lively, opinionated, headstrong. And very attractive. I really fell for her."

"So what happened? How come you left?"

Mark looked at his hands and then at Margot. "Well, it's a long story, and I don't think this is the time to go into it. I will. I want to know what your mother told you about me, and I want to tell you how the situation looked to me. But I don't want to do it now. I don't think it would be appropriate."

"Your music was really beautiful, Margot," said Patty, changing the subject. "I love the cello. Maybe you and Lionel could play some duets for us sometime. And didn't I hear something about a music camp this summer? Are you going?"

"I don't have any money, so I guess not."

"Don't worry about the money, Margot," said Mark. "If you'd like to go, I think I can work it out. Tell me about it."

"It's the first three weeks in July some place in the San Juan Islands. The kids who've gone say it's really awesome, and they learn a lot and get a lot better. They have a big concert at the end, and people play solos and stuff. It sounds really cool. My orchestra teacher told us about it."

"Well, Mark, if you're saying you'll pay for the camp," said Anne, "that's a really generous offer. I don't think I can afford it, and I know it would mean a lot to Margot. We really appreciate it."

"Yeah, thanks," said Margot, glancing briefly at her father. The room was silent for a moment.

"For dinner we are having shrimp . . . louie . . . you call it?" said Mikhail. "Is all ready, except I must put shrimp on and serve. Would you like to eat later—maybe six thirty?"

"Sounds good to me. That gives us time to finish cleaning up and to chill some wine," said Chuck. "I think we could all use a glass of wine tonight. I'll take care of that. Mark, you're welcome to stay."

*****

Anne wandered around the house after dinner, touching the flowers, breathing in the scent of lilies, carnations, roses. Pausing in front of an arrangement in the living room, she said, "Mark, would you like to take some of these flowers to the apartment?"

He stood looking out a window while Margot paged through some music on the piano.

"Thanks, Anne, but I think it would be a waste. I'm flying back to California tomorrow to pack up my stuff. I'll be back on Wednesday. I've arranged for someone to drive my car up, and I'll just use a rental until it gets here. So the only issue is getting Margot to school from here while I'm gone. I'm hoping she'll live with me in her own room until school's out, and then we can decide where to go from there." He looked at Margot, eyebrows raised. "What do you think, Margot?"

"I want to stay here," she said. There was a long pause.

"Well, I don't know how possible that is," he said. "While I'm gone, I think you should talk with your grandmother about what options you have, and their pros and cons. There's a lot to think about, and other people to consider too." He picked up his jacket from the back of the sofa. "It's time for me to go. I've got an early flight. Thanks for including me."

Anne accompanied him to the door. "You're trying hard, Mark, and I know she'll appreciate it one day. But it's probably going to be hard for a while. Giselle wasn't an easy person to be around, as you know, and she was Margot's role model. So maybe we should expect some bumpy periods."

Mark gave her a hug. "We'll work it out. She's got a great grandmother for a role model too."

*****

The next morning, Patty found Lionel sitting in a director's chair on their little backyard patio. "Isn't it lovely? I do get tired of the gray, but it makes me appreciate the sunshine so much more," she said.

"Yes, we Seattleites really appreciate sunshine," he said, with a perfunctory smile.

"May I join you, or are do you need some solo time?"

"No, I'd enjoy some company." He gestured to a chair across from him. "Please, have a seat." He waited while she settled herself. "I've been mulling over regrets and how to deal with them. Giselle's death, and Anne's remorse about their . . . estrangement got me thinking.

You know how you're supposed to say 'I'm sorry,' 'I love you,' and 'Goodbye' to the appropriate people before you die?" She nodded, leaned back in her chair, and waited for him to go on. "There's one big apology that I've resisted making for thirty-five years. I just push it away when it comes to mind. But at my age, I can't do that anymore, I need to get on with it." He looked over at her, and she nodded again.

"About five years after we were married, my wife had an affair with one of my colleagues in the math department—I think I told you that. Everyone but me knew for quite a while, and then when she told me she was leaving me for him, I was pretty upset, even though I tried to act . . . 'adult' about it. He was younger and not tenured yet, and when he came up for tenure, I blocked it. I ostensibly had good reasons, and I tried to keep it from looking like I was getting back at him, but I was. He left for another university and he did get tenure, but way later than he should have. He should have had it when I blocked him." Lionel sipped from his coffee mug. "For years, I've felt righteous—he deserved it. But grudges are heavy, you know? I'm tired of carrying it around. And the old 'two wrongs don't make a right' adage stares me in the face every time the memory comes up. So, I'm trying to resolve to apologize to him."

"'Trying to resolve'? You can't apologize until you've forgiven. And you haven't really forgiven him, right?" Lionel didn't answer, so she went on. "Does he live around here?"

"I think so . . . No, I know he does. He retired, and they moved back to Seattle. Greta died two years ago. I saw the obituary in the paper."

Patty considered this information, and then asked, "What do you think forgiveness is?"

He thought for a while. "I think it means the wrong you did is . . . maybe no longer an issue between you and the . . . forgiver. Not that what you did was OK after all, but that the thing you did is no longer something you're hanging on to. Both of you acknowledge that a wrong was done, there's regret, and then you move on. You don't keep replaying it and wallowing around in it. Does that make sense?"

"Yes, I think it does. But why is it so hard to acknowledge you've done something wrong, and why is it hard to forgive? I've thought about this a lot—I've screwed up and had to apologize a lot! So I've had some practice." She laughed at herself. "It's all about fear of losing love, isn't it? At least the apologizing part. We don't want to admit we did something wrong because it would make us less lovable."

"Sure, but at the same time, people respect someone who acknowledges that he screwed up. People might be more willing to like you or love you if you can apologize for your mistakes. As for this specific apology that I need to make, I don't think I'm doing it because I want him to like me. It's a matter of respect: respect for him, and respect for myself because I've tried to do the right thing. It was wrong of me to block his tenure application."

"This sounds very cerebral, Lionel."

"Well, I think I've forgiven him for having an affair with my wife, in the sense that it's no longer an issue between him and me. But there's still some emotional baggage around this, and it finally occurred to me that it's about the loss. I've been alone all this time, afraid to try again. They took something away from me." His eyes began to fill. "Greta's and my relationship wasn't all that great, in retrospect, but I thought it was at the time. It was their fault I suffered a loss, but it wasn't their fault that I didn't get over it and move on. That was my fault." He dabbed at his eyes.

Patty reached over and took his hand, and they sat, soaking up the morning sun beside the brilliantly green grass and the blooming azaleas, pondering mistakes and forgiveness amidst the faint smell of daffodils.

Man to Man

Lionel climbed the steps to Chuck's studio later that afternoon, a cup of coffee in his hand. "Am I interrupting you?"

"Not at all, Lionel. C'mon in and have a chair. I'm just messing around."

"I've been wondering how your eyesight is, Chuck. But I've been afraid to ask."

"Sorry about that. I was pretty bummed when I first got the news, and I guess you and Annie and Patty got the brunt of it." He leaned back against his worktable and continued cleaning some brushes.

"I'm trying to get adjusted to the idea of going blind," Chuck said, "and it helps that there actually hasn't been much deterioration yet. So I go back and forth, waiting for the inevitable and getting depressed, and then hoping it won't happen and feeling good about what I've still got." He put the brushes away and stacked some small framed canvases against the wall. "I've been trying some things, trying to get a feel for what it might be like. The other day, I put on some really strong reading glasses that made everything blurry. Then I experimented to see what kind of effects I could get. You know, it was kind of interesting. And I Googled 'blind painters'— you wouldn't believe how much came up. One of the things I found was this poem. I copied it out." He reached into his shirt pocket and pulled out a crumpled sheet of paper. "Here, read it. It's about how Monet's blindness might have affected his painting in a positive way." He handed it to Lionel.

Lionel held the paper in his lap. When he was done reading, he gazed out the window at the tub of purple and yellow tulips on the patio. "What can you say about a poem like this?" he said. "Nothing that would do it justice. The images are so vivid, the artist's reaction to his predicament so . . . unpredictable, and yet so insightful."

"Yeah, I had the same reaction. It gave me lots to think about," said Chuck. "One thing I can tell you though. I don't take my eyesight for granted anymore. Every day I think about what it would be like not to see clouds, not to see colors and be aware of how they make me feel, not to see other people's artwork, the expressions on people's faces. I really have a fresh appreciation for my sense of sight.

"Hey, want to walk over to Broadway with me? I thought I'd go get some sunglasses. I'm tired of Annie nagging and, besides, we've got to take advantage of a rare sunny day."

"Sure, I'm up for a walk," said Lionel. "I'll just get my jacket."

They walked through Volunteer Park, enjoying the rhododendrons and azaleas and the broad expanses of lawn. "Bless the city council that hired the Olmsteds all those decades ago," Lionel said, gesturing at the surrounding park. "What a legacy! How many people have enjoyed this place all these years, do you think? Must be thousands."

Twenty minutes later, they were at a drugstore on Broadway. Chuck scanned a rack of sunglasses as he slowly turned it. "Jesus, how many styles of sunglasses does the world need?"

"Here's just the thing," said Lionel, grinning and holding up a pair of granny glasses.

"Yeah, right," said Chuck, putting them on. He looked in the little mirror on the turntable and said, "Makes me look like an ancient John Lennon." He took them off and put on a pair of aviators.

"Oh," Lionel said, "so you prefer the ancient Tom Cruise look—right out of *Top Gun.*"

They both laughed, and Chuck put the glasses back on the rack. "How about these?" He put on a pair of black horn-rimmed glasses.

"They'd go well with this," said Lionel, plucking a fedora off a nearby shelf and plopping it on Chuck's head. "You're supposed to wear a hat too." The gray hipster hat, of some synthetic made to look like woven straw, was too small.

"Man, I'm really stylin', dontcha think, Lionel? The women are going to be all over me!"

"Dream on," said Lionel, laughing. "I don't think that's really your look. How about this?" He handed Chuck an Aussie-style hat, with one side of the brim folded up. "And try these on too."

Chuck put on the hat and some wraparound glasses with a mirror finish. "God almighty—sign me up for the Australia highway patrol! The hat's OK, but find me some different glasses."

As they walked down Broadway on their way home, Chuck kept checking his reflection in the store windows. "Yeah, I think this'll get Annie off my back," he said, adjusting his hat brim.

"Chuck," Lionel said, "I've been wanting to talk to you about something, a personal matter." He hesitated. "It's, uh, kind of awkward. I don't really know where to begin."

"Well, spit it out, man. We're pretty good friends. I doubt there's anything you could say that would shock me."

"You know how I've talked about not caring so much anymore what people think, and how I've said I wanted to get rid of my inhibitions?"

Chuck nodded.

"Well, I'm finding out it's not so easy after all. It's about sex. I haven't had much of a sex life, and I'd pretty much given up on that, but I've been thinking maybe it's not really too late. I want to do something about it, but I don't know how to start. God, I feel like a teenager!"

"Well, I agree with you that it's not too late. It won't be like it was, or could have been, when you were younger—I'm sure you know that. But it's still pretty good, just different. You mind my asking why you think you're inhibited?"

Lionel was encouraged by Chuck's matter-of-fact response and continued. "No, I don't mind. Talking about it might help me sort it out. My family was very straight-laced. They weren't particularly religious, but they were pretty traditional in their values. Sex wasn't talked about, except to make it clear that it wasn't supposed to happen before marriage. 'Good girls' didn't do it, and 'good boys' didn't ask them to. And yet I could see it was going on all over the place. I had the same urges as any normal guy, and I'd listen to the locker-room talk, and . . . it was just really confusing. So, like a dutiful son, I followed the 'rules' and tried not to be attracted to girls, to suppress my wants and desires. I think I did such a good job that I can't get out of that box now."

"You were married, weren't you, Lionel? What happened there?"

"She finally got bored with me and had an affair. So we divorced. But you know, I think the reason she married me to begin with was because I was a challenge. She knew I was uptight, and she wanted to reform me, or make me over or something. But she didn't appreciate how deep my inhibitions were. We had sex, but it wasn't the wild-abandon passionate stuff you read about in novels."

They turned the corner and walked up the hill toward the park. Lionel was so absorbed in the conversation that he barely noticed the profusion of tulips and daffodils blooming around them.

"You've had lots of experience with women, haven't you, Chuck? I don't want to pry, but I can see that women like you and you're easy around them. How did you get that way?"

Chuck pulled a long piece of grass from a rockery they were passing and wound and unwound it around his finger as they walked. "Our backgrounds are sure different, Lionel. Maybe your family was a little uptight, but it sounds like they tried to teach you right from wrong. My old man was a drunk, and my mom hung out with whoever would buy us some groceries. My brother and I pretty much had to fend for ourselves. No one was telling us any rules. So I just followed my instincts. And there were plenty of girls who were willing to do the same." He dropped the grass in a shrub and glanced at Lionel. "My mom did do right by me on one thing, though. She made sure I knew about condoms and what a huge problem it was for a girl to get pregnant. Even though I was pretty wild, at least I was careful about that."

They walked through the park, Lionel feeling exposed and uncomfortable.

"I feel bad I don't have any advice for you, man," said Chuck. "I'm racking my brains, but let me think about it some more." He gazed up at the old brick water tower above the reservoir. "Have you considered going to some kind of therapy or something?"

"Yes, and I'll consider that more if I can't get anywhere on my own. But I thought I'd read some books and do some research on the web first, and see what I come up with." He chuckled. "Jeremy and I are reading the same stuff."

"I looked at those books the other day. There's some good information in there—I read some stuff I was glad to learn."

They walked on, companionably.

"You know," Chuck said, "it's pretty amazing that we're even having this conversation. How many men would be so . . . honest? I don't think I've ever heard men have an adult conversation about sex. It's always bragging, locker-room stuff, et cetera."

"Yes, I was just thinking the same thing. I think we can talk like this because we're older and we aren't trying so hard to impress everyone like we used to—or at least like *I* used to. And because I trust you. I know you're not going to make fun of me. I know you're not going to be gossiping about my insecurities."

"Yup," said Chuck. "This conversation is just between us." He slapped Lionel on the back as they climbed their porch steps.

Mixed Feelings

That night, Lionel was awakened by a scream from Patty's room. He jumped out of bed, ran across the hall to her door, which was slightly ajar, and knocked gently. "Patty, are you all right?"

"Lionel, is that you?" called a quivering voice. "Come in."

He saw her, in the dim glow of her alarm clock, sitting straight up in bed. "Are you OK?" he asked quietly, moving across the room. "I heard a scream or something."

"I had a nightmare, and it woke me up. There was something in the room. It was like a little wispy cloud, and it was floating toward me." She shivered and clasped her arms across her middle. "It sounds so silly! How could that be scary? But it was!" Her voice still shook. "That cloud—it was like a presence. I'm just petrified!" She reached for his hand. "Would you stay with me for a while?"

"Sure," he said, sitting down on the bed, and taking her trembling hand in his. "Do you want to tell me more about it?"

"No, not now. Maybe in the daylight. It was such a strong feeling that something or someone was in the room. Have you ever had a feeling like that?"

"Yes, a couple of times. It was just so unusual, which made it a little scary, but there was no feeling of . . . malevolence or evil or anything like that, and I was really curious about the whole thing. So it didn't bother me too much."

"I'm sorry to be so . . . wimpy, but I've still got gooseflesh all over my body."

"It's OK. No need to apologize. I'll keep you company till you feel safe. Scoot over." He took some pillows from the adjacent chair, propped them against the headboard, and sat beside her, feet on the bed.

She took a deep, ragged breath and lay back, close to him. A few moments later, she popped up again. "Oh, you'll get cold. I'll get an afghan."

She was out of bed before he could protest, crossing to an armoire, from which she removed a cotton throw. She was wearing a thin knee-length cotton nightgown, with little sleeves and a scoop neck. Very fetching.

After spreading the afghan across his lap and legs, she got back in bed beside him.

Now they were both wide-awake. Patty's fear of the nightmare seemed to be receding, and the reality of both of them in her bed in their nightclothes began to loom in Lionel's mind. He wanted to stay, and not just because of the nightmare. He lay there quietly, trying to figure out what to do next, how not to be awkward, how not to make assumptions about the situation, wondering where this strong sense of desire had suddenly come from.

Lionel found himself unusually muddled, as questions and conflicting thoughts crowded into his mind and jostled around. Could this turn into the opportunity he thought he wanted? Was it possible that Patty might want to have a physical relationship with him—or at least try it out?

The clock showed that fifteen minutes had passed.

"Are you comfortable?" Patty whispered.

He didn't reply immediately. Then he said softly, "I'm amazingly comfortable beside you on your bed."

After a moment, she said, "I'm not scared anymore, but . . . I'd kind of like it if you, um, wanted to stay."

Lionel smoothed the bedspread. "I do want to stay, Patty. But part of me is saying, 'Is this wise? What if it doesn't work out?' Then another part is saying 'Are you nuts? You're in bed with a lovely woman, and she wants you to stay!'"

He stayed.

*****

Patty didn't immediately open her eyes when she awoke in the morning. She tried to be aware of how she felt. She hadn't slept so well for ages, and she had a pleasant feeling of languor, of satisfaction. The fright of the nightmare was forgotten in the glowing remembrance that she hadn't slept alone for the first time in years.

But Lionel was gone. She was disappointed. Why wasn't he still there? She clicked out of awareness and into thoughts. Her mind immediately began to examine the possibilities. He was embarrassed—but was it a regretful embarrassment or a happy one? Or maybe he wasn't embarrassed—she knew he was an early riser. Maybe he thought *she'd* be embarrassed or regretful. Maybe he just wanted time to think about their night together and what would come next: How would they be with each other? Would they pretend nothing had happened? Would they talk about it? Would he want to sleep with her again?

Her thoughts turned to her body. Would he be more likely to want to sleep with her if she lost some weight?

She was, after all, about twenty pounds over what she should be, and her doctor was urging her to get more exercise. She was amazed, really, that Lionel seemed to like her body. *Maybe it's just because men are hardwired to like women's bodies,* she thought. Whatever the reason, she wanted to look as good as possible. *Doesn't this ever end?* she wondered. *This deep need to attract the opposite sex?* It was biological, she knew, and the need to attract didn't seem to go away, even when the reproductive capacity did. For most of history, people died before they were too old to have children. But now, with our long life spans, we were stuck with these urges and needs that seemed absurd. Was there anything more ridiculous—or sad—than seventy-year-old men and women trying to look like twenty-five-year-olds?

There was a quiet knock, and a bathrobed Lionel appeared, carrying two cups of coffee. He nudged the door shut and came to the bed, where Patty began piling up pillows for them. In her relief, she gave him a happy smile, which he returned, handing her a mug.

"Thank you," she said. "And good morning."

"You're welcome. And, yes, a very good morning!" Still smiling, he sat down beside her.

"Mmm, coffee in bed," she said.

"All we need are some croissants."

"Yes, that would be nice," she said, settling back against the pillows. "Except for the crumbs. Crumbs in the sheets are not so nice."

They sipped their coffee in companionable silence. Then Lionel sat up and said, "Patty, I didn't even think—do you want me here? I was just so blown away by last night I've been assuming you felt like I do . . . But maybe you don't . . ." He looked embarrassed. "I don't want to take anything for granted."

"Lionel, I don't have any regrets! I'm deliriously happy to hear that you . . . you . . . um . . . don't seem to have any regrets either."

They looked shyly at each other, smiled again, and relaxed into their pillows.

"You know," Patty said, "I could easily overthink this. I've already been thinking too much, wondering this and that, in the ten minutes I've been awake. What I'd like to do is not to think too much, to just *be* instead. Just see how it goes and not worry about it."

"What is there to worry about?" he asked.

"Oh, a million things." She ran her finger around the rim of her mug as she spoke. "What if it doesn't work out? Will you get tired of me? Will you be attracted to someone else, and wouldn't that be awkward? Should I go on a diet and buy some new clothes? All sorts of silly stuff."

Lionel took her hand. "You're right—you're thinking too much. Let's not analyze. Let's just be happy with right now. Let's just enjoy how we feel and not worry about the future." He kissed her fingers.

That night, when they sat on the sofa for their evening meditation, Patty was conscious of their proximity: Were they too close or the same distance they'd always been? Did it matter? Yes, because closeness meant something different now, and it was interfering with her meditation.

So many thoughts, so many more than what was normal for this quiet time in her day.

Margot's Options

Anne was willing to drive Margot to school until they sorted out her living arrangements for the last few weeks of the school year. "I know you want to stay here right now, Margot," she said as they merged into the freeway traffic Monday morning. "But there're a lot of things to think about. First, the room you're staying in is supposed to be for our fifth housemate. We just haven't found him or her yet. Our budget depends on having a fifth person. I can't afford to pay two shares, instead of one."

"I think we should wait to decide until we know how much insurance money there is," said Margot.

"We don't know if there *is* any," Anne said, "let alone how much. Another factor is my housemates. They seem to like you and you seem to like them, but occasional visits are different from living together. It would be up to them to decide if they want a teenager living with us, even if you could afford your share. We all like young people. We want to be around them—we think it helps us stay young. But I can't assume it will be fine with them for you to just move in. It's their decision, not mine and yours." She checked the rearview mirror as she changed lanes. "Next exit, right?"

"Yeah," answered Margot. "You're my, like, guardian or something, aren't you, Gramma? It seems like we ought to live together."

Anne sighed. "Margot, I don't know why your mother didn't want to marry your father. After she left home, she didn't talk to me much about her personal life. But the fact is, you have a father and he'd like to be in your life. If he wanted to, I'm sure he could make a legal stink about the guardianship arrangement. But that's not the way to begin a relationship with you, as he knows very well. I think you should be glad that you have a father as well as an aging grandmother to take care of you." She glanced over at Margot, who was wearing a scowl that looked remarkably like her mother's.

They pulled into the loading area, surrounded by SUVs and vans depositing teenagers in front of their school. "Have you got your bus pass?" Margot nodded. "This might be a difficult day, Margot. As you know from the memorial service, people don't know what to say. They're sorry that you've lost your mom, but they feel awkward. Some will pretend nothing's even happened, because they don't know how to talk about it. But the awkwardness will go away after a few days. People will forget, even though you won't. Be brave, sweetheart. I'll see you at dinner. I volunteer at the day care this afternoon."

Margot got out and moved slowly up the sidewalk toward the building. She turned and gave Anne a quick wave, then disappeared through the doors.

*****

Margot had plenty of time to think on the long bus ride back to Capitol Hill that afternoon. She went back over the various interactions and feelings she'd had that day. People seemed to be looking at her who never had before. Or maybe she just thought they were. Her two best friends had already talked to her on the phone, so it was cool being with them when she could. One guy who was in her biology class told her his dad had died the year before, so he knew what she was going through. He offered to talk with her, if she ever wanted to talk. She didn't really know him, and thought it was . . . what? . . . kind and brave of him to say what he said to her, someone he didn't know. Nice guy. And there was a note on her locker from the school counselor, inviting her to come talk if she wanted to. The worst moment was overhearing two girls bitching in the restroom about their moms. At least they had moms.

Margot got home from school just as Jeremy was arriving for his piano lesson. "Hi," she said, as they walked up the stairs together.

"Hi. How's it goin'?"

"Oh, OK. Hey, sometime could you tell me about the Garfield music program? I'm thinking about transferring next year."

"Sure. Want to talk after my lesson, about five o'clock?"

"OK, I'll see you then." She planned to be there early to listen to him play.

In the kitchen, Mikhail offered her five options when she asked if there was anything for a snack. "Wow, what a choice. I'll take the leftover piroshki, please. Thanks, Mikhail."

From the kitchen window, she saw Chuck walking up the stairs to his studio. She followed and found him taking a beer out of a little refrigerator. "Hi, is it OK if I come in?" she said. "Want some piroshki?" She held out the plate Mikhail had given her. "These are fantastic!"

"Yeah, he's a great cook—we're lucky. Sure, come in and look around, if you're curious. Ever paint?" he asked, taking a couple of piroshki.

"Just the usual grade-school stuff. Why do you like to paint?"

"Mmm. That's a hard one. Why does a horse like to run? Just seems like the natural thing to do."

Margot wandered around the studio as he began stretching a canvas onto a frame. "You've sure got a lot of paintings here, she said. "Is it OK if I look at them?"

"Fine, go ahead. Just ask if you have questions," he said, stapling canvas to one side of the wooden frame.

"Is it hard to paint?" she asked. "How do you decide what you want to paint?" She looked through the canvases leaning against the wall in orderly piles.

"Sometimes it's hard to get it to look like what you want. You just know it isn't right, but you're not sure what to do to make it like you want it. So you have to experiment. Then you sort of get a sense when it's done. And maybe you feel like it's good, for a while, and then after a while, you're tired of it and ready to get rid of it."

"What do you mean, get rid of it? Sell it, give it away?"

"Any of those things, or just toss it in the garbage or take it to the transfer station. You can't keep stuff around forever, especially if you don't think it's well-done and no one else wants it. If you ever want to give painting a try, just let me know. I think everyone should do something creative."

"Thanks. Maybe I will. I like to write. I try to write poems. They aren't very good, but it's fun to write them."

"Well, good for you. We should have a house poetry reading again. We haven't done that for a while. We all bring our favorites. Something someone else has written, or something one of us has written. It's interesting . . . and for me, anyway, challenging."

"Well, I have to go now," she said. "I want to go listen to Jeremy play—he's really good. I'm just going to sit in the library, so he won't know. Thanks for talking to me."

"Sure. Come back any time."

Margot went back into the house and crept quietly into the library, sitting out of sight of the piano. She was impressed with Jeremy's skill in the technically difficult pieces, and with his phrasing and interpretation of the less "flashy" pieces. She was interested to hear his and Lionel's discussion of where improvement was needed or where he had done something particularly well. Maybe she'd get a lot better if she could go to music camp this summer. Practicing her cello was one thing her mom never had to push her to do. Homework, cleaning her room, helping with housework—yes, there had been lots of pushing, but not for practicing. She heard Jeremy and Lionel talking about next week, then Jeremy walked into the library.

"Oh, hi. I didn't know you were here."

"I haven't been here long, I hope you don't mind if I listen."

"No, it's OK. Sometimes I stay after my lesson and read."

"What're you reading? Homework?"

He turned bright red. "Sometimes I do homework, or I read novels. They have lots of different things, and Mr. B said it was fine for me to read here. It's quieter than home. I have five brothers and sisters."

"Wow! I'm an only child—must be really different having all those people around!"

"Yeah, I guess. But I'm used to it, so it doesn't seem different." He sat down as far away as he could get from the stack of books he'd been reading. "So, you're thinking about switching to Garfield? The music program is really good. We have two orchestras, and they even go abroad sometimes. And we have three levels of jazz band. The top band almost always goes to the national competitions. The parents are really supportive. They raise money and stuff like that. Are you going to live here?"

"Uh, I don't know yet. I asked my grandmother if I could live here, but she says it's not her decision; it's a group decision. My dad wants me to live with him. But I don't really know him, so that could be a bummer."

"You don't know your dad?" His eyebrows rose in a surprised look.

She looked down, fiddling with her bracelet. "Yeah, he ran out on us when I was a baby, and just showed up again when my mom died. Maybe he thought there was some money or something."

"Wow, that's really hard to believe! But if it's true, he must be a real jerk."

"Yeah, so anyway, I'm going to try to talk Gramma and her housemates into letting me stay here. If I can, I'll go to Garfield next year. It would be really cool to play in the orchestra there."

"What do you play?"

"Cello. I've taken lessons for about four years. It's the only thing I really like. I'm not very interested in school. But I don't mind practicing my cello. How long have you been taking piano?"

"Let's see, since I was six, so about ten years."

"No wonder you're so good. That's a long time."

"Well, thanks," he said, and then it seemed like he couldn't think of anything else to say. "Guess I ought to get home. Maybe I'll see you next week?"

"Yeah. Well, I hope so. I mean, I don't know if I can stay here or not."

"Good luck—I hope it works out, Margot."

*****

By the third week in April, Mark had gotten settled into Giselle and Margot's apartment and was now meeting Anne for afternoon coffee at the mansion. "Thanks for cleaning things up at the apartment, Anne. I'm glad I didn't have to go through the process of asking Margot about every little thing. She seems to have a grudge against me, so it was probably best that we didn't have to start out by getting into an argument about what to keep and what to get rid of. What a ton of stuff Giselle had! What was all that about, anyway?"

"I don't know, Mark. Giselle seemed to have a grudge against *me*, so we didn't talk much, and it always seemed to degenerate into recriminations." Anne rubbed her forehead absently, her face strained. "Anyway, she was apparently in debt and occasionally asked me for money. But when I saw what she was spending her money on, I balked. I don't have unlimited funds. Which brings up the subject of Margot. I think it would be better for her to live with you than with a bunch of old people. I'm not sure I could give her the attention she should have—not because I don't have time, just because I'm too old, the wrong generation to be raising a young person. And I don't want to put my housemates in the awkward position of appearing not to be supportive, if they'd rather not have a teenager here. Of course, if you weren't in the picture, the whole situation would be different. I'd just have to make do."

Mark reached across the breakfast room table and covered Anne's hand with his. "Your housemates have all been really supportive, Anne. I would never think they didn't want to help out. But I agree with you. I think once we get acquainted, it would be best for Margot to live with me. And not just for her—for me too. I've been out of the picture too long, and I feel guilty about that. I want to know my daughter—not just know her but be a father to her. I suppose it's possible I could have other children, but the odds get worse every year, so I want to have as good a relationship with Margot as I can."

"I've been thinking about this a lot," Anne said, "as I'm sure you have, Mark. Here's an idea—tell me what you think. Let's have Margot stay here, maybe three days a week, until after her music camp in mid-July, assuming my housemates agree. The other four days she could be with you. She could pick the days. I'd think she'd want consecutive days, so she wouldn't be moving clothes and things back and forth all the time. That would give you two time to get acquainted, and some 'spaces in your togetherness,' as they say."

Mark nodded, thinking about Anne's idea. "Sounds like a good option to try. I also think she should eventually get a job, don't you? It's not that I need money to support her—I've got plenty. I just think it would be better for her to see how much work it takes to earn a little money. And the discipline of having to get there on time every day. Well, you know all the things a person learns from having a job."

"Yes, I completely agree. But I think she should be able to choose what she does. We don't have to decide. I was wondering if she'd like to be our lawn-care person. We were going to pay a service to mow and edge, and she might as well have that money, if she can do the work—and wants to."

"But what about the long run?" said Mark. "If she wants to change schools, it would make sense for us to move closer to wherever that is. If she chooses Garfield, I hope it's not just a ploy to stay with you and avoid living with me." He sighed and played with his coffee cup. "I'm afraid she's got the wrong impression about why I wasn't in her life. She hasn't said anything specifically, but I wouldn't be surprised if Giselle . . . led her to believe that I didn't want to be involved. But it was exactly the reverse—Giselle cut me out, made it really clear that she didn't want me around. I could never figure it out. But I shouldn't have agreed. I know that now, looking back. Anyway, here we are. I have to go on from here and hope we can develop a relationship."

"I thought Giselle was crazy not to marry you, Mark." She got up to pour them some more coffee. "It was some kind of 'I'll show you, I can go it alone' thing. Why she needed to do that, I don't know. It made life harder for her and Margot. And even if she didn't want to marry you, she could have let you be in Margot's life. That would have been good for both of them. Well, I guess we'll never know. You're right. We just go from here. I'll talk to her tonight about splitting her time between here and—what do we call it? Her old place? The Shoreline place? I'll think of something."

*****

Margot walked into the kitchen and dropped her books on the island. "Hi, Chuck. Hi, Gramma. What's happening?"

143

"Hi, Margot," said Anne. "I'm just washing some early strawberries."

"Not much going on with me," said Chuck. "What's happening with you?"

"School's a drag," Margot said." My best friend has a boyfriend now, so she doesn't have time for me anymore. I have a ton of homework to catch up on, and it's so boring. And half my stuff is at the . . . other place, so I keep wearing the same things. People must think I'm weird or something."

"So you think people notice what you wear and look down on you for some reason," Chuck said. "And you feel uncomfortable?"

Margot's grandmother placed a bowl of strawberries in front of her.

"Yeah, I guess that's right." She ate a strawberry, and then another. "These are really good—thanks, Gramma. But you know, I don't remember ever noticing if somebody wore the same thing two times in a week. If somebody wore the same thing every day, I'd notice."

"What would you think of that person?" asked Chuck.

"Maybe that she was poor. Or didn't care about clothes."

"I wore the same thing to school almost every day." Chuck bit into a big strawberry. "We didn't have a washing machine, and my mom just couldn't quite get to the laundry once a week. We had hand-me-downs from the neighbors or stuff from the thrift store. I know some of the kids looked down on me and my brother. Maybe that's why we were so wild. But I still had enough friends."

"Well," Anne said, "speaking of clothes, this is a good lead-in to something I wanted to discuss with you,

Margot. I talked to your father today, and we'd like to suggest that you spend three days a week here, and the other days with him until after your music camp. And then we'll see where we go from there."

A frown appeared on Margot's face. Chuck left to work on some sketches in his studio.

"Why can't I stay here, Gramma? There's enough room."

"We've talked about this before, Margot. Your staying here is a temporary situation. Our plan has always been to have five people living here and sharing expenses, and now that we have Mikhail and Karina, we're ready to start searching for our fifth person." Anne straightened the hand towel on the towel rack. "We'd like to have someone who will be with us for a long time. Even if you were living here, you'd only be around for a couple of years. Then you'd be off to college." She sat down on the stool next to the island.

"But that's not the point, Margot," Anne said. "Your father would like to be in your life, get to know you, be a dad. He may not have another child—you may be it. And you should get to know him. It's good for children to have two adults raising them, preferably at the same time, but serially is better than only one. You need to see that people look at things differently, care about different things. You missed out on having a two-parent family, so you didn't get to see a couple interacting, compromising, helping each other, disagreeing. Of course, as a child, your mother missed that too. Maybe if I'd had a partner . . . Well, I didn't. And that certainly shaped Giselle's life. Anyway, you have a chance to have a dad in your life, and I think you should give it a try."

"Why did he show up now, Gramma? Did he think Mom had some money or something? If he really cared about having a kid, where was he all those years?"

"That's something you have to ask him, Margot. He's told me a little about why he was absent for so long, but I think it's better for you to hear it from him. In any case, I can't believe he came back for money. He hasn't asked anything at all about Giselle's estate, and he's offered to pay for your summer camp—and school, if you want to go to a private school. Besides, he told me he has plenty of money. I don't know what that means exactly, but I think you can safely assume he isn't here to try to grab your inheritance, whatever it might be."

"When will I know about that?" Margot asked, taking another strawberry.

"I hope this week. I have to speak to the personnel people at Giselle's office about her benefits and so on. And I need to go to her safe-deposit box and see if there's anything there."

"If there's some money for me, will I get to have it, or will someone else, like, control it?"

"I don't know, sweetheart. If there is any, you probably wouldn't get it until you were at least eighteen, maybe twenty-one. Now, let's get back to your living situation. It's only about three weeks until school's out, and then another month until your music camp. I think that's a good amount of time for you and Mark to get used to each other and work out your routines. I was thinking that if you stay there Monday through Thursday, you can take the bus to school and then he can bring you here on Thursday night and I can drive you to school on Friday. Then you can bus back here for the weekend."

"How about Tuesday through Friday with . . . Mark?" Margot didn't want to miss seeing Jeremy on Monday afternoons. "You could drive me to school Monday and Tuesday mornings. It's better than five mornings, and there's only three more weeks of school. Please, Gramma."

Anne sighed. "Well, I need to check with my housemates to make sure they won't need the car. Assuming that's not a problem, I guess I can do it for three weeks. All right, Margot."

Margot got up and gave her grandmother a hug. "Thanks so much, Gramma!"

The doorbell rang. Jeremy was here for his lesson. Margot went out to sit on the front porch and listen to Jeremy play.

In a little over an hour, he appeared. "Oh, hi," she said, closing the biology textbook she hadn't been reading.

"Hi. How's it going?" He sat down on the steps beside her.

"OK, I guess. Things are kinda up in the air. Gramma wants me to split my time between my dad and here, at least till I go to music camp in July." She studied the chipped black polish on her bitten fingernails.

"It could be worse, couldn't it? I mean, what if you didn't have a grandmother, or a dad? I know you don't know him yet, but maybe he's a nice guy. There's at least a fifty-fifty chance, isn't there?" He fiddled with the zipper on his backpack. "Hey, want to get gelato at Vios?"

They walked the few blocks to the neighborhood restaurant and sat at a sidewalk table, chatting and eating their gelato.

"Well, I've got to get my bus," he said, thirty minutes later. "Nice talking with you. See you next week."

"Yeah, and thanks again for the gelato. See you soon."

He's a nice guy, Margot thought as she walked back to her grandmother's. *Red hair and brown eyes make a nice combination.*

*****

Anne sat down as Mikhail set the side dishes on the table—salad and a casserole of roasted Brussels sprouts.

"Oh man, pork roast!" Chuck looked ecstatic. "Hey, Mikhail, you're happy here, aren't you? If not, you just let me know and I'll take care of it. We got to keep you happy!"

"Yes, very happy, Chuck. We are blessed to be here." He looked at his wife, and they both smiled shyly and nodded as the serving dishes traveled around the table.

"Tell us about your new job with the caterer, Mikhail," said Patty. "The last few days have just evaporated, and we haven't had time to hear what you think of it."

"I think will be very good experience." Mikhail put down his knife and fork. "Ms. Carlisle is very nice and works very hard. She is good with people. But I think she could do some things . . . to make it easier, and to spend less money, so there would be bigger profit."

"Are you comfortable talking to her about your ideas?" asked Lionel.

"Not yet. I must wait until I have more experience and know her better. Perhaps I am wrong. I will be working this Friday and Saturday evenings, and Wednesday for a business lunch, called a retreat. What is this 'retreat'?"

Lionel answered. "It's when a group goes out of the office and away from their usual routine and thinks about how they could do better—like change their procedures, or be clearer about priorities. Or just get to know each other better. It's a morale boost for the employees when the company takes them to a nice place and gives them good food, and they get to talk about how they could be more effective."

"Ah . . . very American. Not very Russian," he said, smiling. "I will try to listen as I serve."

"And how is your job going, Karina?" asked Anne.

Karina sighed. "There is not much to do, and Mr. A is sad. It seems he has given up on life, though he is very nice to staff. The good thing is that I have lots of time to work on my studies. In few weeks, I will be ready to take exam and get my certificate as nurse's aide."

"I was wondering if I could live here with you guys," Margot said, completely ignoring the flow of conversation, "since . . . my mom died. You're really nice, and it would be like having six grandparents." She looked up from her plate and beamed at everyone. "And you've got room."

Anne was speechless. Chuck leaned back in his chair and said, "What do your dad and grandmother think of this idea, Margot? Have you discussed it with them?"

Margot's smile faltered. "Well, I've talked to Gramma about it."

"And what did she say?" Lionel asked, helping himself to some more vegetables.

"Uh, she thought I should live partly here and partly with my dad for a few weeks, and then we could decide."

"Well," said Patty, "Anne hasn't had an opportunity to talk to us about your request. Don't you think it would have been better to let her do that, rather than bringing it up yourself?"

Margot sat up taller and plunged ahead. "She gave me a bunch of reasons why she didn't think it would work, and I just wanted to ask you myself."

"There's a football term for this, Margot," Chuck said. "It's called an 'end run.'" He returned his attention to his pork roast.

Anne had finally gathered her wits. "Margot, we have a house meeting on Wednesday night, and we'll talk about your request then. There was a steely tone in her voice. "Meanwhile, we'll continue as you and I discussed. I'll take you to school tomorrow, and then you'll be with your father for the rest of the school week."

Dinner with Dad

"Margot, I need to tell you how I feel about what you said at the dinner table last night," her grandmother said as she drove.

Margot tried to keep a nonchalant look on her face, though she had been dreading this conversation.

"I felt that you were ignoring what we had discussed because you didn't get what you wanted," Anne said, "and that you were trying to put me in an awkward position in order to have things your way. And I think my housemates felt that too. Is there some other explanation I should consider?"

There was a long silence. Margot was biting her fingernails when her grandmother glanced over. "No, I don't have another explanation," she finally said.

"In my experience," Anne said, "people who try to manipulate others to get what they want don't have many real friends, and they aren't respected or trusted either. I hope you'll think about that if you're ever tempted to try manipulation again." She pulled into the parking lot at Margot's school. "Got your lunch and bus pass? Don't forget you're not coming to Capitol Hill tonight."

"OK, Gramma," Margot said, hoisting her backpack from the floor. "I'll see you on Friday night or Saturday."

"Call and let me know." Anne tucked a stay tendril of hair behind Margot's ear. "All is forgiven. Have a good day, sweetheart."

Margot got out of the van and waved goodbye as her grandmother pulled out of the parking lot. *Yeah, have a good day,* she thought. *No mother, no friends. I have to live with a guy I don't even know—just because he says he's my father. What if he's a jerk—or worse?*

Margot was preoccupied during her classes and paid even less attention than usual. She took her time getting home, finally arriving about five o'clock.

She didn't say anything about the tidy living room and kitchen, the new flat-screen TV, and the big desk with a futuristic chair in front of it. A vase of pink gerbera daisies was centered on the kitchen table, set for their meal.

"Hey, Margot—welcome home," her dad said. "I'm making spaghetti for dinner, one of the three things I can cook. Do you suppose Mikhail would give me some cooking lessons?" He stood in front of a salad bowl, with a kitchen towel tucked into his pants to serve as an apron, a knife in one hard and an avocado in the other. "How was school, by the way?"

"It was OK. Boring as usual. Katy—that's my best friend—she's dumped me for her new boyfriend. Orchestra was the best part today, even if it isn't a very good orchestra. People are more into sports than music at my school." She trudged down the hall toward her bedroom. "I guess I'll practice my cello until dinner's ready."

About six, there was a knock on her door. "Dinner's ready," Mark said.

He was putting the plates on the table as she came into the kitchen and sat down.

"The flowers are nice," she said. "Mom liked flowers. You've probably noticed there's a ton of vases around here."

"Yeah, I've noticed some things, but I'm not sure what to make of them. I could just infer, but it would be nice if you would fill me in. I know this is going to be a tough transition for you, Margot, and I want to make it as easy as I can. So if you can just tell me about your life—what you like and don't like, stuff like that—it would help me a lot. And if there are things you want to know about me, feel free to ask."

She looked up from buttering her French bread. "You said you'd tell me why you didn't marry Mom and why you left us. I'd like to know about that."

Mark sighed and sat down at the table. "I've thought a lot about how to talk about this, and I'm not sure I'll do it right, but I'll try." He took a sip of wine. "Oh, would you like some wine?"

"Sure," she said, amazed. Her mom had never offered her any kind of alcohol. He got a glass from the cupboard and filled it about one-third full.

"Giselle and I had been going together, or been a couple, or whatever you want to call it, for about six months. She was twenty-five, and I was twenty-seven. We were in some of the same classes at UW, but we didn't get together until we met again at Microsoft. She was 'the one,' as far as I was concerned. I hinted at marriage a couple of times, but she ignored me." Mark stopped to put more salad on his plate. "Then she got pregnant. I never could figure out how that happened. She was taking birth control pills, or so she told me. But I didn't always use a condom, and it happened. I take my share of the responsibility. Anyway, I asked her to marry me, and I thought for sure she'd say yes, faced with a pregnancy, *and* I thought she loved me. I had a good job, I was ready to be a husband and a father, and I loved her. I couldn't believe it when she turned me down." Mark had a faraway look, as if he were remembering conversations and arguments with her mom. He took another sip of wine and looked over at Margot.

"She said she didn't want to marry me and she could take care of the baby herself. I tried to reason with her, and I know your grandmother did, but she was determined to do it her way. And she never would tell me why she wouldn't marry me. At one point, I asked her if the baby was someone else's. She said no, but it made her angry that I thought she might have slept with someone else, and it was a good excuse to tell me goodbye. She made it very clear she didn't want any child support and she didn't want me around, 'interfering' in her life, as she put it. I was really pissed. I felt jerked around, rejected, dumped on—you name it. So I left, moved to California, and was angry for years. But I knew about you, Margot. A mutual friend sent me your birth announcement. I knew I had a daughter."

Margot sat with her elbows on the table, her fork halfway to her mouth, through most of this revelation. She didn't know what to believe.

"Would you like some more spaghetti?" Mark asked.

"Oh, it's really good, but no, thanks. I'll have some more salad." She emptied the remains of the salad bowl onto her plate. "I don't know what to say. It's so different from what Mom said. I'm not accusing you of lying, but I've just had this other picture for so long of why I didn't have a father, and, like, what kind of person he must have been."

"I know this is really hard, Margot. So why don't we just take it a day at a time and get to know each other. Don't you think it's better to rely on our own experience, rather than what someone else said?"

She kept eating her salad, eyes on her plate. "Yeah," she said. "I guess so."

A Teenage Housemate

Mikhail passed out plates of chocolate cake as Anne and the other housemates assembled for their regular business meeting on Wednesday evening. Dusk was falling, and the doors were open to the fresh lilac-scented air.

"So, what's on the agenda for tonight?" Chuck asked, settling himself in a comfortable chair, his long legs on an old leather hassock that Anne thought looked like it had come from Turkey about a hundred years ago.

"We need to talk about Margot's request to live here," Anne said curtly. "I would just reject it out of hand, but I told her we'd discuss it. So that's one item." She folded her arms across her chest.

"We were scheduled to talk about finding another housemate, and I think Margot's request fits right in with that discussion," said Lionel. "Why don't we start with a review of the guidelines or criteria, or whatever we're calling it, for making a decision on a new housemate. Patty, do you have the list? You always have good notes about things like this." Anne noticed the smile that passed between Lionel and Patty, and that Patty was sitting a bit closer to Lionel than she usually did.

Patty turned on the floor lamp next to the sofa and opened the blue manila folder in her lap. "Yes, I brought them. Shall I read them?" She looked over her reading glasses to see her housemates' nods. "OK, number one: Shares our values and purpose. Meaning they believe that life is about growth, up until the day you die, growth is hard work and not always pleasant, but we'll keep at it, and we're living together to help each other grow and live more fully. Number two: Is complementary rather than being just like us, in life experience, personality, and interests. And number three: Willing to accept the rules of the house."

"We put this together after we had all found each other," said Lionel, "so we didn't formally go through these guidelines ourselves. This'll be our first time trying to apply it—should be interesting. Mikhail and Karina, you're part of the family now. Do you have any thoughts about how we choose a new person?"

The couple looked at each other. Mikhail shook his head, and Karina said, "Maybe we will have thoughts after we hear yours. If we do, we will speak then."

"Well, how does Margot fit the criteria?" asked Chuck. "Assuming she'd be willing to accept the rules of the house, she's certainly complementary—different from us in a lot of ways." He took a bite of cake.

"She's a *teenager*, for Pete's sake," Anne replied. "There was no discussion of teenage housemates when we all got together."

"Yeah, I know, but maybe we ought to be more open-minded. A lot of times, rules don't work quite the way you thought they would when you try to apply them. So maybe we should reconsider our criteria. Do we want to exclude teenagers? Or people under sixty-five, or over eighty, or what?"

"I can't believe we're even considering this!" sputtered Anne, attacking her cake with her fork. "Are you just pulling my leg, Chuck?"

"No, I'm not, Annie. I just think we need to be open-minded. Are you going to reject the idea out of hand, even if the rest of us are willing to consider it? Would it be too much of an imposition on you, having Margot here?"

Before she could reply, Lionel interjected. "There are lots of issues, all wrapped up together, it seems to me. One is what it would feel like to Anne to have her granddaughter living here. Another is how it would feel to each of us, having a teenager here—none of us ever considered it before. And Chuck brings up the issue of the age of our new housemate. We've always assumed it would be someone in the latter part of his or her life. Maybe we should talk about that."

Patty looked up from her note taking. "Sure, we should talk about it. And why not take it further and consider Margot *and* Mark? Just theoretically, I mean— like kind of a test case. One of the reasons we wanted to live together is because we didn't want to be in one of those places where everyone's the same: a sea of gray hair in the dining room, a fleet of wheelchairs. We have kids on our street and block parties, and neighbors chatting about elections and stuff like that. Maybe it would be good for us to have housemates who are at a different phase in their lives. That's how it's been for most of history, after all: several generations in one household."

"Yes, but Margot and Mark have their own lives to live," replied Anne. "They don't want to be taking care of old people before they have to."

"You don't necessarily know that, Anne," said Chuck. "In a lot of cultures, people are really glad to have grandparents around. It's natural. It's how it is. Grandparents help out with the parenting, and the kids get to see that all adults aren't like their parents. And why their parents are the way they are. Seems kind of healthy to me. I know it's not the norm in our country, but maybe we'd all be better off it were happening more."

The conversation paused as everyone considered this new approach.

"I have to say, I'm feeling pretty touchy," admitted Anne, setting her coffee cup down. "I'm embarrassed that my granddaughter did something inappropriate. And maybe I just don't want to go through the teenager experience again—it was so painful with Giselle. I really need to sort out my feelings. Part of me really does want to spend more time with Margot."

"No one's going to force anything on you, Anne," said Patty, putting her pen down on top of her folder. "I completely get not wanting to be actively parenting again—who's got energy for that! But I like to help out, I like to have something to do with my grandkids. It's good for them and for me." Patty got up to refill coffee cups. "If Margot were here, it's like she said, she'd have six grandparents instead of one—assuming we were all willing to take on that role. And what a relief for Mark, to have other adults around, and not have to be a single parent."

Lionel finished his cake and set the plate on the coffee table. "What if he got married? He'd probably like to. If he and Margot lived here and then she left for college and he married and moved out, we'd be looking for another roommate when we're in our mid to late seventies."

"That could happen whether Mark and Margot are here or not," said Chuck. "We all know we're living on borrowed time now. Cancer, heart attacks, strokes— that's all waiting in the wings. And as careful as we are, we might choose someone who didn't work out, and left before he was carried out. So I think we should be open to Margot and Mark, even if they only stayed for a couple of years."

There was another silence while people mulled over what had been said. "Well, now what?" asked Anne. "What should I tell Margot?"

"I think we should all think about the points that've been made, consult our feelings, and so on," suggested Lionel. "We don't have to decide right now. Can we talk again Friday night before we watch our movie? Then Anne could talk to Margot and Mark and see what they think. One of them would have to use the guest room in the basement, which would leave us without a guest room. That's another consideration."

Anne said, "Yes, we shouldn't rush into this. Margot should have some time living with her dad, trying that out. I don't want her to just eliminate that possibility, without seriously trying it. I'll call and tell them we need a couple more weeks before we can give them an answer."

"Well, lots to think about," said Chuck. I'm fine with talking again Friday night, and all of us giving it a lot of thought between now and then. Do we have any other agenda items?"

*****

The next day, Anne took her cell phone out to the backyard patio and settled herself in one of the director's chairs. She heard the sounds of gardeners mowing and edging and leaf blowing in the surrounding yards. The garbage truck came banging down the alley and moved on to the next block. Finally, it was quiet and she could enjoy the big old cherry tree with its new leaves, the first round of rose blossoms, and the expanse of soft green grass.

The sun was warm on her back as Anne called her granddaughter's father and asked him to tell Margot that they would be considering her request over the next couple of weeks. "I'm sure you understand, Mark, this is something we don't want to rush into. Also, I think it will be good for Margot to get into a regular rhythm and get used to being with you. I don't want her to think the option of living with you is off the table."

"Makes sense to me, Anne. I'm sure she wants what she wants right now, but I agree there's a lot to consider—for all of us. There's no reason to hurry."

"Good, we're agreed," Anne said. "We'd like you two to come over for dinner in a couple of weeks, and we can all talk together. But I'll call before that to give you an idea of what's been discussed."

Anne sat for a while longer in the sunshine, thinking about how some of Margot's mannerisms reminded her of Giselle. She ached for her lost daughter.

*****

She took the next step a week later. "Hi, Mark. This is Anne. Do you have some time to talk? I just wanted to fill you in on our conversation about Margot's living with us." Anne sat at the island in the mansion's sunny kitchen. "It's taken a rather surprising turn, at least to me. My housemates are all thinking about what it would be like to have *both* you and Margot here on a permanent basis. We were looking for another housemate anyway, and now this possibility has presented itself. So we're exploring it individually and as a group, and we want to invite you to think about it too."

"Wow!" Mark said. "This is a surprise—I don't know what to say!"

"Well, that's only natural," she said. "It was a surprise to me when this idea came out of our initial discussion. We can talk about it on Saturday night, when you come to dinner. But in a nutshell, here are the possibilities as I see them. One is that we continue the option of three days here, four days with you. Another is that Margot stays with you permanently, once you two get better acquainted. A third is that Margot moves in with us. And a fourth is that you both move in here. We absolutely won't be offended if that's something you don't want to consider, Mark. So please don't worry about that, if it's not something you want to pursue. It would be kind of an odd thing for a guy your age to do, given that you might find a partner you'd like to live with."

"This is pretty much blowing my mind," he said. "It's not that I reject the idea out of hand, but I've never thought about a group-living situation. I haven't done that since college. So there's lots to consider."

"I couldn't agree more! So let's give ourselves plenty of time to think about it. I'll leave it up to you how to bring it up with Margot. I just don't want her to think I was brushing off her request."

Fatherhood

Mark put down his phone and leaned back in his chair. *What a bombshell! Isn't it enough that I'm living with a teenager? Do I want to live with a bunch of old people too?* He looked at his watch. *I don't have time to think about this now—got a deadline tomorrow.*

But Mark's attention kept leaving his programming project, and he kept thinking about all the reasons why what Anne proposed was a crazy idea. He was middle-aged; they were old—really nice, but old. Who would want roommates again? He liked having his own space, playing his own choice of music, not having to interact if he didn't want to. He kept pushing away these thoughts until he was finally reabsorbed in his work.

He was at a good stopping point when Margot arrived home about five. "Hey, Margot," he said, pushing his chair away from his computer. "Want to go out for fish-and-chips tonight? I've been so focused on this deadline I didn't think about dinner, and it's my night to cook."

"Sure, I'm always up for fish-and-chips," she said enthusiastically.

A half hour later, they were sitting across from each other at Ivar's Seafood Bar, dipping their steaming chunks of cod in tartar sauce. "Oh, this is so good!" said Margot. "I can never wait for it to cool a bit, so I get 'fish mouth'—you know, like 'pizza mouth,' when you burn your mouth on hot pizza?"

Her dad laughed. "Yeah, I remember that. I've had plenty of 'pizza mouth' in my life." He took another bite and then said, "Margot, there's something we need to go over. Anne called today to talk about your request to live with her. She had an interesting proposal." Mark explained the options that Anne had offered. "So we have a lot to think about and discuss. They invited us for dinner Saturday night," he said, dipping a French fry in ketchup, "so we should have some kind of response by then."

Apparently, Margot had a fish-and-chips routine: three little containers of tartar sauce were open and lined up on the table, and next to them were two open containers of ketchup. She didn't answer immediately, seeming to concentrate on her food. After a few more bites, she looked up and said, "What do you think? What do you want to do?"

"Well," he said, "it partly depends on what you want. I don't think either of us should stake out positions at the outset, or anything like that. Let's just toss around the pros and cons. For example, a variation on the alternative of your splitting your time between Anne and me would be if we moved closer. The lease here is up at the end of the summer, and if you want to switch schools, we could find an apartment on Capitol Hill or someplace where it would be easy to get to school and to Anne's by bus. It would be nice to be closer to them, even if you were with me full-time. And I like the Capitol Hill vibe." He leaned back in his chair and took a sip of lemonade. "You know, Margot, we're only talking about two more years. After that, you'll be off to college. And those two years are going to go so fast you won't believe it. Anyway, I think it's too soon for you to know how you'll like the back-and-forth option. If you want to keep doing that, I'll bet it would be all right with them, at least for a while."

"What about you? You haven't said anything about living there yourself," she said, stirring her Coke with her straw. "I'm getting that you aren't interested."

"Let's go for a walk at Carkeek Park and talk some more," he said, standing up and piling his trash on his tray. "I need some exercise."

There was no conversation as they drove to the park, Mark still thinking about how he felt and how to express his feelings.

They parked and started down one of the wooded paths toward the beach. "It's really beautiful here," Mark said, pausing by Piper's Creek to admire the stream and the intensely green plants on its bank. "It's so peaceful and quiet—a nice break from the traffic noise."

Just then, there was shouting from somewhere down the trail, male and female voices, an altercation of some kind. "Leave me alone, you bastards!" Mark heard as they neared whoever was shouting.

"Uh-oh, I think we'd better check this out," he said, increasing his pace, Margot right behind him. "Hey!" he shouted. "Anyone need some help? We're coming!"

They rounded a sharp bend in the trail to find a woman in jogging shorts and a T-shirt confronting two young men holding cans of beer and blocking her path. Mark motioned Margot to stay behind him. "Is there some kind of problem?" he asked, coming to a stop about ten feet from the guys.

"These jerks are harassing me—they won't let me by!" answered the woman, jogging in place, her face red and sweaty.

"Aw, come on, lady," said the bigger guy. "We weren't harassing you—just having a little fun."

"Blocking the trail and making sexual remarks qualifies as harassment, you creep! If I had my phone, I'd take your picture and report you to the police."

"I've got a phone," said Margot, stepping from behind Mark. As the two turned to see who was speaking, she snapped their picture. "You want me to call nine-one-one?"

"Hey, wait a minute," said the other guy, alarm in his voice. "We were just having a beer, having some fun. We weren't going to hurt anybody. We're outta here. No need to call the cops." He shoved his friend past the woman, who was still jogging in place, and they disappeared down the trail.

"Are you all right, miss?" asked Mark. The woman had dark hair in a ponytail, with loose, damp tendrils around her face and neck. He couldn't help but notice a very attractive and fit body. She was probably in her thirties.

She stopped jogging in place, her shoulders slumped, and tears appeared in her eyes. "I'm not hurt, just scared. I jog here all the time, and I've never had a problem. Now I'll never feel comfortable here again. It just makes me furious! What right have they got to ruin this nice spot for me and make me afraid to jog anywhere?" She wiped her eyes with the backs of her hands.

"I'm sorry this happened. Wish I could do something to make it go away," he said, "but . . ." His shoulders shrugged, and his hands opened in the universal "what can I do?" gesture.

"Oh, don't worry, I'll be fine. And of course it's not your fault. I'm just glad you were here! Thanks so much for helping out. I really appreciate it." She stuck out her hand. "I'm Claire. Thanks again."

"I'm Mark Nevins, and this is my daughter, Margot." He turned to Margot and put his arm lightly around her shoulder. "Quick thinking, by the way, Margot. Nice job with the camera." He smiled at her.

"Yes, it *was* quick thinking. Thank you, Margot," said Claire. "Well," she added, "I think I'd better get home and get cleaned up."

"We can walk back to your car with you," offered Mark, "or wherever there're more people."

"OK, thanks," Claire said. "I'd appreciate that. I'm sure I'd be fine, but I'm still a little shaken up."

They made small talk as they walked back up the trail, all the while Mark mentally scrambling for a way to stay in touch with her.

"Looks like we're both Volkswagen people," he said when they reached her aging VW Golf, parked right next to his late-model Audi. Reaching into his hip pocket, he pulled out his wallet and removed a business card. "Here. If you want to follow up with the police, you can reach Margot through me. She'll keep the photo for a while, in case you want it." He turned to his daughter. "OK, Margot?" She nodded.

Claire took the card and got in her car. She smiled up at both of them. "Thanks again. I'm glad to meet you, and really glad you were there to help out." She waved as she drove out of the parking lot.

Margot glanced at her phone. "I think we should go home," she said. "I've got a test tomorrow."

"Yeah, this whole episode kind of got me out of a reflective mood," he said. "We can talk some more tomorrow night about living arrangements. I don't think we have to decide right away. Anne said they weren't in a hurry. She just wanted to get back to you because she'd told you she would. Do you have time for us to stop and get groceries? Your turn to cook tomorrow night."

*****

Mark spent the next morning at a client's office in Pioneer Square, going over the project he'd been working on. The client was pleased with his progress, and there was another project in the offing with the same company. After lunch, he decided to walk to Pike Place Market to stretch his legs.

When he returned home with a latte in the midafternoon, he noticed the answering machine blinking. He punched PLAY and heard a male voice saying, "Hey, Margot, so you're going for older men now, huh? Just wanted to tell you to ditch that photo you took yesterday or some talk might get around at school about the stuff you did at Heather's party. Know what I mean? I think you do. See ya around, ho."

Mark was dumbfounded. His sixteen-year-old daughter apparently had done something she wouldn't want her classmates to know about, and she was being insulted and blackmailed! His mind raced through a list of unsavory possibilities he'd seen during high school and college parties. It didn't seem so bad at the time. Well, mostly—there were a few over-the-top occasions. But it looked very different now, to think that his *daughter* could be involved in drinking and random sex. *Jesus Christ! One false move and it could be pregnancy or an STD or rape. What the hell kind of mothering had Giselle been doing?*

Thoughts like this continued as he paced the living room. He finally got hold of himself and tried to calm down. He needed to approach this with Margot as rationally as possible and hear her side of the story. He played the message over a couple of times to make sure he hadn't missed something and tried to think how to bring it up with her.

She arrived home about four thirty. "Hey. OK if we eat about six?" she asked, dropping her backpack on the sofa. "I'm making pizza tonight, and I've never made the dough from scratch. Might take me a while." She surveyed the cans and bottles in the fridge and chose a can of flavored sparkling water.

"Before you start on the pizza," Mark said, "there's something we need to talk about. Sit down for a minute."

She looked at him questioningly.

"No, not about living at your grandmother's. It's about those guys we ran into on the trail yesterday. Did you know them?"

Her face became guarded. "I know who they are. They go to my school—they're seniors. Why?"

He punched the PLAY button on the answering machine and watched the expression on her face change from shock to horror. There was a long silence. Margot didn't look at him, but she etched a square into the tablecloth with her fingernail, over and over.

Finally, Mark said, "I don't want to dump on you or assume anything bad, but I can't just let this go. This asshole is threatening you and your reputation. He's blackmailing you, for Christ's sake!" He got up and circled the room before coming back to sit down. "I'm sorry. I didn't mean to swear and make this any worse than it is."

She still wouldn't look at him. Her shoulders were hunched.

"So I need to know three things," he said. "First, what is he talking about—what did you do, and what were the circumstances? Second, does anybody else know besides him? And third, do you care about other people knowing, or is this something you'd rather people didn't know?"

She seemed to be trying to act nonchalant. "It wasn't so bad—lots of girls do it—but I'd just as soon not have people talking about it. I don't think anyone else knows. We were in the bathroom, and the door was locked. It's not like we were having sex or something."

"What *were* you doing, then? I'm sorry if this is embarrassing for you, but I need to know what happened in order to deal with the situation appropriately. And when did this happen?" He waited.

"It was a party at Heather's, about four months ago. I think it was January. Her folks were out of town, and a lot of kids came and brought beer and stuff. A lot of people got pretty drunk."

"And were you drunk?"

"I had some drinks, but I wasn't drunk. I remember what happened."

"And what happened?" he asked quietly.

There was a long silence as she continued to etch her square in the tablecloth. "It was nothing. Like I said, a lot of girls do it. He just wanted me to suck him, and I did. No big deal."

Mark looked at his hands intently, cracked his knuckles, gazed at the ceiling, crossed his legs, and uncrossed them. Margot stole a look at him and quickly went back to her tablecloth project.

"But why did you do it?" he said. "Did you like him, or did he pressure you, or were you trying to prove something, or did you just want to see what it was like . . . or what?"

"Well, he's kind of hot and he's a senior, a really good football player. I thought maybe he'd like me or ask me to the prom or something. But he had a girlfriend . . . They're still together. So I guess . . ."

"Also, I thought you said you didn't have sex with him."

"That wasn't sex! Sex is when you can get pregnant— I'm not that dumb!"

"No, you can't get pregnant from giving some guy a blow job, Margot, but it *is* sex and you can get STDs— from doing it, including AIDS. Don't they teach this stuff in school? Didn't your mom tell you, for Christ's sake?" He got up and started pacing again. "I'm sorry," he said. "I should leave your mother out of this. It's just that this is information I would have thought you had. But you have it now, so let's go from here." He went to the fridge and got out a beer.

"OK," he said. "Let's think about this: This jerk might have bragged to his friends—that's what a lot of guys do, Margot. They just use girls to make themselves feel good, to get what they want, and they don't care about the girl's reputation. In fact, they think that if a girl will do that and she's not their girlfriend, she probably doesn't care about her reputation and doesn't deserve a good one." Mark took a sip of his beer. "On the other hand, he might not want his girlfriend to find out. She probably wouldn't like knowing that her boyfriend was having random sex with a sophomore, so we can hope that he didn't talk about it." He stared at the floor, deep in thought. "Do you know if he's going to college and if he got a football scholarship?"

"Yeah, we had the awards assembly last week, and he got all kinds of awards. I'm pretty sure he got a scholarship to UW."

"OK, this is what I'm thinking, Margot. What I'm going to do is call him back and tell him that if one word about what happened between you two gets out in your school, not only will his girlfriend know, but so will the university's athletic department, which just might endanger his scholarship. I'll also say that the photo will definitely be sent to the police and that we'll ask the woman they were harassing to file a complaint. That last part is kind of a bluff, because we don't know how to reach her, but he doesn't know that."

"I got a photo of her license plate," Margot offered. "So I think we could find her."

Mark plopped down on the kitchen chair and took another drink. "It's amazing to me how sharp you can be in some ways and how . . . naïve you are in other ways. I guess that's normal for your age, but it's all new to me. Anyway, got any comments on what I plan to say?"

Looking relieved, she said, "I'll think about it, but so far it sounds OK." She stopped and then added, "And thanks for trying to help." She got up and pulled an apron out of a drawer. "Guess I'd better start on the pizza."

*****

As she rode the bus to school the next day, Margot thought about the guy who had tried to grope her at the movie on their first—and last—date, and the drunk guy at the party her freshman year who had begged her give him a hand job. She gave an involuntary shudder of disgust and was very glad her dad didn't know about those incidents.

That evening, she told her father that in the hall at school she'd seen the guy who'd left the phone message. He said only, "I won't say anything if you don't." So she assumed, uneasily, that the matter was settled.

She lay in bed later that night thinking about her father, whom she had now known for about a month. She no longer suspected him of using her to get money from her mother's estate. She could see that Anne and her housemates liked Mark, and she respected all of them, so she was cautiously more accepting of him than she had been initially. She liked the order of their new household, her father's willingness to share the housekeeping, how he treated her more like an adult than her mother had. She liked the absence of uproar, which had seemed to characterize her relationship with her mom. Yet tears dampened her pillow as she felt the huge hole in her life that was the loss of her mother.

Blowup

For about four weeks, Karina and Amparo monitored the flow of their elderly patient's sleeping pills. Sure enough, they were disappearing at a rate faster than the prescribed dosage would allow. Karina came up with a plan to talk to the doctor at his next biweekly visit, whether Mrs. A wanted her to or not.

She arranged with Amparo to come late one Friday when the doctor was scheduled to arrive, so that Karina would have the excuse of covering for her. Mr. A was more alert than usual as she read to him, and they were laughing about an article when the doctor and Mrs. A came in.

"Oh! What are you doing here, Karina?" asked Mrs. A, frowning.

"I'm covering for Amparo. She called about three o'clock and asked if I could stay for an hour. She had family emergency." Karina stood up and shook hands with the doctor. "Hello, Dr. Benson. I'm Karina Azarov, Mr. A's day nurse."

"And a very fine nurse she is," put in Mr. A. "She reads me interesting things, and we laugh and talk a lot."

"Well, you certainly sound very chipper this evening, Frederick," said Dr. Benson. "Is there anything I need to know?" Turning to Karina, he said politely, "Anything you'd like to report, Ms. Azarov?"

"Something has been puzzling me. I have noticed that Mr. A's sleeping pills are disappearing faster than they should. I questioned Amparo, but she keeps track of pills she gives Mr. A and she's following prescription closely. So I wondered if you could check with pharmacy to see if prescription has been refilled according to schedule. I can't understand how this is happening. Also, I've noticed that he's less . . . groggy on days you come than on other days."

"Karina," said Mrs. A sharply. "This is the kind of thing that you should have discussed with me. It's not your place to talk to the doctor."

Karina ignored her. "Dr. Benson, I would also like to suggest some changes to Mr. A's diet. I think that might keep him from being groggy so much. I volunteered to cook. I don't have much else to do, so it's no trouble. And it might help him." She turned to look directly at Mrs. A. "But Mrs. Augsburgh told me I couldn't do that."

"This is entirely inappropriate," Mrs. A said, her voice a notch higher. "Dr. Benson and I will decide what's best for my father-in-law. You are not in a position to know."

Karina burned her bridges. "I am in better position than you, Mrs. A." She turned to Dr. Benson. "I was ER nurse for twenty years in Moscow—in this country, the same as an RN. I study geriatric nursing on my own, and I prepare to take the nurse's aide exam here in this country. I have some knowledge of what might help Mr. A enjoy a better life, even though Mrs. Augsburgh does not think so."

Dr. Benson was caught in the middle. He wouldn't want to offend his patient's daughter-in-law. However, he seemed to instinctively trust Karina.

"Well, well," he said jovially. "Maybe it's time I take another look at Frederick's regimen. We need to reevaluate long-term care measures periodically. What do you think, Frederick?"

"I feel like I'm in a fog most of the time, Clark. But I'd sure like to try some of Karina's cooking. If she cooks as well as she reads, I should be feeling better in no time." He smiled at her.

"Karina, you may wait in the kitchen," Mrs. A said frigidly. "I'll speak with you after Dr. Benson's visit."

"One more thing before you go," Dr. Benson said. "I'll have my consulting nutritionist send over some recommendations and recipes. And thanks for your concerns for Frederick. We've been friends for decades."

"He is very fine man. I have enjoyed being his nurse." She smiled at Mr. A and went downstairs. She got her jacket and waited for Mrs. Augsburgh, who came into the kitchen about fifteen minutes later.

"We will not be needing your services any longer," she said. "I will not tolerate help who disrespect me and question my judgment. Do not ask me for a reference."

"A reference from you would not be of any use to me," Karina said. "And I am not 'help.' I am professional nurse, who swears to promote health. You are not professional, and you are not promoting your father-in-law's health. I hope that Dr. Benson will pay more attention now, because I truly love Mr. A. Goodbye, Mrs. Augsburgh." Karina slapped the key she had been given down on the kitchen table and left.

Patty and Lionel

Saturday morning, Lionel lay in Patty's bed, watching the room lighten as the sun rose, its rays striking the cut-glass perfume bottle on her dresser, the robe draped over the corner of the bathroom door, the book in her chair. He still couldn't believe how suddenly and dramatically his life had changed; he felt almost dazed. For over a month, they had been sleeping together——sometimes in her room, sometimes in his—not every night, but often. He felt so energetic! He was playing the piano more, working in the garden more, throwing away old files and things he'd stuffed in the back of his closet to deal with later. He'd even gotten out his old camera and was rereading some of the photography books he'd bought long ago. Patty wanted him to take photos of Chuck's artwork for a new website.

He took in the woman sleeping beside him, the mussed gray-blond curls, the plump arm lying across his chest, the ample bosom beneath the décolletage of her nightgown. If they'd been married for fifty years, would he be as excited lying next to her as he was now? Surely not.

In a while, she stirred, pushed herself up to sitting, and yawned. She smiled at him sleepily. "You're looking at me in that way I've noticed lately. What is that expression?"

"Lust!" he said, reaching for her. "How does it feel to make an old man lusty?"

"Powerful! Energizing!" she said, laughing and falling into his arms. "I think I'll make new curtains for my bedroom today. Something boudoir-ish. Or maybe I'll go out to Chuck's studio and do some watercolors. I just feel like creating something. See how you affect me?"

"How would you feel about creating a cup of coffee? I think it's your turn," he said, running his hand up and down her arm. "But not quite yet."

An hour later, they sat in the sunny breakfast room eating cinnamon rolls, which Mikhail had baked the night before. The smell of freshly brewed coffee filled the kitchen. Outside the windows, the rhododendron blossoms nodded in the slight morning breeze.

"I've been meaning to ask you," Patty said, "did you ever talk to your former colleague—the one you wanted to apologize to?"

"Yes, I did," he said. "I'm glad I did it, but it was a rather odd experience. I thought I'd be really embarrassed, or he'd be angry or something. But he was the one who was embarrassed. After I'd made my apology, he said something about consequences for stealing another man's wife and went on to talk about what a great job he had after he left—lots of accolades, et cetera. He was sort of letting me know that he'd been successful in spite of me. So I guess he accepted my apology."

"Well, I'm glad you got that off your chest. Not to change the subject, but do you think the others know what's going on—I mean with us?"

"I'd guess they do or they have some suspicions," Lionel said. "Should we bring it up or just see what happens or what?"

"I don't want to make a big fuss," Patty said, "but at the same time I don't want to act like we don't want anyone to know, like it's a secret or something. So I think we should just acknowledge it when the time seems right, when an opportunity arises. What do you think?"

"Makes sense to me. I wonder what they'll think," he mused, cutting another small piece of cinnamon roll for each of them.

"They'll be happy, just like we are," she said, giving him a sunny smile. "Now I want to catch you up on what I've been thinking about to launch Chuck into the art world. You've got your assignment: learn how to take photos of artwork and then take them. I've researched the Capitol Hill Art Walk and scouted some potential sites for Chuck's paintings. And I've looked at several artists' websites, to see what they should look like and how other people make their work known. One thing Chuck could do is donate art to charity auctions— someone's always having an auction. And there are all kinds of shows and competitions that he could try for. And I'm going to ask Mark tonight if he'd be willing to create the website. He could probably do it in a couple of hours." She looked at Lionel smugly.

"Well, busy lady, those are pretty good ideas. You can be Chuck's agent or representative, or whatever they call it. I'm sure he'd welcome someone to do all the non-art stuff."

"Thanks!" Patty said. "On another topic, I thought we had a good discussion last night about the possibilities of Mark and/or Margot living with us. I didn't detect any unexpressed reservations, did you?"

"No, I didn't," he said, "and we've all been together long enough now that I trust people to be honest if they have concerns about things. Besides, if whatever option is chosen doesn't work out, then we can do something else. Change is OK." He leaned back in his chair and wiped his sticky fingers on his napkin. "I know a lot of older people don't like change—maybe younger people too. But I read this book by Betty Friedan years ago. It was called *The Fountain of Age*. She did all this research about aging, and one of her primary conclusions was that a secret to happiness in old age is the ability to change. It wasn't health, or where you live, or financial security, or having family nearby. It was how adaptable you are, how willing to change. I think this group is pretty good at that. We reinforce each other. This Margot thing is a case in point."

"Well," said Patty, getting up to make a fresh pot of coffee for the next breakfasters, "It'll be interesting to see what Mark and Margot decide.

The Crayons

Anne was sitting in the dining room that evening with her granddaughter and the housemates, the remains of dinner scattered around the table. The front door was open to let in the warm evening air, and she could hear the neighborhood children playing kickball in the street.

"I'm gonna go first," said Margot. "I'd like to go on like we have been until August—four days with . . . Mark, and three days here. I'll be gone at music camp for three weeks of that time." She was wringing her napkin as she talked. "And then we're going to get a new apartment here on Capitol Hill, so I can be close to Gramma and go to Garfield and be in the music program there. That will give Mark and me time to get used to each other some more. I really hope that will be OK with you."

Mark went on. "Margot and I want to thank you again for your generous offer," he said, "and for being open to so many possibilities, but I've decided that a group living situation isn't what I want at this stage of my life—even with people as special as you." He smiled. "And I'm not just BS-ing—you are an amazing group! But I'm still hoping I'll find a partner, and maybe have more kids, and I want to stay open to that possibility."

Margot gaped at her father, a stunned look on her face.

"Don't look so surprised, Margot," said Anne, laughing. "Your handsome father's plenty young enough to get married and have more kids, and he'd be a good catch. Having a wife and family is totally within the realm of possibility."

"Wow," Margot said. "I'll be a stepsister! How cool is that?"

Everyone laughed.

"Let's not get ahead of ourselves," said Mark. "I've been looking for quite a while, and I don't have much of a track record."

Chuck stood up and grinned at him. "Hey, man, she's out there somewhere, just wondering where the hell you are. You gotta get out and about so you can find each other." He headed for the kitchen. "Anyone else want some more of that fine rhubarb stuff Mikhail made?"

"I think Chuck's right," Anne said. "Keep a positive attitude. I can't believe some lovely woman hasn't snapped you up yet." She smiled at him and patted his hand. "But I want to get back to our earlier topic. I just want to confirm with my housemates that we're all in agreement that Margot can stay here three days a week until the first of August."

She saw nods of agreement around the table.

"OK, Margot," she said, "you're in!"

Margot jumped up and hugged her grandmother. "Thanks so much, Gramma—and everyone. I promise I won't be any trouble!"

After they did the dishes, Chuck, Patty, Lionel, and Margot got into a cutthroat game of Scrabble in the library. Mark and Anne sat in the living room, talking quietly.

"Just before we came over tonight," Mark said, "Margot told me she needed some new clothes. Then she burst into tears and ran into her room. I finally got it out of her—she and Giselle liked to shop together for clothes. Now they can't do that, of course, and she knows they'll never be able to do it, and her mom won't see her in her prom dress or her wedding dress. So she's feeling pretty sad. I'm glad you all were willing to let her stay here a while longer. And I think we're getting along fine. She seems more comfortable with me every day. But I think she'd really like to spend time with you, Anne."

"Oh, Mark, I wish she didn't have to be sad—but that's reality for us now, I'm afraid." Anne studied her hands, and then said quietly, "I'd love to take her shopping, or do anything she'd like to do with me. I'll ask her what she'd like, and if you have other suggestions, I want to hear them. I'm so glad to finally have time with Margot. I'm hoping that spending more time together will help both of us through the grief."

The Scrabble players came into the living room and flopped down into chairs, laughing and joking. "'Turpentine'! Chuck got 'turpentine.' Like, who would ever think of that!" said Margot. "It's not fair."

"Well, it's just as fair as 'oxymoron,'" Chuck said. "Who would think of that? Only a professor, not an ignorant painter like me. And it has an 'x'!"

Patty sat down next to Mark on the sofa. "Mark, I wanted to ask you about building a website for Chuck, to help him sell his paintings. Could you help us with that? I've been looking at artists' sites online, and I have some ideas. And Lionel is going to make photos of Chuck's work so we can use them on the website. What do you think? Would it be very expensive?"

"If you're not in a hurry, I'd do it for free," Mark answered. "I don't imagine you want something really fancy, and this would be kind of a fun project—more artsy and less high-tech than what I usually do. I could fit it in between my other projects. We could probably have it done in less than a month." He leaned forward, hands clasped, and asked Chuck, "What did *you* have in mind? I assume you want people to be able to purchase online, have a little bio, an artist's statement, a gallery of photos of your work. Something like that?"

"Whoa! You guys are really into this," Chuck said. "I'm not so sure this is a good idea, and I don't want you to do a lot of work for nothing."

"What do you mean, not a good idea?" Patty huffed. "Of course it's a good idea. It's a must. All artists have websites nowadays! For heaven's sake—how are you going to sell any of your work if people don't know about it?"

"Well, I've sold some work over the years. I can go on like I have been," he said, sounding a little cranky.

"What's going on, Chuck?" asked Anne. We talked about this the other night, and you were fine with it."

"Well, I didn't think it would really happen."

"Wait a minute, wait a minute, folks. I think we're coming at this the wrong way," said Lionel. "It feels like we're pushing Chuck in a direction he doesn't want to go." He looked at Chuck. "You're pleased when you sell your art, right?" He paused, and Chuck nodded, barely. "You'd like to have more income, and you're running out of space in your studio, so it would be good if you sold some work. Right?" Chuck shrugged a reluctant yes. "So your hesitation or resistance, or whatever it is, is something else, maybe something not rational."

They sat quietly, waiting to see what Chuck would say.

After a couple of minutes, he shifted in his chair and said, "When I was little, about five maybe, the lady who lived in the trailer next to us gave me a little box of color crayons. She was real nice, like I thought a grandma would be, always doing little things for me and my brother. Man, was I proud—my very own box of crayons. One row, you know, but brand-new. She also gave me a piece of tablet paper and I drew a picture, and then I ran home to show it to my mom. She held it up and turned it all around." He mimed a person turning a piece of paper around and flipping it upside down. "And she said, 'What the hell is this?' Then she tossed it on the table with all the junk mail and cigarette butts and other trash." He sat slumped, his legs crossed at the ankles, and his hands dangling off the chair arms. "I know that was a long time ago, and I know I have talent and I do good work. I know that in here." He tapped his head. "But I'm still pretty uptight about people's reaction to my art. I know why, and it's old stuff, but it's easier just to not get any reaction at all. If you don't put it out there, you don't get any negative feedback."

There was another long silence, which Patty finally broke by saying, "Chuck, you've come so far, overcome so much to get where you are—bless your heart! That took a lot of guts, besides hard work and talent. With just a little more guts, there's a chance you'll achieve financial success too."

"I need to think about it, guys," he said. "I know you're trying to help—and I appreciate it. See, I get this pain in my innards when I think about promoting myself and getting mixed up in the professional art world. But I'll think about it." He got up and ambled out of the room.

"I don't understand," said Margot. "Did he just say he didn't want to make money because of something his mom said when he was five years old?"

"Not quite, sweetheart," answered Anne. "He's afraid to do the things he has to do to make money because it involves people's judgments about his work. If his work didn't sell or he got bad reviews or some 'authority' said he wasn't very good, that would hurt. It would feel like he felt when his mom said what she said, which was just . . . cruel."

*****

Before bedtime, Chuck showed up in the kitchen at the same time as Margot, both looking for a snack. He poured them each a glass of milk while Margot got out the cookies.

"Chuck," she said, "I just want to say, if somebody doesn't like your artwork, then screw them! It really doesn't matter what a few people think. Even if you didn't make awesome artwork, you're a really neat person. You're fun to be around. You help those guys in juvie. You make my gramma happy. It doesn't matter what some random douchebag says about your art!"

"Thanks, darlin'," he said, kissing her on the top of the head. "You just made my day. Sleep well, Margot."

When Chuck got back to his room, he found Anne sitting on his bed. He stretched out beside her and offered her a cookie. "You know, that granddaughter of yours is something else." He repeated what Margot had just said to him. "So. Your granddaughter says I make you happy. Is that right?" He put his empty glass on the nightstand, dusted the cookie crumbs off his hands, and turned to face her. "Hmm?"

"You could say that, I guess. Yes, you could definitely say that," she said, trying not to smile. "I cannot tell a lie."

"Well, why don't you come a little closer, and I'll do my 'make you happy' thing, he said, pulling her over on top of him.

"OK," she said, slipping her arms around his neck. "Do your thing. I'll only give you eight hours, though."

Nature Fix

"Where are we going for our nature fix tomorrow?" asked Patty at the dinner table. I heard some suggestions last week: Discovery Park, Tiger Mountain, was there another?"

"How about Deception Pass?" suggested Chuck. "It'll take a couple of hours to get there, but, hey, we're retired, we have plenty of time. I'd like a beach and the smell of salt water. I haven't been to the beach for a long time.

"What's your 'nature fix?'" asked Margot, reaching for the fruit salad.

"Well, I keep running across articles about how important it is for people to be in nature," Patty said. "They've actually done studies now about how people can remember things better after some time in nature, compared to when they haven't been. And children behave better if they have time outdoors—not just on an asphalt playground, but walking in the woods, playing in real dirt. So I convinced my housemates—it didn't take much convincing, actually—that we should get out in nature on a regular basis. We set up one day a month that we'd go for sure, and we try to go more often. Tomorrow's the regular day."

Margot was on her last rotation at their house. She wanted to go with them on their outing, so the next morning all seven of them stuffed themselves into the van and drove up the interstate and then west to the northerly end of Whidbey Island.

As they drove, Patty described a book she was reading about how technology and nature affect the mind. "Some people say that all this technology is great, that people can learn tons more than they ever could, that they aren't stopped by distance or weather or time. Others say that younger people—the ones who use all this technology—aren't any better educated than the older folks. Just having the technology doesn't mean they use it to get educated. And I read all kinds of stuff about how people actually relate less to each other because of the use of smartphones: too many texts and emails, no body language to help interpret what's being said, junk communication instead of real communication."

"One day, I was having brunch with a friend in a restaurant," Anne said, "and this couple came in and sat down across from us. They were thirtyish, attractive, and both sat through the whole meal looking at their devices, or whatever you call them. Even when they were eating! They hardly spoke to each other, but they didn't seem to be angry or ignoring each other. They just seemed more interested in their phones than each other. I thought it was sad. Anyway, continue."

"Well," Patty said, "the upshot of all this is that nature experiences stimulate learning and inspire creativity. They affect our senses, and now they think that we have a lot more than the five senses we all know about. For example, ever heard of proprioception? It's your sense of where your body is in space." She shifted in her seat and tugged at her seat belt, as if trying to get comfortable in the crowded car. "Anyway, all this time with technology is about visual and intellectual learning, but not about learning with the other senses. So this guy says that we need to keep our connection with nature so we can learn and function in other ways than just with the left brain. And since we're getting old and our senses don't work as well as they used to, being in nature is really good for us."

They parked in a lot surrounded by giant fir trees; they could hear the breeze ruffling the branches as they unloaded their day packs and walking sticks and started down the nearest trail. It meandered through the woods, and the smell of kelp and salt water became stronger as the trail led them to the beach.

They were walking along the water, dodging the waves, when Chuck pointed to their right. "Look at the driftwood up there. There's a Nessie Monster—see that log? The whole beach looks like a pile of pick-up sticks. The waves toss it all around and create things, and then people come along and create things too: artwork, shelters, bonfires, furniture. Have you ever seen a beach with driftwood that didn't have a structure of some kind, or art? Seems like humans just have to do something with driftwood."

"Come on, Chuck, let's make something," said Margot, running up to the high-water mark, where a twelve-foot-wide ribbon of driftwood stretched down the beach as far as they could see. Mikhail and Lionel joined them. Anne and Karina started a driftwood project of their own, and Patty gathered rocks and shells to make a mosaic design in the sand.

An hour later, Margot was shouting, "Gramma, come see what we made!" Anne and Karina walked down the beach to view a tall . . . something.

"Well, it's very . . . impressive! How did you get it to be so tall?" Anne said, grinning. "And dare I ask what it is?"

"It's a sculpture, of course!" Margot said. "We're going to have a contest to name it. What do you think we should call it?"

"How about 'Tree Rocket'?" Anne said.

"Hmm, not bad. But what do you think, Karina? How about something in Russian?"

"'Plyazhnaya Skul'ptura'?" suggested Karina. It means 'beach sculpture' in Russian."

"Oh, that's good too. What did you and Karina make, Gramma? Let's go see it."

"Oh, cute!" said Margot when they got to Anne and Karina's creation—a little dollhouse, complete with a seaweed doll. She took a picture with her cell phone. "Let's go see what Patty did."

Patty was just finishing up a five-by-five-foot two-dimensional tree made of beach rocks. Lionel was standing beside her, admiring her handiwork. "Isn't it amazing how many beautiful rocks there are?" he said. "Whenever I go to the beach, I can't resist picking up a rock that I think is just the greatest rock in the world. And then two steps down the beach, I find another one. I finally quit picking up beach rocks. They never look as good at home, all dried out." He dropped several rocks he'd been carrying. "But there's a nice one—maybe I'll make an exception." He stooped to pick up a rock and fell over.

"Lionel! Are you OK?" Patty said as Karina bent to help him up. "What happened?"

"I don't know," he said. "I guess I just lost my balance on the uneven beach. But I'm fine. Nothing broken." He gave them a bemused smile.

"Maybe Lionel needs food. *I* need food," said Margot. "That little picnic wasn't enough. Can we stop for hamburgers on the way home?"

Dinner Discussions

"Hey, everyone, good news," Anne said as she passed the marinated asparagus to Lionel. "Mark and Margot have been looking at apartments around here. She's pretty excited about possibly being in a new place, close to Garfield, and that he's considering her opinion. He seems to have enough disposable income to buy some new things for her room too. Giselle couldn't really ever do that. Anyway, I think Margot will decide to stay with Mark full-time. So I think it's safe to start looking for our new housemate."

"Well, that's really good news, Anne. Glad to hear that they're getting adjusted to each other," said Lionel. "As far as the new housemates, I think we should do what we did the last time—let's start talking to people. Why don't we come up with a list of names and run them by each other, and if no one objects, we can initiate some conversations."

"Good," said Patty. "We've settled that. Now, I've got an idea I want to bounce off everyone. I think we should have a one-man show of Chuck's art here at the house. I was thinking we could do a benefit for the low-income preschool where Anne volunteers, and a percentage of the sales would go to the school."

In her enthusiasm, Patty didn't seem to notice Chuck's back stiffen, and his close examination of the napkin in his lap.

"We could have some door prizes and a raffle," she went on, "with the proceeds also going to the preschool.

193

Jeremy and Lionel could play background music, and maybe Margot too. Mikhail could do the food, of course. What do you think?"

"I am thinking like you, Patty," said Mikhail. "I want to start catering business. If I could have party here and invite all your friends and ours—we don't have so many—this would be good chance to show what I can do. Would this be OK?"

"Terrific! We could launch three businesses at once," said Lionel. "Chuck's art business, Mikhail's catering business, and Jeremy's party-music business. Did I tell you Jeremy and I have been talking about a little business for him of playing at parties? Aren't we the entrepreneurs! I like your idea, Patty, and the way it's developing. What do the rest of you think?"

"Well, it sounds like a nice idea for Mikhail and Jeremy, but it's not my kinda thing," said Chuck. "Go ahead and plan a party, but don't plan on me." He gathered up his dishes and left for the kitchen.

The enthusiasm whooshed out of the room like a popped balloon. "Oh dear," said Patty. "Guess I should have talked to him first. Anne, do you think we can change his mind? It would be such a great party with Chuck's art, Mikhail's cooking, and Jeremy's music! And it could be really good for Chuck's sales."

"I don't know," answered Anne. "He's pretty stuck in this anxiety about what people think of his work. But I'll try talking to him."

*****

On her way to bed, her steps quiet on the Oriental rug, Anne admired the beautiful old staircase yet again; she could vaguely smell the furniture polish they used on the shining woodwork. As she did almost daily, she marveled at her good fortune to live in this beautiful house. She felt cared for here, by the house itself, as well as by her housemates. She stopped at Chuck's room and knocked.

As if expecting her, he called, "Come on in." She found him sitting in his favorite chair, sketching on a big tablet as the summer evening light faded. "So. You coming to sweet-talk me into making a fool of myself?" He didn't look up.

Coming up behind his chair, she leaned over, put her arms around his neck, and nibbled on his ear. "Well, I hadn't thought about that strategy, but it sounds like a good one." There was a smile in her voice.

"Annie, just leave me alone! We've been over this before. I just don't want to be out there pushing my art. *I* know it's good enough, and that's good enough for me. I just want to do art. I don't like all this marketing shit."

"You're stuck. I *know* you know it. One of the reasons we're together is to help each other get unstuck. I can give you all kinds of reasons why Patty's party idea's a good one: It's very low key—you don't have to be in a fancy gallery. All our friends and neighbors will come, and you know they'll be supportive. You might sell some work, and you'd be helping the preschool and Mikhail and Jeremy. It's not just about you. What's the worst that could happen?"

"What if nothing sold?" He threw down his pencil. "What would that say about my work?"

"Probably nothing! Maybe your prices are too high. Maybe people didn't bring their checkbooks, because they're used to paying by credit card and you don't accept them yet. Maybe they don't have any space for art. Maybe they don't have any taste, or can't recognize good art when they see it. Besides, who'll know whether you've sold anything except us? And, Chuck, I know you're worried about money. This little event could help." She kneaded his shoulders.

"But even more importantly, you need to get through this stuckness. What's most important? What *you* think of your art or what other people think? If some people don't like it, does that mean you're a bad person, or a failure or something? Is that why you don't want to put your work out there? Because it might make you look to yourself like a failure? You need to give this some serious thought!" She kissed the top of his head and left the room, closing the door quietly behind her.

*****

Chuck gazed out his window at the stars, trying to find some calm to counteract the roiling in his stomach at the idea of hordes of people looking at his paintings and sketches. He knew Anne was right; this would be an easy way to show his work and possibly sell a few things. He did need the money. Did he care too much about what people thought of his work? He'd never believed that about himself, but now he saw that it could be true.

He got into bed, tossed and turned, and heard the clock strike midnight before he finally fell into a restless sleep.

*****

Chuck finally, grudgingly, conceded to their plans. His work was accepted for the Capitol Hill Art Walk, and

Mark created a website, which awaited only Lionel's photographs.

Lionel was enjoying the technical challenge of properly photographing Chuck's paintings and drawings. One afternoon toward the end of July, he was in Chuck's studio, experimenting with the lighting for some watercolors when he lost his balance and fell into a pile of paintings stacked against the wall.

"Oh, no! I didn't ruin anything, did I?" he said, shaking his head, as if dazed.

"No, no. No problem, Lionel. But are you OK? What happened? Did you trip? You just seemed to fall over for no reason." Chuck stooped to help Lionel to his feet.

"I don't know what happened—all of a sudden I was on the floor." He sat down in Chuck's dilapidated easy chair. "I don't feel dizzy or faint or sick. I've never had any balance problems. Maybe it's just old age," he said. "I know people start to get a little tottery when they get older." He stood up. "Well, I feel OK now. Let's get back to shooting those watercolors."

*****

That evening at dinner, Chuck said, "Did anyone hear that piece on NPR today about ageism? Man, it's outta control! We neglect our old people, and they feel useless. Women fill their bodies full of chemicals, because they think it makes them look younger. People get discriminated against in jobs because of their age—it goes on and on. Pretty damn disgusting!"

"The other day, a young man got up and gave me his seat on the bus," said Anne. "That's a first for me, and it was a bit of a shock."

"Was it a shock because he had manners, or because it made you realize some people think you're old?" asked Chuck.

They all laughed. "Both," said Anne. "Could I have some more dessert, please? I don't mean he was engaging in ageism—I just realized that to some people I look old."

"What's 'old,' anyway?" asked Lionel, passing a berry-and-goat-cheese tart to Anne. "Is it an objective condition? I don't think there's much agreement when we're talking about humans. Maybe everyone would agree that eighty is physically old, but before that there's a big age range that different people would define as old, probably anywhere from sixty to seventy-five."

Patty served herself a slice of tart and said, "Yes, and what about objects, especially when there's planned obsolescence? When is a PC old? A car is old at twenty-five years, but a house isn't old for decades. You know that toaster we're using? I found it at an estate sale, and it was just like one I got as a wedding present fifty years earlier. Works much better than the new ones."

"When I was working in the art supply store with Patty's husband," Chuck said, "he used to complain about the younger people he hired. He said a lot of them didn't have a work ethic, weren't as dependable as the older people. He'd always go for the old-toaster people, rather than the spiffy new model, when he had a choice." Smiling at his wordplay, he put another piece of tart on his plate. Guess I fall into the old-toaster category."

Lionel pushed his plate away. "I think when we're talking about people, it seems to be as much a matter of attitude and demeanor as physical years. Some eighty-year-olds look younger than some fifty-year-olds," he said. "Life experience surely has something to do with it.

If you'd lived through the Cultural Revolution in China, or civil war in Sudan, you'd probably look older than people who hadn't. But for people who haven't had those harrowing life experiences, who've lived what we'd call a fairly 'normal' life, why do some look much older than their peers?"

"Like you said," Chuck answered, "attitude and demeanor. You can bitch and moan about the fact that you can't see or hear as well, that sex isn't what it used to be, that your hips ache—whatever. But what mattered when you were younger still matters: family, friends, doing something creative, food, parties, reading, art, sex. All that stuff is still there, so why do so many people focus on what they've lost, rather than what they still have?"

"Fear," said Patty. "Fear of ending up strapped into a wheelchair and being force-fed in a nursing home. Or even if it's not that bad, fear of being alone and unloved. We're lucky. We have each other, and pensions and social security, and some of us have children who aren't going to abandon us. But that's not the case for an awful lot of people. And even if they have money, they don't necessarily have friends and family."

"Let's go back to the people like us," said Chuck, leaning back in his chair. "People who don't have the financial worries and do have families and friends—but who get all bent out of shape about getting old. I still haven't heard an explanation of why that is."

"Well," said Patty, "lots of people have their self-worth wrapped up in things that're affected by age. Like women are so conditioned to the importance of being physically attractive, and you just can't compete with younger women. Men typically define themselves by their careers, and at some point they get passed by younger people or they have to retire, and then who are they?"

"I think that's true—for our culture." Lionel leaned forward on his elbows. "But we know that in other cultures, getting old isn't viewed as a bad thing. In Asian cultures, the aged are revered, and in general I think they look forward to being old—it's a happy time. And in the Hindu tradition, the last phase of life is about spirituality. Why is it a happy time or an important spiritual time for those cultures and a time to be dreaded in ours?"

"Because for us, death isn't really viewed as a natural thing," Anne said, "even though nothing is more normal than birth and death. When we're older, death is closer. It's not so easy to ignore anymore." She looked around the table. "Maybe two-thirds of your life is gone, and you feel time speeding up, and you realize life as you know it isn't going to go on forever. That's scary, so people try to stay young, to put it off."

The conversation paused while the mellow tones of the grandfather clock struck the hour. Then Chuck said, "Yup, I think you nailed that one, Annie."

*****

Lionel was reading in Patty's bed later that night when he took off his glasses and laid them on the bedside table. "Patty," he said, "do you worry about competing with younger women? I wouldn't have thought so, but I was just wondering . . ."

She put her glasses on the other bedside table and snuggled up beside him, resting her head on his shoulder. She sighed. "Yes, I have to admit I do, I'm afraid. It's kind of involuntary. At least now I catch myself doing it and can tell myself to knock it off: that's progress." She smoothed the wrinkles in the blanket. "The other day when we were walking to the drugstore, I saw you noticing a sweet young thing walking down the street in short shorts and a halter top, and I had this little flash of . . . something . . . I don't know, like fear or sadness or something. I know I'll never look like that again . . ." She hugged him closer. "But then I remind myself that you're sleeping with me, that you like my body—you can't imagine how much that means to me, Lionel."

"Oh, sweetheart," he said, running his fingers through her hair, "you can't imagine how much it means to *me*, being able to make love with you, having this chance so late in my life. Don't think anything about those stray glances. Men are just programmed to notice women—it's pretty much unconscious. I'm not comparing you with other women, or even thinking about what it would be like to go to bed with some girl I see on the street. It's nothing more than an appreciation of a lovely thing, like a nice view or a pretty flower."

"That's kind of what I thought. But it's reassuring to hear you say it, all the same. Women have been conditioned all their lives that they have to be attractive. The culture says that the signs of normal aging are unattractive, and it's hard to tune out that idea as you get older."

"Well, my dear, how about some more reassurance?" He turned off the light.

New Prospects

Bright August sunlight flooded the big room at the community center where Anne taught a movement class for children. She stood by the door, watching the interaction between a little girl and her grandmother. She'd noticed them before. They seemed very close—lots of hugs and giggling between them. The little girl wanted to play on the climbing equipment before they left, so her grandmother was standing beside the window watching.

"I assume Mai is your granddaughter," said Anne.

"Yes, I'm Lin Chan. Mai really likes this class."

"I'm Anne Aikens, her 'teacher,' if you can call it that. She's a pleasure to have in the class, a real sweetheart."

"Yes, she's a joy all right. I'm so happy I can pick her up every day. It's about the only time I get with her—her parents have her so highly scheduled. It would be a pretty dreary life without her."

"Are you retired, Lin?"

"Oh, no, I have to work to make ends meet. I'm an ESL teacher at Seattle Central. There are a lot of Chinese students coming to America, so the demand is there. But it doesn't pay very well." She stopped to wave at her granddaughter. "Do you happen to live around her, Anne? I'm looking for an apartment so I can be near the college. I'm out in the North End now. That's a long bus commute, and it's expensive to drive and a hassle to park."

"I live just a few blocks from here. Why don't we go out for coffee sometime and chat about what you're looking for."

"What a nice offer. Thank you—I'd like that. How about the café at Elliott Bay Bookstore?" Smartphone in hand, she looked at Anne. "Let's see, Monday about two?"

"Perfect."

They exchanged phone numbers, and Lin and Mai went down the path toward the parking lot, Mai skipping and chattering alongside her grandmother.

*****

When Lionel went into Victrola for his tall double-shot decaf skim latte with almond, the coffee shop was full, as usual, so he asked if he could share a table. "Sure. Welcome," said the table's occupant, gesturing to the chair across from him. "Gets pretty crowded in here about this time of day."

"Haven't I seen you in here before?" asked Lionel, sitting down and sneaking a peek at the title of the man's book. "You always seem to be reading something."

"Yeah, I come here before I start work every day and just hang out. It's a friendly place, even though most people have their noses in their laptops." He shook his head as if to say "These crazy people with their laptops."

Lionel couldn't imagine where this well-spoken, distinguished-looking man with graying temples could work in this little business district of shops and restaurants. "Where do you work, if you don't mind my asking?" he said, but he immediately realized he was bordering on impolite, so he added, "Oh, am I interfering with your reading? I guess I am. Sorry."

"No, you're not disturbing me. It's nice to have someone to talk to. I work the night shift at the supermarket across the street. I used to be a detective with the Seattle Police Department, and the store people like the idea of a big black former cop bagging groceries near the front door. I'm supposed to scare off the shoplifters and troublemakers." He grinned again.

"A former cop who's reading Kant before he goes to his job bagging groceries. You must have quite a story! By the way, my name is Lionel Blackburn."

"Abe Thomas. Glad to meet you, Lionel." The two men shook hands across their coffee cups. "I've seen you in here before, I think. Are you a regular too?"

"Yes, I am. I could save a lot of money and make a latte at home, but I like to support the local businesses and just sit and watch people. I also enjoy the walk from our house, and sometimes I meet interesting people like you."

"Well, it's convenient that I've met you," Abe said. "I'm looking for an apartment so I can be near this job. I'm out in the North End now. It's a long ride on the bus, but driving is expensive and parking is a real hassle. So, if you have any suggestions, I'd be happy to hear them." He put a leather bookmark in his book and set it on the table. "You said '*our* house.' Are you married?"

"No, I live with three other people about my age in a big old house a few blocks from here. We decided to be an 'intentional family' and grow old together. We have a cook and a really splendid situation. It's working out very well. I expected us to have more problems adjusting to each other, but it's been remarkably smooth so far."

"That takes some guts at our age—you must be a really interesting bunch!"

"Let's chat again," Lionel said. "Will you be here Friday about this time? I have a doctor's appointment right now, so I have to run."

"Friday it is, Lionel. Nice to meet you." They shook hands again.

Another Diagnosis

"The ophthalmologist said there's nothing wrong with my eyes," Lionel announced at dinner, "so it must be something else causing my eyesight to get fuzzy. He said I need to see my GP for further tests. I'll make an appointment tomorrow. Would you pass the vegetables, Anne?"

A week later, Lionel saw his doctor, who ordered an MRI and arranged an appointment with a neurologist.

"Isn't this overkill just for fuzzy eyesight, Jim?" Lionel asked his doctor of twenty years.

"We just need to eliminate all the possibilities, Lionel. Don't want to take any chances."

After the MRI, Lionel got a call from the neurologist's office, asking him to bring a friend or relative with him to his appointment. Then he began to worry. It was now early September, and Patty was busy getting ready for the first day of school. He hadn't told her about his appointments, and she'd been away often enough not to notice their frequency. The night of that call, after their meditation, he asked her to come with him to see the neurologist and filled her in on all the tests he'd been having.

"Oh!" she said, with a look of consternation on her face. "I wish I'd known." He watched her replace the consternation with a carefully composed smile. "But maybe I'm glad I didn't know. I'm such a worrier. This will be a good exercise for me, Lionel, trying to support you without worry. What good is worry anyway? The news may be bad, or it may not, and we'll just have to make the best of it." She stopped and sighed. "That sounds like such a cliché. Well, it is a cliché, but it's also true. And no matter what, I love you." She touched his cheek.

He stood, took her hand, and they went in to dinner.

Later that week, Lionel sat with Patty in front of the neurologist, Dr. Putnam, trying to be prepared for the worst but hoping for the best.

"I'm afraid I don't have good news for you, Mr. Blackburn." He showed them the results of the MRI. "You have what appears to be a brain tumor, called a glioblastoma multiforme. The treatment involves surgery, radiotherapy, and chemotherapy." He launched into a lengthy explanation of the type of tumor he suspected, and what the treatment involved, but Lionel hardly heard anything as questions spiraled through his head.

How accurate is this MRI? It must be malignant or they wouldn't be talking about chemo. I've got a brain tumor?

"I suspect you're having a hard time taking all this in," the doctor said. "It's completely understandable. I've had to share news like this with many patients, and it never gets any easier. But it's not like there's no hope. There are treatments that can help." He seemed to be speaking more to Patty than to Lionel, though he made eye contact with both of them as he talked. "We have a great deal of printed information, and we can refer you to some good websites if you'd like to research this condition further yourselves. We'll spend as much time as you like explaining the diagnosis, treatment options, and your prognosis. I've got a folder of information for you to take with you, and my assistant will schedule a follow-up appointment in a few days. That will give you time to read all this material and compile a list of questions."

"There's one aspect you haven't mentioned, Dr. Putnam," said Lionel. "What's the long-term outlook for this type of tumor?"

Dr. Putnam shifted in his chair and straightened the papers on his desk. "Well, that depends on a lot of things: the success of the treatment regimen, the lack of complications, the health of the patient going into the treatment process."

"If there's a prognosis for this type of cancer, I'd like to know what it is. I do better with certainty than uncertainty."

Again, Dr. Putnam shifted in his chair. "I'm afraid, Mr. Blackburn, that this is the most common and most aggressive form of malignant brain tumor. I want to emphasize that the survival rate can vary a great deal from individual to individual. But even when all the therapies are used, the median survival rate is about fourteen months. Only about three percent of people with this diagnosis survive for two years."

Patty gasped, and Lionel sat back in his chair.

After a moment, Lionel stood and said, "Thank you for your candor, Doctor. I know this isn't easy for you either. We'll look over the information and make the follow-up appointment." He extended his hand.

"Let's go home and have a nice shot of Scotch, shall we?" Lionel said to Patty with a weak smile as they left the doctor's office and began their walk home. "And let's order tickets for the ballet and the opera. Let's get expensive seats, right up front, while I can see. If I've only got a little time left, I want to enjoy every minute."

They walked the rest of the way home in silence.

When they climbed the front porch steps, Patty said, "Oh, Lionel, I don't know what to say, or think . . . I'm so shocked! I'm going to my room . . . I have to try to sort this out. I don't want to cry in front of you and make you feel worse."

It was his turn to be shocked—he couldn't help but feel she was deserting him!

*****

Patty slumped down into the faded rose armchair in her bedroom and turned on the table lamp. This morning she was so happy, even euphoric, and now what was she? Disbelieving. Numb. A woman whose chance for new love had been wrenched away. *Why did this happen?* Her thoughts came and went in no order.

She began her mantra, hoping to find some calmness in meditation. Though the thoughts continued, under them she could feel the familiar steady, centered place, and after a while, a word came to her: "compassion." Her thoughts began to quiet and become more orderly. She realized that she'd been thinking only of herself, and not at all of what Lionel was facing, and then she felt selfish and ashamed. *No, I'm not going there. It's OK for me to be disappointed and shocked. But I'm not doing the shame thing. I just need to think about Lionel and what he needs—that's the priority. I can talk to him tonight.*

She met him in the hallway on the way to their meditation time. "Lionel, I'm so sorry I ran away. Will you come to my room after dinner so we can talk?" He nodded and followed her into the living room.

It was a quiet dinner; everyone seemed preoccupied, and there wasn't the usual lively conversation. After the dishwasher was loaded and the kitchen cleaned up, everyone scattered. Lionel followed Patty up the stairs to her room, each of them carrying a cup of coffee. After shutting the door, she took his cup and put both cups on her night table.

Putting her arms around his waist, she rested her head on his shoulder, "I'm so sorry I ran off and left you," she said. "I can't believe I did that! I think it was the thought of losing you. You've come to mean so much to me, and I've been so happy since we got together." She stopped and pulled away from him. "Listen to me—I'm still doing it. I'm still babbling on about *me*! I'm disgusting. I didn't think I was so selfish!" She sat down on the bed, covered her face with her hands, and burst into tears.

Lionel sat down beside her and put his arm around her shoulders. "It's really confusing, isn't it? But I'm doing the same thing: thinking about what it means to *me*, and then thinking I should be thinking about *you*. It's real and it's not real. I've been all over the place today—disbelieving, angry, afraid. Even accepting, for a few seconds. I expect all this confusion is perfectly natural, but knowing that doesn't make it much easier. I think we just have to live with it for a while and gradually we'll become more settled, we'll see what we're up against." He hugged her tighter.

Patty pulled a tissue from the box on her nightstand and dabbed at her face. "This is one reason I love you so much—you're so calm and reasonable." She touched his cheek. "Even when you're talking about . . . about . . . your death." Tears again flowed down her cheeks, and she collapsed against him.

When she finally had herself under control, they arranged themselves against the pillows on the bed and talked. They needed to look at the materials they had been given to read. They needed to research his symptoms and how they were expected to change over time. What were the treatment options and the pros and cons of each? Would he consider alternative medicine? They talked until midnight and fell asleep in each other's arms.

Telling the Others

It was the middle of September by the time Lionel was ready to share his bad news with the housemates. They were sitting on the backyard patio, enjoying the warm evening air, having their after-dinner coffee and tea. "What's on the agenda tonight, Lionel?" asked Chuck. It was the date of their monthly business meeting.

"Not too many items, but I do have something difficult to share with you. I don't know quite how to start, so I'll just plunge right in." Lionel looked around at everyone. "I have a brain tumor—that's what all the falling and fuzzy eyesight is about. I've only known for a couple of weeks. Patty too. I wanted to wait a bit before telling you, to see if I could get some kind of . . . what? Equanimity or something. But I haven't . . . It will probably take quite a while. Anyway, there you have it." He looked around again at those who had become his family.

There was a long, shocked silence.

"Can you tell us prognosis?" Karina asked gently.

"It's not good," Lionel said. "They can do radiotherapy and chemotherapy, but not surgery, in my case. I'll probably be blind before the end. And the average life expectancy for this kind of cancer is twelve to eighteen months. Only about three percent of people with this kind of cancer survive for two years."

A strangled cry came from Anne. "Oh, Lionel, can't they do better than that? They do such amazing things these days." She groped for Chuck's hand.

"Well, we can hope for a miracle, but I'm trying not to go there. I'm trying to focus on living each day, each moment, as fully as I can. I know that will get harder as time goes on, but that's what I want to do. I'll consider all the treatment options, allopathic and alternative. So many of the mainstream medical treatments are so damaging to your body and your quality of life. Maybe I'd rather have a shorter life than live a longer life being miserable. I don't know yet." He studied the coffee mug in his hands, then looked around at everyone. "I'm so glad I've got all of you to help me. I know if you put yourselves in my place, you'd feel the same way about our group. There's no one I'd rather face this with than you. But it's going to be hard for you too. I've thought about what it would be like for me, watching one of you facing a pretty fast decline, and I know it would be really difficult." There was another long silence.

"Well, shit, Lionel," said Chuck, rubbing his chin. "It oughta be me. I'm older, and all the drinking and smoking and carousing I've done . . . Sometimes I'm amazed I'm still alive. And you've been such a clean-living guy. Life is really strange. And not real fair."

Tears were running down Karina's face. She leaned over and hugged Lionel, cheek to cheek. "You won't need to hire nurse," she said. "I am available whenever you need me." He patted her shoulder, and she went inside.

"I do not have any words," Mikhail said, standing. "But we will take very good care of you." He followed his wife into the house.

"I guess we won't have a business meeting tonight. I kind of blew that out of the water," said Lionel. "But I'm glad to have this all out in the open now."

The good friends sat there in silence for quite a while longer. Lionel could hear the children playing in the street, the piano practice of the little girl next door, a siren in the distance, a lawn mower on the next block.

"There's something I want you all to consider," he said. "I've been thinking that maybe we should tell Lin and Abe what's up and invite them to visit with us on a regular basis. Now that I'm going, we'll have room for two, eventually, and I think they'd both be a really good addition to our group. We're lucky we won't be in the position of having to choose between them."

"I don't think 'lucky' is the word," said Chuck. "But it's a good suggestion. Let's think about it for a few days though." The others nodded.

"When shall we tell Margot and Mark and Jeremy, Lionel?" asked Anne.

"Soon. I think their feelings would be hurt if we kept it from them, even if our intention was to . . . spare them unhappiness."

*****

As he rode the bus to his piano lesson, Jeremy thought about his senior year. One more year and he should be able to get away from home. He'd applied to several colleges; his test scores and grade point average were high, and he had good references from Mr. B and his teachers. He was saving his money from his part-time job helping the custodian at his church. Things were looking good. There was even a remote possibility of a girlfriend: Margot always seemed to be around when he was there for his lesson, even though she was living with her dad now. He took that as a good sign, though he had no expectations that she was interested in him—just hopes.

Sure enough, she answered the door when he rang the doorbell. "Hey," she said. "How's it goin'?

"Fine," he said, but he noticed that her eyes were red and she had a tissue wadded in her hand.

"Come on in. Lionel's waiting for you. I'll talk to you after your lesson," she said, and she disappeared into the kitchen.

"Hi, Jeremy. Lovely day, isn't it?" Lionel was seated in his customary place next to the piano. Jeremy sat down and took his music out of his pack.

"Yeah, I love this time of year. Fall's my favorite season." He looked intently at his teacher. "Mr. B, is something wrong with Margot? She looked like she'd been crying."

"Um, I'm not sure," he said. "But I have an idea what it might be. Let's talk about it after we finish, OK?"

Jeremy didn't play as well as he usually did; he was unsettled. Lionel also seemed a bit preoccupied; he said nothing about Jeremy's mistakes. But they continued with the lesson, as though nothing were wrong.

"I guess that will do it for today," Lionel said. "I'm sorry if I seemed inattentive. Basically, you're doing fine." He paused and adjusted his position in his armchair. "But there's something I have to tell you."

Jeremy had a sinking feeling in his stomach as he gathered his music into a pile and stuffed it into his pack. He turned to face his teacher.

Lionel looked out the window at the golden sunlight coming through the maple leaves, and absently fiddled with the crease in his pants. "This is hard. There's just no good way to say it." He looked at his pupil and took a deep breath. "Jeremy, I have an inoperable brain tumor. I just found out a few weeks ago, and I just told Margot and Mark last night. I think that's why Margot's been crying. It's a lot for her. It hasn't even been a year since her mother died, and we've all kind of become grandparents to her. Now she's facing another loss."

"But so am I!" he blurted out. "You're like a grandfather to me too, or an uncle—way more than just a piano teacher." His voice broke, and tears appeared in his eyes. He wiped them away on the back of his hand. "Are you sure? Isn't there something they can do? Can't you have chemo or something? It's no big deal to lose your hair. There must be something they can do." His knee was jiggling up and down as he looked desperately around the room.

"Yes, there are treatments, Jeremy, and I'll consider all of them. They *can* prolong life, but it can be a miserable kind of life, and that's not how I want to spend my final months."

"Months! Just months? You're going to be here when I graduate, aren't you? I've been looking forward to that so much. You're the reason I've worked so hard. You've gotta be there!"

"Jeremy . . . Jeremy, my boy . . . I'm very touched that you . . . you care so much. You know I'll be there if I can. I'll do everything within my power to be there when you walk across the stage to get your diploma . . . and all the awards I'm sure you'll get. Nothing could make me happier." He paused.

Jeremy didn't say anything; he was looking at his hands.

"Now. We've got the hard part over with—it's out in the open. Let's talk about where we go from here. I want to continue with your lessons as long as I can. It gives me such pleasure to see your progress. You're a very talented young man, but I've given you about all I can give. You're ready for more than I can offer. However, we still have lots of sessions ahead, so let's just really enjoy them. We can start right now." He turned around and picked up a plate of chocolate chip cookies from the table behind him. "Here, have some cookies. Margot just baked them. Put some in your backpack for your trip home. And I'll see you next week."

Margot was sitting on the front steps when Jeremy left the house. "Hi," she said. "OK if I walk to the bus with you?"

"Sure, it'd be nice to have some company. Mr. B just told me. About the tumor. He said he told you and your dad yesterday."

"Yeah, he and Patty came over to our apartment after dinner last night. I'm totally freaked." They walked silently down the tree-lined street, past the big old houses and manicured lawns, past the children playing jump rope and hopscotch.

"I've never lost anyone I cared about," said Jeremy. "I mean, none of my relatives have died except my dad's father, and I didn't even know him; he lived in Texas. Mr. B is like a father or a grandfather or uncle or something. I care about him more than . . ." His voice broke, and he took a deep breath. "This must be hard for you too. I know it hasn't been very long since your mom died."

"Yeah, it's weird, isn't it? She died, and all of a sudden I had a whole family: a dad and six grandparents. And now one of *them* is going to die. What's next?"

At the end of the next block, she said, "It's like being in some alien place. Nothing seems real. Just like it felt when my mom died, all over again. It's kind of scary." She glanced up at Jeremy and then looked off down the street as they continued to walk.

"I know what you mean, about it not seeming real. I just can't get my head around the idea that he won't be here. How can that be?"

Jeremy stood with Margot at the bus stop, feeling lost and wondering what was coming besides the bus.

The Launch

The radiation started immediately, and Anne noticed that Lionel's energy level dropped dramatically; he managed to continue with Jeremy's music lessons but otherwise read and slept a lot. Still, he was adamant that they should proceed with the "startup party," as they had come to call it. He said he wanted life to be as normal as possible for as long as possible.

They decided on a date in mid-October. Anne took care of the arrangements with the preschool; its board was delighted with this fund-raising opportunity and offered to send an invitation to everyone on its mailing list. From Chuck, she pried a list of people who had bought his paintings over the years; she used the internet to track down as many as possible. They already had a list of neighbors, and Patty and Lionel gave her the names of other friends and associates to be invited.

"Why are you inviting people who don't even live around here?" Chuck asked Anne on the way back from the lumber store where they had just purchased wood for the frames he was making.

"We just want them to know you're still painting and have work available. Someone may have a new house with walls just calling out for new art. Or maybe someone needs a gift. Or maybe they'd just like to know you're still alive and kicking. And this is a good way to let them know about the website. The invitation can serve more than one purpose."

He looked dubious. "OK, Annie, whatever," he said. "You do your thing. I've got to keep focused on the frames. Lionel and I are going through the house this afternoon to decide what artwork we should take down and what should be put up and where we could fit some more in. This is so weird. Except for the days he has the treatments, he seems the same as ever, and yet I know he's not. It's kinda surreal." He parked the van in their driveway.

Her hand on the door handle, she said, "Yes, I know what you mean. I think we're all finding it surreal." She sighed. "I'll make sandwiches while you unload."

In the kitchen, Mikhail was sitting at the island with a cup of tea, working on menus for the party and a handout the guests could take away with them. He showed them to Anne.

"Mmm, looks yummy!" she said. "I'm sure people will enjoy these hors d'oeuvres, Mikhail."

"I am asking Margot to help with the . . . 'handout,' you call it? She will make it look nice. She can do amazing things on computer. And Mark has made wonderful website for me. I can hardly believe all these things are happening! We have not been here a year, and we have beautiful home, new family, very good work, and now I am starting my business. Such blessings!" His faced clouded over. "If only Lionel . . ."

Just then, Lionel came into the kitchen and sat down at the island. "Sandwiches! Just what I wanted. I've just been looking at potential places on this floor for more of Chuck's art. And we could use the stairway too." He noticed the menus. "Oh, these look like menus. Can't quite read them, but I'm sure they're good." He moved the sheet of paper closer to his face, then farther, trying to read the words, then put it down. "Mikhail, I really like the name we came up with for your catering business, after all that silliness. I don't think I've laughed so hard for ages—all those crazy names we were trying out at the dinner table the other night. I think you're going to have a very good niche. Different, but not too different." They had decided on "Mikhail" as the name of the business, with a tagline of "Catering Mediterranean and Balkan Specialties."

Anne finished making the last turkey-and-Jarlsberg sandwich, added it to the others, and pushed the plate into the middle of the island. "OK, everyone, help yourselves."

Chuck came in from his studio, took half a sandwich, and joined his housemates at the island. "I'm going to start making frames after we tour the downstairs, Lionel. I've got to get hopping to finish these in three weeks. I'll probably be working on them right up until the party starts." He took another bite of sandwich. "Where's Patty? She subbing today?"

"No, she's at the copy shop getting the invitation printed. She should be back soon." Lionel looked at his watch. "What time is it, anyway?"

"About twelve thirty," said Anne, as she pretended not to notice that Lionel couldn't read his watch.

Everyone left the kitchen but Anne and Lionel, who sat staring at the crumbs on his sandwich plate. He looked up at Anne and said, "We all know we'll die, but most of us don't know when. It's amazing how much difference it makes to know when."

*****

Patty was in the garden later that afternoon, taking out the spent impatiens and replacing them with purple mums and ornamental kale and cabbage. She yanked out the dead plants and dumped them into the garden cart. Jabbing a hole in the bag of potting soil, she mixed some of it into the earth where she was going to set the new plants.

Her thoughts were mutinous. *I am so pissed off! Why should I have to go through a death again? Why shouldn't Lionel and I have some happy years together? Why do we just get a few months? Why should something like this happen to such a good man? It just makes me furious!*

She spaced the plants where she wanted them, dug them in, and watered them. After crushing the papery plastic containers the plants came in and throwing them in the garden cart, she stomped savagely on the cardboard boxes from the garden store. Gathering up her tools, she wheeled the cart around the house to the recycle and yard-waste bins and threw all the trash away, slamming the lids.

She sat down on the back steps and cried tears of frustration. *This is too hard,* she thought. *I can't do this.*

But she knew she could, and she would. She just didn't want to.

*****

The Sunday afternoon of the launch party was a glorious fall Seattle day. Yellow and red leaves sprinkled the green lawn, and from inside the house, Margot noticed that the windows made a perfect frame for a variety of maples and other deciduous trees blazing in the last sunshine of the day. Bouquets of dahlias and chrysanthemums from the yard were scattered about the house, along with strategically placed stacks of business cards for Chuck, Mikhail, and Jeremy.

In between sets of playing with Jeremy, Margot helped Mikhail and Karina pass the hors d'oeuvres and replenish the beverages. Chuck divided his time between his studio and the house, meeting people and chatting about his artwork. Patty and Anne circulated, talking about the low-income preschool that would benefit from the money raised by the raffle and offering tickets. There was quite a crowd, all interested in the art, the house, and their living arrangements. As she walked from room to room, Margot overheard snippets of conversation.

"I'm so glad they had this event—I've always wanted to see the inside of this house."

"The kitchen is to die for! I wonder how much it cost."

"Oh, honey, I love the color of the breakfast room—let's repaint ours this color."

"I really like his paintings. Not the drawings so much, but I never like drawings."

In the crowded dining room, a couple stood in front of one of Chuck's larger paintings. "I don't know what everyone is carrying on about," the man said. "His work seems kind of derivative to me."

"I can't agree," a man standing behind him commented. "This is the least derivative work I've seen for a long time."

"Oh really?" the first man said, embarrassed at the challenge to his apparent attempt to impress his companion with his knowledge of art, which was probably nonexistent.

"I can't believe the art community hasn't discovered Chuck before now. If I were you, I'd buy some of his work before it gets so expensive you can't afford it." Smiling pleasantly, the man walked into the next room to listen in as Chuck tried to answer a question about composition from a group of elderly neighbors. They nodded and smiled, seeming impressed to be talking to a real painter but a bit bewildered about what he was saying.

"Come on over some afternoon," Chuck said, "and we'll play with some paint in my studio. It's a lot easier to show you than to talk about it." They looked thrilled at the offer and moved on to look at the next painting.

"I really like your work, Chuck. Tell me about your art background," said a middle-aged man of average height with sandy graying hair. He extended his hand. "Dave Simmons. I'm new to the neighborhood. We just bought the house at the end of the block, second from the end on the west side."

"Well, welcome to the block," Chuck said. "I hope you like it as much as we do. People around here are real nice. As far as my art background, I'm mostly self-taught, but I did take a lot of drawing classes at Cornish. I was hangin' out with this rich gal who thought I was the new Picasso, and she insisted on paying for my art classes. What could I say?" He shrugged his shoulders, his palms up. They both laughed. "Anyway, she got bored with me and moved on to the next new Picasso, but I got a lot out of those classes."

"Are you represented by a gallery?"

"Naw, I don't do the kind of stuff that's really in right now, so I haven't even tried to find a gallery. But my housemates have pushed me to get a website and look at some different ways of getting my work seen—like this shindig. Maybe it'll help." He shrugged again. "I just want to paint, you know? But I have to say, it's great to sell some work now and then. Helps pay my share of the bills."

Dave looked at Chuck with an appraising glance. "What about the public art competitions? We've got all these great percent-for-art programs in Seattle, and other places in the state. Have you ever submitted work?"

"No, I never have. To be honest, I guess I don't really know much about them." He looked a little embarrassed.

"Well," Dave said, "all these jurisdictions have laws that certain capital projects—like new police stations or electrical substations, or waste treatment plants—have to devote one percent of their project budgets to acquiring art. You should get on their mailing lists so you know when they're going to be making purchases. I really encourage you to pursue it." As he spoke, Dave was looking around the house. "Not to change the subject," he said, "but I've heard from the neighbors that you have a rather unusual living arrangement here. Would I be snooping if I asked about it?"

"No, not snooping at all. We just wanted to get old in a different way than most people do, and we've been lucky enough to find each other and make it happen."

"It must be hard adjusting to living with other people after decades of not living in a group situation. I can't imagine how you do it."

"Well, the alternatives are worse!" laughed Chuck. "Yeah, we have our little frictions, but we were really careful creating the group. We talked a lot before we committed and bought the house." Chuck adjusted the painting in front of them a fraction of an inch.

"I don't want to monopolize you, Chuck. You'd better get out there and circulate with your potential clients. I've really enjoyed talking with you."

"My pleasure, Dave." They shook hands, and Dave wandered off through the crowded room.

"Hey, Margot, can I have one of those, or maybe two?" She sidled up to Chuck with a tray of appetizers.

Margot grinned and handed him a napkin. "Want to hear my spiel?"

"No, just give me some food. All this fraternizing is making me hungry. Who's that with your dad?"

She turned and watched her dad, who was waving while working his way through the crowd. He was accompanied by an attractive woman with long dark hair, who was carrying a laptop bag. She looked familiar. But it wasn't until Mark finally got across the room that Margot realized why.

"Margot, you remember Claire, the woman we met at Carkeek Park? I ran into her up at Victrola and invited her to the party. Claire, this is Chuck—it's his art all over the house."

"Hi, Chuck," said Claire. "I look forward to seeing more of your art. I hope it's all right to crash the party. Looks like one of those 'more the merrier' kind of events." She smiled and turned to Margot. "How are you, Margot?"

"Oh, just fine—nice to see you again." She gestured at her tray. "I'm kind of busy right now, though. Maybe we can talk when there aren't so many people." She smiled shyly at Claire. "Here's a napkin. Try some appetizers. Mikhail's awesome—that's the chef. He's teaching me how to cook."

*****

Patty was on her way to sell more raffle tickets when Lionel stopped her. He was talking with a handsome man about his age. "Patty, I want you to meet my old friend Antonio Diaz. He teaches piano at UW. He and I did some community projects together, and we've stayed in touch. Antonio, this is my housemate, Patty."

"I'm very pleased to meet you, Patty. I was happy to get your invitation. Lionel and I don't see each other as much as we'd like." Antonio had wavy dark hair streaked with gray; dark-brown eyes; and a very appealing smile.

"Well, we can fix that easily enough," she said. "Would you like to come for dinner sometime, you and your wife?" She had noticed his wedding ring.

"I'd love to come for dinner, but my wife died two years ago. I know she'd have enjoyed meeting you, though. Lionel's been telling me about your 'intentional family.'"

"You can expect an invitation," she said, smiling. "Now, I've got to sell some more raffle tickets. I'm glad to have met you. See you soon, I hope."

By seven, the last of the guests had gone and the residents were collapsed in the living room, evaluating the party.

"Oh, my feet hurt," moaned Patty. I've been running around or standing up since two o'clock. She kicked off her shoes and put her feet in Lionel's lap, hoping for a foot rub.

"I'm tired too, but I think it went well, don't you?" said Lionel. "I went around to where the business cards were, and at least half of them are gone. How much money did we make for the preschool, Anne?"

"I don't know yet," Anne said. "Chuck sold a lot of paintings, but I still have to add up the prices to determine the cut for the preschool. We did really well on the raffle, I think. I did a quick count and came up with about five hundred dollars."

"There might be a few more sales," Chuck said with obvious satisfaction. "Some people were interested in the bigger, more expensive pieces but wanted to think about it."

"So how's your gut, Chuck?" asked Anne. "Was it really so awful to talk about your work? Looked to me like you were kind of having a good time." It was clear she couldn't help needling him affectionately.

"OK, OK," he said. "It wasn't so bad. And I had a good talk with our new neighbor. Seems like a real nice guy. "

"Oh, good!" said Patty. "I was hoping he'd come. He's the chair of the art department at UW. Who knows how that might be helpful to you?"

"Jesus!" said Chuck. "Glad I didn't know that when I was talking to him. He was pretty complimentary. Said I should enter the percent-for-art competitions. I really enjoy public art, but I just never thought about that as a possibility for me."

"Mikhail," said Patty, "how do you feel about the party? What kind of feedback did you get?"

"I have two events to cater. One is neighbor's cocktail party, and another cocktail party for preschool. Called 'fund-raiser.'" They all cheered. "I gave many cards. People liked what we were serving. So I think it went very well."

"How was it for you, Jeremy?" asked Lionel.

Jeremy, sitting on the couch next to Margot with a plate of leftover appetizers in his lap, raised his hand to signal his mouth was full, but gave them a thumbs-up.

When he could speak, he said, "All of my cards are gone, and I talked to two people about playing for them. One was background music; the other was accompaniment for a singing party. I was a little nervous at first, but I got over it. Most people weren't listening very carefully anyway."

"I decided I don't want to play at parties," Margot said. "I'm not as good as Jeremy. I'd rather cook with Mikhail. So maybe I can become his apprentice or something." She popped one of Jeremy's appetizers in her mouth.

Mikhail beamed. "You are good student, Margot. I will need helper when business grows, so we can practice now. I will be proud to show you my special dishes and how to be good chef."

"Hey, folks, one more bit of good news," said Chuck. I haven't told you all this yet, because I wanted to be sure, but I think my eyesight is actually getting better. I'm going back to the doctor to have it checked, but the fuzziness has gone away. They told me this could happen. I guess the vitamins they give you can have a really good effect for some people. Seems to be working for me. Man, what a relief!"

"Fantastic!" said Lionel. "The best news of the day! Now that you've told us, I realize that you've seemed more at ease the past few weeks, more your old self."

"Sorry if I've been a pain in the butt," Chuck said. "I *am* really relieved, but you know, I learned a really good lesson. Not only do I not take my eyesight for granted, but I've started thinking about all the other things I shouldn't take for granted. So you could say this eyesight problem was a good wake-up call."

The Unwelcome Visitor

In mid December, Mark and the housemates sat in the living room of the mansion, admiring the decorations and enjoying hot buttered rum while the rain drove in from the southwest and the windblown branches tapped against the windows. The mantel was draped with boughs, among which nestled small poinsettias and red glass balls.

"I'm glad we could all agree on the type of Christmas tree we wanted," Patty said, rehanging an ornament in what she must have considered to be a more advantageous location. "I really like the old-fashioned unsheared Doug firs."

"Yeah, they really smell good," said Chuck. "That's the best part of the tree thing—that smell. Some of the other types of trees *look* really good, but it's more important to have the smell than a perfectly shaped tree, at least to me."

"I like our decorations," said Karina. "Is good that each person made something or gave something. My favorite is Patty's bubble lights. I sit and watch them bubble and bubble. And Chuck's . . . What do you call them, Chuck?"

"Oh, I don't know," he said. "Swirls or whirlpools or something. It was fun to paint the paper and put on the gold-and-silver overlay and then see what happened when I cut them out. I'll make more next year—you always get better the second time around. What's your favorite decoration, Mikhail?"

Mikhail looked around the room. "All are beautiful," he said, "but I like best the menorah in the kitchen window. I light the candles while I am preparing dinner and remember seeing them at our neighbor's house when I was child."

"I've never really had much in the way of Christmas traditions," said Anne. "Since my parents lived in New England and we didn't have much money, Giselle and I would usually spend Christmas with other friends who didn't have family around. We had a tree and presents and some photos with Santa, but that was about it."

"Sounds like my Christmases," said Lionel. "But I didn't have the tree and presents, except for housewarming gifts, or an office gift exchange. I was always glad when the holidays were over."

"Me too," said Chuck. "I had a few good ones here and there, but it was kind of a relief when it was over, so I wasn't being reminded of what I was missing. No family and all that."

Patty tucked the afghan more snugly around Lionel's legs. "Well," she said, "we had all the family and tradition and the whole nine yards, for over thirty years, and I can tell you it was a mixed bag. In the early years of my marriage, there were the frictions among my husband and my siblings about who would host the dinner, and who would go the parents', or would the parents come to the kids. And then it had to change when there were more children and too many to fit into one house. Then there was the whole bit about what the children wanted, and could you find it or did you want them to have whatever it was, and how much you should spend. Not to mention the cooking and cleaning and decorating and Christmas cards—all that on top of the rest of life." She threw up her hands. "Nothing else seemed to stop. We just piled Christmas on top of regular life. I used to be so anxious, wanting it to be happy for everyone else, wanting it to be a certain way for myself. I enjoyed the special food and fancy meals, but I must say, Mikhail, I'm really looking forward to your being in charge and not me!" She looked over at him with a smile of relief. "But I'm happy to help. Helping would be fun, not work!"

"I am happy you want to do French dinner," he replied. "That will be fun for me, to try something different."

"You're sure you wouldn't have preferred to do something traditionally Russian or Ukrainian?" Lionel asked.

"I will make some traditional appetizers for Christmas Eve, but I like to do something different. Life is different for us now. I am not holding the past, the old.

"What kind of Christmas memories do you have, Mark?" Anne asked.

"Mostly good," he said. "Especially when I was little. I remember lying under the Christmas tree and looking up through the branches, the favorite ornaments I liked to hang up each year. But every year, my Mom faithfully hung up some god-awful things that we'd made. Finally, when we were teenagers, we told her she could retire those." He laughed and went on reminiscing. "My family's from California, so even after I left home, I was never too far away to get back for Christmas. But I can sympathize with what Patty's saying. When I got older, I could see how much work it was for my parents, especially my mom. I think she's relieved now that she can go to a daughter and son-in-law's house and not host the whole thing herself." He took a sip of his drink.

"Margot and I talked about Christmas," he said. "What she liked about it, didn't like, what she wanted to do this year. She finally decided she was up for meeting my family, so we agreed to spend Christmas Eve here and fly to California early on Christmas Day. We'll be there in time for the big to-do at my sister's."

"Speaking of Margot," said Anne, "where is she?"

"She's out Christmas shopping with Jeremy," Mark said. "They were busing downtown to meet at Westlake Center. And she's going to church with him on Sunday."

"That'll be a new experience," said Anne, her face taking on a pensive look. "I don't think Giselle ever took her to church. Giselle and I used to attend the Congregational church near where we lived. They were nice people, very inclusive, not big on doctrine, but when Giselle was about twelve, she decided she didn't like church anymore and refused to go. I never figured out what changed. Maybe it was just the preadolescent thing."

"How are you doing, Anne?" Patty asked gently. "Is Christmas a harder time for you this year?"

Anne sighed, absently braiding the fringe on her pashmina shawl. "It seems like I'm sad all the time. I don't feel sadder because it's Christmas. It's just I think of different things to be sad about: The arguments Giselle and I had about money. Her not wanting to be with me or do things with me, especially at the holidays. How little Christmas time I had with Margot when she was a child." There was a catch in her voice. "And now it's too late."

"It's not too late for Margot," said Mark. "She really wants to be with you. With all of you. She's really clear that family is something she wants. You probably noticed how much she enjoyed decorating the tree. She and Giselle didn't have a lot of decorations, but Margot kept the ones they had and dug them out of the bottom of her closet a couple weeks ago. She knew right where they were. And she's sure into those crochet snowflakes you taught her how to make, Anne. If she doesn't stop making them soon, we won't be able to see the tree for the snowflakes!"

The doorbell rang repeatedly. "That'll be Margot," laughed Anne, getting up to let her in. "She must not have got enough doorbell ringing as a child. She can never stop with one ring."

Margot and Jeremy burst into the room, laughing, cheeks pink, carrying Christmas shopping bags and dripping umbrellas.

"Oh, the tree smells so good!" Margot unwound her scarf and shrugged off her jacket, dropping it on a chair. "Wait till you see what Jeremy got for his little sister—it's so cute!"

Jeremy picked up her jacket and took it to the hall closet, along with his. Then he flopped down on the sofa.

"Man, everybody in Seattle must have been downtown tonight," he said. "We stayed and watched the indoor snow at Pacific Place. It was really cool!"

"Could we have one of those?" Margot pointed at Anne's hot buttered rum and looked at her father. "What are they? They must be good, or you wouldn't all be drinking them."

"Sure," said Mark. "It's hot buttered rum. Come on in the kitchen and I'll show you how to make it. But you only get one."

Margot dragged Jeremy off the sofa, and they followed her dad into the kitchen.

"I think it's so cool you let me drink," she said. "Mom never let me have anything, except a sip of her beer or champagne." She and Jeremy settled close together on the stools at the island.

"Well, I guess she and I would have disagreed about that," Mark said. "I think kids ought to learn how to drink at home, so it's not such a big deal—some forbidden thing you have to go out and do to rebel against your parents or whatever. And you can learn how to drink different things and appreciate them, not just chug something in order to get drunk." As he talked, he got the butter-and-sugar mix and a lemon out of the fridge and began measuring ingredients into their mugs. "I assume you want one too, Jeremy?"

"Uh, sure. I've never had any rum—or any kind of alcohol. My parents wouldn't approve. But I don't think like they do about everything, so, yeah, I'd like to have one. Sounds good."

"I hope I don't get in trouble, serving alcohol to minors, but I'll trust you two to be discreet," said Mark, eyebrows raised in warning.

"Jeremy," Lionel said as the three of them went back into the living room with their drinks, "we were just saying we'd like to sing. Would you play for us? There's a file folder of Christmas music with my other music. Second shelf from the bottom, on the left."

"Sure, Mr. B," he said, and he went to get the music.

"We were just talking about Christmas traditions," Anne said to Margot. "Since we get to make up our own," she said to the group, "I'm wondering what everyone is thinking about gifts. None of us need any more stuff, and I often found gift giving to be kind of stressful. What if it didn't fit or she didn't like it or already had one. You know . . . ?"

"I know what you mean. I've felt all that too," said Patty. "But I also really enjoy giving gifts. It's such a nice feeling when it's just the right thing. Why don't we think about consumables or experiences, or things we make ourselves? We could give something to the group as a whole or give individual presents—whatever feels right."

"Found it, Mr. B," said Jeremy, waving the folder of music at Lionel. He sat down at the piano, and Margot went to sit beside him.

"I'll turn the pages for you," she said with a flirtatious look.

After they'd sung several carols, Lionel asked Margot to play "Ave Maria."

"Sure," she said. "I've got lots better since music camp, and Jeremy knows the accompaniment."

She got out her cello, and they were about to start when there was a loud banging on the front door. Chuck got up to answer it.

"Where's my son?" an angry voice said. "I came to get my son and take him away from you people trying to corrupt him." A man of medium height with disheveled hair staggered into the living room, his soaked parka dripping on the floor. "There you are! Come on, Jeremy. You're coming home with me." He moved toward the piano.

"Dad! What are you doing here?" Jeremy was standing now, clearly shocked. "You can't just barge in here like this!"

"Oh, yes, I can! You heard me—let's go." His speech was slurred, and he walked unsteadily.

Then he saw Margot, sitting beside the piano with her cello, bow in hand. "That's why you're here," Jeremy's father said. "That shameless girl—she's bewitched you.

Look at her! Legs spread, with that thing between them. I've got to get you away from these people or you'll be headed for damnation!" He grabbed Jeremy's shirt and tried to pull him toward the door.

"No!" shouted Jeremy, pulling back. "You're drunk, and I'm not going with you. You come in here and insult my friends, some of the nicest people in the world. You with your booze and your judgments. Get out of here!" Jeremy jerked his arm out of his father's grasp and pushed him. The man staggered, but he caught himself and lunged at his son.

By this time, Mark had overcome his stupefaction at this intrusion, and both he and Chuck rushed to grab Jeremy's father.

"OK, outside you go," said Chuck, twisting the man's arm behind his back using his ex-bartender technique. They manhandled him out the front door to the porch.

Jeremy's father cursed them and yelled about the spawn of Satan. "Let me go, you bastards!"

"Now what?" asked Mark, trying to hang on to the recalcitrant man. "We can't just stand here all night. Should we call the police?"

"Sounds like an excellent idea. A cell should calm him right down!" said Chuck, trying to maintain his hold. "How the hell did he get here anyway?"

Jeremy answered from behind them. "That's our car right there. My mom drove him. He does this about once a month—gets drunk and makes her drive him places. Then he beats her."

"Don't you talk about your father like that," the man said. "A liar for a son. Let go of me, you SOBs!" Working free of Chuck's grasp, he pushed Mark against the wall and stumbled down the stairs. They let him go. He fell into the car, and it drove off.

Chuck put his arm around Jeremy's shoulder and pulled him back into the house. "Come on, son. Let's go inside and figure out what to do next."

Jeremy stood in the middle of the room, shoulders slumped, looking at the floor. "I'm really sorry, everyone. I'm so embarrassed. I don't know what to say." He glanced at Margot and then back at the floor. "I'm really sorry, Margot. What he said was totally off the wall. I don't know where all that came from."

"It's OK," she said. She was sitting on the couch, holding her grandmother's hand, and her voice was a little shaky. "It wasn't you who said it, and he was drunk, so just try to forget it."

"Jeremy," Lionel said, "would it be helpful if Chuck and Mark and I talked with you about what to do next? I don't want to exclude anyone, or make this into a guy thing, but I don't think it's necessary for all of us to be involved in the discussion. I'm sure this is hard enough for you to talk about."

Jeremy nodded. "Yeah, I'd appreciate it. Thanks."

"Dinner will be ready in an hour," said Mikhail. Does that give you enough time? I can serve later."

"That should be fine," Lionel said. "Chuck, can you help me into the library?"

The four of them settled into a circle of chairs. "Jeremy, I'm concerned about your mom," Chuck said. Do you think your father is likely to . . . attack her when they get home? If so, we should call the police."

Mark could tell that Lionel, not having heard Jeremy's revelation, was trying to put two and two together. His face was drawn with worry.

"Has she ever called the police?" Mark asked. "Or has anyone else?"

"No one's ever called the police that I know of," Jeremy said. "Dad's real good about covering it up, and he tells her he'll beat one of *us* if she screams or tells anyone that he's beating her. I've almost called, but she begs me not to." Tears were running down his face. "I don't see how she can keep letting it happen!"

"I had a friend who was abusing his wife—and I know he loved her!" said Chuck. "So it gets real complicated, and I don't think any of us are going to figure it out. The question is, is it appropriate for us to get involved? I can call the police and ask them to go to your house, but I won't have to face any of the fallout. And you probably will, Jeremy. Are you sure you're up for that?"

Jeremy was quiet for a long time. He wiped his sleeve across his eyes and sat up straighter in his chair. "Yeah," he said, "it's time for me to do the right thing. I'm tired of feeling like a coward. He's been doing this for years— gets drunk, then starts hitting her. I don't know why he wouldn't do the same thing tonight. I'll call the police and tell them what I think is happening."

"I don't want you to feel that we're pushing you to do this," Lionel said. "It's likely to cause a lot of uproar and unpleasantness, and it's easy for us to think the right thing to do is involve the police, but it may not be."

"No, I don't feel like you're pressuring me. I feel like you're supporting me . . . like you're helping me do something I wanted to do for a long time but was afraid of. Can I use your phone?"

Lionel nodded.

Jeremy dialed 911. "Hello, my name is Jeremy Freeman and, uh, I think my dad is beating my mom right now. Uh, he does this once a month when he gets drunk, and he was just here, drunk, at my friends' house, and my mom drove him home. So could you send someone over?" He gave his home address and Lionel's phone number.

Lionel gestured to Jeremy to give him the phone.

"Just a minute," Jeremy said to the dispatcher. "My friend wants to talk to you." He gave the phone to Lionel.

"This is Lionel Blackburn. Jeremy's father was just here, drunk and making accusations about the people who live here. It took two of us to get him outside. Please call me if you need any corroboration of Jeremy's story." Lionel repeated his phone number and gave the operator his address. "Also," he said, "we can take Jeremy home or to the police station—whatever is needed. And he can stay here tonight if that would be advisable. Will someone call us back and let us know what we should do?"

While Lionel finished up with 911, Jeremy paced around the room, picking up books and setting them down. "Uh, I think I'll go get some water," he said, and he left for the kitchen.

"What was that shit about Margot?" said Chuck. "What a weirdo that guy is!"

"I think it's worse than weirdo," said Mark. "Margot told me he was really strange when she went over there for dinner that time. She said he looked at her funny— whatever that means. And when she went to the bathroom, he was standing outside the door when she came out. Sat a little too close when they were playing Monopoly after dinner too. My take on it is that he's lusting after her and he's blaming her for his lust. What a disgusting SOB!" Mark slammed the armrests of his chair. "Poor Jeremy. It's a wonder he's such a nice kid, given what he's had to put up with."

They were halfway through dinner when the doorbell rang. Chuck went to answer it and came back to tell them that two officers were waiting in the living room. He and Lionel went with Jeremy.

"Margot, I think we should go home soon," said Mark. "It's getting late, and we've got work and school tomorrow."

"Can't I stay here tonight?" she said. "I want to talk to Jeremy, and make sure he knows I'm not mad at him or anything."

"We don't know whether Jeremy will stay here tonight or not," said her grandmother. "And it may be awhile before we find out. Besides, I think he might like to have some time alone. His feelings are probably all over the place: anger, embarrassment, fear—"

"I know! That's why I want to stay. To tell him it'll be OK."

"Margot," said Mark, "I think Anne's right. Why don't you talk to him before we leave, or Anne will talk to him later and make sure he knows you're not upset with him. And you could send him a text to reassure him, or leave a message on his cell. It's not that we're trying to keep you apart. It's just that he probably needs some space right now. I think it would be best for us to go home."

All during this conversation, Margot's face was a panorama of emotion: indecision, defiance, worry, bewilderment. Mark figured she felt ganged-up on by the adults, but he was convinced Jeremy would be relieved that he didn't have to face her again right away after what his father had said.

Dinner finished without much conversation, and Margot and Mark left before Jeremy had finished talking with the police.

Coping

Patty watched Lionel silently from the library doorway, tears in her eyes. She had found a lightweight wheelchair at a neighborhood garage sale, and Lionel now needed to use it. He was awkwardly pushing a wooden chair away from the desk so he could maneuver his wheelchair in front of the PC.

The printer was out of paper. He struggled to get a ream out of the desk drawer with his right hand alone; his left was almost useless now. "Goddamn it! Can't even get paper in the printer—and it's going to get worse." He slammed the package of paper down on the desk.

Patty wiped away her tears and walked into the room. "Googling already?" she said brightly.

"I'm sure glad it's so easy to make the print big. Otherwise my computer-using days would be over already," he said, equally brightly. "I found a really good poem at the poetry site I frequently visit. Here, read this." He handed the page he'd just printed to Patty.

She sat on the desk, her hand on his shoulder, and read "Losing My Sight" by Lisel Mueller. When she'd finished, she said, "It has a lovely tone, doesn't it? Some gentle humor . . . a sense of discovery . . . an appreciation of the good things about a new situation. And all the time in the background is the loss, but it's not mentioned. What are you noticing, as your sight gets worse?"

He played with the ivory-handled letter opener on the desk, looking out the window, then he looked back at her and smiled. "I've got everyone's walk down. I can tell

243

who's coming through the foyer or down the upstairs hall. Not that I can't see them, but I'm just more aware of sounds. And when we watch the news on TV, I notice the accents and inflections, the laughs, because I can't really see their faces very well." He stopped talking and looked around the room at the comfortable furniture, the Oriental rugs, the shelves and shelves of books, the artwork. "This house has its own night noises, you know. I notice not because I'm losing my eyesight, but because I'm awake so often when everyone else is asleep."

*****

Chuck walked into the kitchen to find Anne staring off into space in front of the open dishwasher. He came up behind her and put his arms around her. "How are you feeling, Annie?" he asked gently. "You seem a little distracted, like sometimes you're here and sometimes you're not."

"I miss her. So many things remind me of Giselle: Every time I go past the flower section in the grocery store, or a florist. When I smell French fries—she was a French fry addict. I notice the photo of her and Margot on my nightstand several times a day. And I know there's no chance to see her again, not in this life anyway."

Chuck pulled her closer to him.

"And, at the same time, I get so angry!" she said. "Angry that she kept carrying that chip on her shoulder, that she tried to make me feel guilty for the way I'd raised her. So when it seems like I'm 'not here,' it's probably because I'm rerunning all these old tapes." She gave him a weak smile. "Now there's a dated metaphor, if I ever heard one!"

Christmas Eve

Lionel was happy to have Abe and Lin at the mansion for Christmas Eve. Lin would spend the next day with her daughter's family, and Abe had been invited to stay the night, since he didn't have any family nearby.

"Are you sure I should be here tonight and all day tomorrow?" Abe asked Lionel as they sat in front of the fire after dinner. "I don't want to intrude, and I do have some invitations from other friends to drop in tomorrow."

"You're not intruding. You need to see us in our pajamas with bedhead." They both laughed. "And besides, you're halfway to being family now, and this is our family's Christmas time. Patty will be going to spend part of the day with her children and grandchildren tomorrow, and Mark and Margot are flying to the Bay Area first thing in the morning for a few days with Mark's family. He's been up here for, let's see, eight months now, but his folks haven't met Margot yet. And Mikhail and Karina will be spending part of the day with his cousin's family. So this is our time to all be together."

Abe got up to poke at the fire. "Lionel, do you know about the status of Jeremy's family? I haven't heard anything since you filled me in on the phone about what happened the other night."

Lionel sighed. "It's still difficult, but I think there's hope for some improvement. Since Jeremy's father was assaulting his wife when the police arrived, they took him to jail and kept him for two nights. He's agreed to go for alcoholism and anger-management treatment, and to work with his pastor. So we're crossing our fingers. I gather things are a little strained, but Jeremy is back at home, after staying with us the night of the . . . incident."

*****

Anne came in from the kitchen, followed by Patty and Lin carrying trays of *bûche de noël.* "Ah, Mikhail's traditional French Christmas Eve dessert—I can hardly wait!" said Lionel. "I'm so glad the chemo is over for a while and I can enjoy eating again. Got to get fattened up for the next round!"

Then the rest of the family trailed in, Chuck and Karina carrying the tea and coffee pots and Patty's china cups and saucers.

Mark sat down on the sofa. "Man, I'm stuffed—I don't have to eat for a week. But I did save room for dessert. Dinner was fantastic, Mikhail."

Mikhail's smile was as discreet as ever, but Anne knew him well enough now to know he appreciated the praise.

"Where did Jeremy and Margot go?" asked Lionel.

"They went downstairs to play Ping-Pong," said Mark. "I'll go get them."

"Is it time for presents yet?" asked Margot, coming into the room hand in hand with Jeremy. "Jeremy and I have a present for everybody." She was practically bouncing with energy and enthusiasm. "Shall we do it now?"

"Don't you want your dessert?" asked Anne.

Margot looked at Jeremy, who smiled and shrugged. "I can wait." He sat down at the piano.

"We'll have dessert after," said Margot. "We've been practicing some music for you." Her eyes sparkled as she flounced over to her cello. She tugged at her fuzzy red sweater, tucked her long dark hair behind her ear, and arranged herself and her instrument. She nodded to Jeremy, and they were off with "He Shall Feed His Flock," and "Come unto Him All Ye That Labor," from *Messiah*, followed by a rousing version of the "Hallelujah Chorus," accompanied by those who could sing it or could at least hum along.

"Splendid, splendid!" cried Lionel, tears running down his cheeks. "Oh, what a marvelous present—thank you so much!"

Anne had tears in her eyes as she went to give Margot a big hug. "Oh, sweetie, I wish your mom could have heard that. She'd be so proud."

Jeremy and Margot stood, bowing and grinning to all the applause until Patty said, "Well, you certainly deserve your dessert. You get two pieces each for that!" She delivered a plate of the Christmas cake to each of them, with lots of whipped cream.

"Hey, Margot," Chuck said, "since you aren't going to be here tomorrow, shall I give you and your grandmother your present tonight?"

"Oh, yes," Margot answered. "Let's have it now—I love presents!"

"Yes," Anne said. "No better time."

Chuck left the room and came back with a large package wrapped in brown paper.

"Oh, the paper's beautiful," said Anne. "It's too nice to rip it off. We have to save it and see if we can use it again."

"Oh, go ahead and rip it," Chuck said. "I can always paint you some more bows."

Anne patted the seat beside her, and Margot sat down. Together they started removing the paper. When they saw the painting, neither of them said anything for a moment. Then Anne's tears resumed, and Margot said, "Wow, Chuck, it's awesome! I know which photo you painted it from. How did you get it?"

"I saw it when I was helping Anne bring things home from your mom's place, and I copied it and slipped it back into the box."

"We're dying here!" cried Patty. "Can we see it too?"

Anne turned the frame around.

"Oh, it's breathtaking, Chuck!" said Patty. "How very, very special. I think that should go over the mantel."

"Describe it to me," said Lionel. "I'm afraid I'm not seeing much more than a smudge."

"It's Anne," Patty said, "about to go onstage, sitting on a chair and smiling up at the photographer. Looks like she's tying her toe shoes. It's very Degas-like, impressionistic, except the face is clearly Anne. The colors are creams and pinks and some black. Oh, it's just lovely!"

"Mom had that photo on her dresser for as long as I can remember," said Margot, now sounding sad. "When was it taken, Gramma?"

Anne wiped her eyes and leaned back in the chair. "It makes me so happy to hear that Giselle kept it on her dresser. It was taken by a dancer friend who had a pulled hamstring and couldn't dance that night. She was also a photographer, so she was hobbling around backstage taking snapshots, and this was one of them. She was one of Giselle's favorites of my friends. I'm not sure, but I think that night we were doing *Coppélia*." She looked up at Chuck while the others gathered around the painting for a closer look. "It's really beautiful, Chuck. I don't know how to thank you—it's so special."

"You're welcome, darlin'," he said, bending over to whisper in her ear. "Just being with you is thanks enough."

Mark banged his spoon on his teacup. "May I have your attention please? I don't think I can compete with Chuck's painting, but I have a little announcement to share with you. I'm sorry Claire couldn't be here too. She's with her family . . ."

"Ohhh," squealed Margot. "I bet I know, I bet I know!"

"Guess I'd better talk fast or she'll steal my thunder: Claire and I are engaged!"

New Year's Eve

"So, how was the trip?" Jeremy said. He and Margot were talking on the phone as he bused to the mansion for his piano lesson. "You said you'd tell me all about it when you got home. Was it hard to talk on your cell when you were there?"

"Yeah, we were pretty busy," Margot said, "and I was sharing a room with my cousin Rachel, so I didn't have much private time. Besides, I kind of wanted to soak stuff up and think about it before I told you about it."

"Where were you?"

"Mark's family's from a really neat place called Tiburon," Margot said. "We took BART—that's their commuter train—from the airport to downtown San Francisco, then we got on a trolley and rode down to the waterfront, and then we got on a ferry to Tiburon. It's a lot like Seattle—except warmer and the plants are all different, and it's *so* developed. You know how you take the ferry to Bainbridge, and all around Seattle and Puget Sound there're lots of trees? Well, around San Francisco Bay, it's all buildings. Lots of plants too, but it's basically all built-up. Kind of scary. I've never been in a place with so many people. I hope Seattle never gets like that!"

"Yeah, I was only there once, but I remember how crowded it was. How was Mark's family?"

"Oh, really nice—I like them. It's kind of weird suddenly having aunts and uncles and cousins and more grandparents. But they were awesome, really happy that Mark and I had finally gotten together—and that he got engaged. Rachel's a year younger than me, and her family lives in San Diego. She invited me to come visit and go sailing with them. We had fun riding bikes around Tiburon and hanging out in the touristy places in San Francisco. I know I said it was too built-up, but it really is a cool town!"

"Yeah," he said. "I remember Fisherman's Wharf from that trip we took when I was only five or six. And Chinatown. That was cool."

"So how was Christmas at your house?" she asked.

There was a pause. "It was OK . . . A little tense. But we're trying to get back to normal. I don't know if that's the right word. Probably not." He pulled the cord to signal he wanted to get off at the next stop. "Hey, want to go to a movie New Year's Eve?"

"Um, I was going to ask if you wanted to come over for dinner. I want to practice some recipes Mikhail's been teaching me. And we could watch a movie here. Mark and Claire are going to some kind of business thing, so they won't be around."

"That sounds good," he said, exultant at the possibility of a night alone with Margot.

"Great! Want to come about six?"

*****

"Margot, there's something I wanted to talk to you about." Mark put down his fork and smoothed his napkin across his knee. "By the way, this is awesome stroganoff—you're really learning a lot of good stuff from Mikhail. Um, anyway, what I wanted to say . . . This is a little awkward. Claire and I want to be together more, and I was wondering . . . if you'd feel neglected or something if I stayed at her place some nights. Not every night, of course. Or maybe she might stay here sometimes. How would you feel about that?"

"No problem either way," Margot said blithely. "Of course you want to sleep with Claire. I'm a big girl—I'm not going to feel neglected. *Is* she going to move in with us?"

"We don't know yet. It's a decision we all three have to make together. It's several decisions, really: Should she move in here? Should we get a bigger place—a house maybe? When should we do it? We'd like to have a child, and she's thirty-five, so we don't want to wait too much longer. You'll be going away to college in a couple of years. Lots to think about."

"I'm not sure I want to go to college," Margot said, looking at him over her glass of milk.

"Oh," Mark said. "Well, ultimately it's your decision. But I really think you should give it a try. If you don't like it after a year or so, it's fine to do something else. But it's an important life experience—or it can be—and the odds are better that you'll get good-paying jobs if you go to college. You need to be able to support yourself." He stopped and shook his head. "Listen to me. I never thought I'd be telling someone they have to go to college to get a job! I'm not really saying that. It's true about college grads having better-paying jobs, but that's not the point of an undergraduate degree, in my opinion. It's about life, about seeing what's out there, how people think and live so differently, how to appreciate and get along with people who come from really different backgrounds than yours, how the world got the way it is. If you get a job related to what you study, all the better, but that isn't necessary."

Margot took their plates to the sink, rinsed them, and put them in the dishwasher. "I was thinking it would be awesome to go to France to cooking school."

"Were you really? Wow, that would be terrific! Maybe we could go to France this summer. You could do a language immersion course, and Claire and I could do Paris, or hang out in Provence or something," said Mark, almost bouncing out of his chair with enthusiasm. "Would you like that? You'd sort of be on your own, but not completely. Let's think about it. But something else just occurred to me. You haven't said anything about college entrance exams. Don't you have to take those this year?"

"Yeah, I signed up to take the SAT. Jeremy said I should keep my options open." She put the remaining stroganoff in a container and turned on the dishwasher. "Well, my cello is calling. Time to practice."

*****

Margot was excited at the prospect of an evening alone with Jeremy. She had been scheming for weeks, trying to figure out how to make it happen. And then the New Year's Eve opportunity dropped in her lap. They had been holding hands and sitting close together since Thanksgiving weekend, when they'd had their first official date. But he hadn't kissed her yet. Was it because of his strict religious upbringing, or was he just shy—or maybe both? She didn't know. Maybe she should just kiss him. But what if he thought she was slutty or something? She pondered the situation as she walked home from Central Co-op with the groceries for dinner. She decided she'd just kiss him lightly when he arrived and say,

"Happy New Year!" and pretend it was no big deal. Then he'd know that kissing was OK with her.

At four thirty, it was almost dark and the wind whipped her scarf and chilled her ears. She punched in the door code, walked across the big tiles through the peach-and-terra-cotta lobby, and studied the abstract painting on the wall as she waited for the elevator. She liked the building: the newness, the tasteful design, their corner apartment with southern and eastern views of the mountains. It had been seven months since her mother died, and Margot still couldn't believe how much her life had changed. She missed her mother. But she didn't miss all the arguments and bickering, the perennial problem of money, the amount of time Giselle was gone, working late or out with friends. Still, Margot was sometimes overtaken by a fear of being alone; it just seemed to come out of nowhere. She would think about her grandmother and her father, and the fear would gradually recede.

It meant a lot to her that now she had a dad, and a laid-back one at that. He was reasonable, and he treated her like an adult—at least more so than her mother had. She had a cool apartment, new clothes when she needed them, summer camp, a trip to San Francisco. Was all this worth losing her mom? No way! But it was some kind of . . . compensation, or distraction or something. And better than the stuff, she had more time with her grandmother and her "family," and a dad and a job and a boyfriend. Probably none of this would have happened if her mother hadn't died. But it was hard to know what to make of so much differentness.

"Hi, I'm home," she called, taking her bags of groceries to the kitchen, where she set them on the granite countertop and switched on the lights.

"Hey, Margot. I'm just finishing up a status report on the Henderson project," called Mark from the third bedroom, which he'd made into his office. "Then I have to get dressed and pick up Claire."

When Margot appeared in the doorway, he swiveled around in his chair. "What time is Jeremy coming, and what's the lucky guy getting for dinner?"

"He's coming about six, so I'd better get busy. I'm making salmon and green salad and heavy hors d'oeuvres. It's pretty easy, but it takes a long time."

"Well, tell him happy New Year for me. Oh, wait. I guess I can tell him myself—he's coming to dinner with us tomorrow, isn't he?"

"He doesn't know yet. Depends on what's happening at home," she said. "I'm off to the stove."

An hour later, Mark came into the kitchen. "How do I look? Is my bow tie straight?"

She smiled, wiped her hands on her jeans, and made a minor adjustment to his tie. "You look good in a tux. Wish I could see what Claire's wearing."

"I'm looking forward to seeing that myself!" he said with a big grin. He patted his pants pockets for his keys and wallet. "OK, I'm off. I'll be back late in the morning. Have fun with Jeremy—and happy New Year."

"You too. Hurry up—you're going to be late."

As soon as her dad was out the door, Margot took a bottle of champagne out of the wine rack and put it in the freezer. Then she went to change clothes. She'd been thinking all week about what to wear and had finally settled on silver ballet flats, black tights, a short black skirt, and a clingy low-cut silver sweater that had belonged to her mother. She looked at least twenty-five, she thought with satisfaction.

*****

"Well, if you don't trust me, you've got yourselves to blame—you raised me!" With that parting shot, Jeremy left the house, slamming the door.

The angry exchange with his parents filled his thoughts as he rode his bike to Margot's. They seemed to think he was still six years old. Always asking him where he was going, when he'd be back, who he'd be with— especially if Margot was involved. Just because he didn't want to tell them every detail of his life, they thought he was hiding something, doing something wrong. He could have told them he was going to a movie with his friend Ted, but he didn't want to lie. Better to stand up to them, not let them force him into lying.

He made himself leave those thoughts behind and think of Margot instead. That wasn't hard to do; he was thinking about her most of the time anyway. He still couldn't believe how lucky he was that such a beautiful girl was willing to hang out with him. What did she see in him, anyway? She was hot—no doubt about that. Really, he didn't like that word. "Hot" seemed to be only about looks and sexiness. It was hard to think about Margot and not think about sex, but he also liked her enthusiasm, her directness, her lack of shyness: all the things he didn't have.

A horn honked next to him, jerking his attention back to riding his bike at night in the street.

In about half an hour, he reached Trader Joe's and bought a rose for Margot.

He rang her doorbell exactly at six, and there she was—she almost took his breath away. "You look awesome!" he said. "But I didn't know we were going to dress up. Why didn't you tell me? I'm just wearing jeans. I could have worn my suit."

"You don't need a suit. You're fine. You look comfortable. And you couldn't help me cook if you were wearing a suit. Come in."

He handed her the rose as she closed the door behind him.

"That's really nice. Thanks! No one's ever given me flowers before." She stepped close to him and kissed him lightly on the lips.

Jeremy blushed, startled by the kiss. "Well, I'm glad I got to be the first one."

"Come on into the kitchen," she said.

Jeremy followed her, trying not to stare at her short skirt.

Margot took the champagne out of the freezer. "Have you ever opened one of these?" He shook his head. "I've watched people do it at the mansion, but I've never done it either. Mikhail said not to shake it." She peeled off the foil and unwound the wire holding the cork in. "OK, now you're supposed to turn the cork and work it out." She handed the bottle to him. "Mikhail puts a towel over the end—I'm not sure why. Maybe to keep the cork from flying off and breaking something, or maybe to catch the drips."

Jeremy turned the cork back and forth, trying to wiggle it out. Suddenly it popped out, and the champagne followed. "Oh no," he said, "we're wasting it! Get a glass!" He held the bottle over the sink, dropped the towel, and tried to catch some of the champagne in his mouth.

Margot laughed. "Here's a glass. Pour some in here." She handed him a tumbler. "Maybe I shook it when I took it out of the freezer."

Jeremy poured it too fast, and the champagne fizzed up. "Maybe the bubbles will go away," he said, "and it'll turn back into regular champagne again."

"It'll be fine." Margot giggled. "You looked pretty funny trying to catch the overflow in your mouth."

"Well, there's at least three-quarters of it left, so I think I did pretty well for my first time with a champagne bottle." He pointed at the tumbler. "Do you want to drink out of that glass?"

"No, we've got some real champagne glasses," she said, removing two flutes from a cupboard. "I'll pour mine into one of these, and you can fill up the other one. Then we'll have a toast. What shall we toast to?"

"How about the New Year?"

"That's way too boring. How about a scholarship for you to your favorite college?"

"That doesn't seem like a toast," he said. "More like wishing on a star."

"OK," Margot said. "How about 'To us'?"

"Sure," he said with a big smile. "That's a good toast." They clinked their glasses.

"So, am I supposed to help cook?" he asked, leaning against the stove. "What do you want me to do?"

"Here's your apron," she said. It was a denim apron with BBQ written on the front. She slipped the top of it over his head, then she reached around him to cross the ties in back, bringing them to the front to fasten. "OK, now you look very chef-y." Putting on a flowered apron with a ruffle across the bottom, she said, "We're going to make gougères. They're like a teeny cheesy cream puff without the cream, and they're really good with champagne. You can get out the big cookie sheets and butter them." She pointed at a cupboard beside him. "I'll mix up the batter, and then we can both load up the cookie sheets. I'll get out some other stuff while they're cooking."

After he finished buttering the cookie sheets, Jeremy watched with interest while Margot melted butter and milk in a pan, mixed in flour, and then beat in eggs, one at a time. After she mixed in grated parmesan, they begin filling up the cookie sheets with dollops of batter.

"These are sooooo good. You're going to love them," she told him as she put both cookie sheets into the hot oven and set the timer.

"This is pretty amazing," he said. "How many times have you made these?"

"I've never actually made them," she said, "but I've watched Mikhail make them two or three times. Want some nuts and olives and cheese?"

"Sure, sounds good. Uh, are we going to have something else?"

"Oh, yeah," she said. "These are just, like, the appetizers. We're going to have salmon and green salad. Could you pour me some more champagne, please?" She grinned at him and held out her empty glass.

"Your cheeks are pink," he said. "Is that the wine?"

"Probably." She pointed at his nearly full glass. "You've hardly touched yours. You'd better get going or I'll drink it all."

"Nope, I'm in charge of the champagne, so I'm going to hoard it and make it last through dinner. I'll make sure I get my share," he said, laughing, "but you can have some more."

They argued about whether he had given her enough as she got out the nuts and olives. The conversation got even sillier as the wine disappeared, and then the gougères. "Man, these things are awesome!" he said, popping one after another into his mouth.

Margot was focused on her menu and cooking. He noted the intent look on her face as she made the vinaigrette and ripped up romaine for the salad. It occurred to him that she was going to a lot of trouble—for him. She seemed to be trying to impress him. He thought again about the kiss at the door.

She suddenly threw down the towel she'd been using to dry the lettuce. "Oh, I forgot the cheese!" she wailed. "It was a special goat cheese."

"I'm pretty stuffed. Why don't we forget the salmon and salad? I'm totally happy with what we've got here."

"I'll just put the goat cheese in the salad. I'm almost finished making it. How's that? Then we can watch a movie and, after that, have dessert."

He gave her a thumbs-up and poured a little more wine for each of them.

As she put the salad greens in a bowl and chopped green onions, she said, "Are you coming over for dinner tomorrow? Mikhail's roasting a duck."

"Wow—duck! I've never had duck. Yeah, I'm coming. New Year's Day's not a big deal at our house, so I don't think it will cause a blowup if I'm not there for dinner. I'll go to church with them in the morning." He picked up the silverware and napkins she had set out on the counter and carried all of it to the table. "Hey, how's Lionel? I haven't seen him for three or four weeks now—since before Christmas break. He's got the eyesight problem, and the wheelchair because of the balance thing, but other than that, he seems pretty much the same to me. I keep waiting for something really bad to happen, and then I think maybe it won't be so bad. Maybe he won't get worse. You read about people who just get well—no explanation or anything. I keep hoping for that." He was talking fast, and his voice had tightened. He hoped Margot didn't notice the tic that appeared in his left eye when he got tense.

"I think he's doing pretty well," she said. "But you can see for yourself tomorrow."

Thirty minutes later, they had eaten their salad and most of the gougères, and cleaned up the dishes, and Margot was cuing up a movie on the TV.

"What are we watching?" Jeremy asked as he plopped down on the dark-blue suede sofa.

"*Pride and Prejudice*, the Keira Knightly version. Have you seen it?

"Nope."

"I just loved the book. And the BBC version with Colin Firth," she said, sitting down beside him with the remote. "I'm a Jane Austen junkie."

"Why do you like this story so much?"

She tucked a strand of long dark hair behind one ear, "Oh, it's just very romantic, and Lizzy notices things about people, and she's really funny," Margot said. "And wait till you hear how they talk. These days, nobody could say a sentence as long as the ones they say!"

He took her hand as the movie started, and she leaned a fraction closer to him.

After the movie, she said, "Well, did you like it?"

"I did." He thought for a moment. "I liked the scene where her father says her mother will never speak to her again if she doesn't marry Mr. Collins, and *he'll* never speak to her again if she does! That was pretty funny. And when Lady Catherine is trying to get Lizzy to say she won't marry Mr. Darcy—that was really good. That was like a war with words." Jeremy was amazed that he sounded so normal; he felt intoxicated by the perfume she was wearing. "What's your favorite scene?"

"I liked the scene where he proposes," Margot said, "and she's so shocked and she tells him off. You could see how attracted they were to each other, how they really wanted to kiss, but the words got in the way. And his pride and her prejudice." She looked up at him, her face close to his.

During the course of the movie, he had put his arm around her shoulder and she had kicked off her shoes and curled up against him. But he still didn't have the nerve to kiss her.

"It's only ten o'clock," she said. "What shall we do for the next two hours? Want some dessert?"

Jeremy had read the whole stack of books on sex and relationships that Lionel had assembled for him. He knew all about erogenous zones, and male and female arousal times, and different positions—but he'd never kissed a girl. Margot's nearness, her low-cut sweater, the sexy ending scene of the movie: all had turned him on. His hands were shaking. He thought she wanted him to kiss her, but what if she didn't like it when he did?

He bent his head and kissed her. Then he kissed her again, and she kissed him back.

His voice now husky, he said, "I'll just have you for dessert, OK?"

He got "Mm-hmm" and another kiss in reply.

She leaned against his chest, put her arms around his neck, and lifted her face for another kiss. He ran his hand through her hair, felt its silky softness, smelled the fragrance of her shampoo. He kissed her closed eyelids, then her throat, as his shaking hand reached around her waist, brushing her breast on the way.

She flinched slightly, and he started to draw back, but she said in a sort of drugged voice, "No, no, it's OK. I want you to touch me. I like it. Don't stop. I'm just totally turned on—it feels really good." She ran her fingers through his hair, pressed closer, and kissed him as his arms tightened around her.

Jeremy lost track of time, of everything but the two of them, their bodies, and the sensations flowing through them.

The sound of fireworks brought him back to the outside world. "Gosh! Midnight already! I've got to go home pretty soon," he said, stroking her back and burying his face in her hair. "I don't want to—I could do this forever."

"Jeremy, you could stay all night if you wanted. My dad won't be back until late in the morning."

There was a long silence while he contemplated what she was suggesting.

"Margot, I don't think I should," he finally said. "It's not that I don't want to." He stopped to give her a lingering kiss. "I just don't want to ruin this. I just want to go slow . . . and just, like, soak it up. Make it last. You're so beautiful. I can't believe a girl like you would even look at me! So I just want to . . . I just don't want to go too fast. In my head, that is. The rest of me is ready to head for the bedroom!"

She giggled and snuggled closer. "OK," she said. "I'm all right with that. We don't have to be in a rush. We've got time."

They were quiet for a moment, and then she said, "Part of me wants to go to bed with you, but part of me is scared. I've never done it, and I want it to be good for both of us." She fiddled with the buttons on his shirt.

"Yeah, I know what you mean," he said. "I've thought about it a lot. You want it to be great, but you hear it isn't always so good the first time. That's a bummer."

"Well, happy New Year, J. We've got a lot to look forward to!"

Connectedness

Lionel sat in the living room with Karina and Patty as they met with a hospice social worker, Janice Stone. The lamps cast a warm light that warded off the gloom of the gray late-February afternoon as they drank their coffee and talked about what could be expected in the course of Lionel's illness. Lionel wanted to know as much as possible while he was still competent to make decisions.

Janice, a middle-aged woman with warm brown eyes and an equally warm manner, was explaining how the hospice process worked. "A person is eligible for hospice services within six months of when death might occur. Of course, we never know when the end will come—some people live much longer than the doctors expect they will. But you're wise to start the process, because the earlier you do, the better relationships you'll have with your team. We're here to support all of you: you as a patient, Lionel, Karina as the caregiver, and Patty and the rest of your housemates."

They talked about services offered, visits of the hospice staff, how things are paid for, who does what. "I'll leave some printed material that I hope will be helpful to all of you. It includes some books and websites that you might find useful," said Janice. "It's my experience that the people who have more information, who know what to expect, deal better with the difficulties of the latter stages of an illness. Some people don't want to think about it. Other people want to try to control everything." She turned to Lionel. "This will be a very challenging time for you, emotionally as well as physically."

"Yes, that's what I'm expecting." He blew out a long exhalation. "I'm really paying attention to my Buddhist practice of 'letting go.' I've always tried to, but now it's clearer to me what that's all about. I'm hoping all my years of meditation will help me."

"You're doing very well for someone at this stage of your illness, Lionel," said Janice. "And I'm not just saying that to make you feel good. You're seeing some alternative practitioners, aren't you?"

"Yes, I am," he said. "Although I don't think my neurologist puts much faith in alternative practices, so I don't talk about them much with him. But I think they help, and I'm the one who matters. I've also been working with a neighbor who's a yoga teacher, so I do that every day, and I meditate more than I used to. Also, I changed my diet. I read about some studies that show that a high-fat, high-protein diet with no sugar can stop the cancer, at least for a while. It's not definitive yet, but I figure it can't hurt. Mikhail, Karina's husband, is our cook, and he's just . . . well . . . words fail me. He comes up with these wonderful meals for me and different wonderful meals for the rest of us. We're so blessed to have him." Lionel reached over and patted Karina's hand.

"It's kind of interesting," Patty said to Janice. "We're all doing yoga now, and we've dramatically cut down on sugar. So Lionel's illness has made us all healthier. And thanks for reminding us how well he's doing. It's so easy to get focused on the negative—the nausea, the weight loss and sight loss, the hair loss—all that stuff, rather than the positive. It's really helpful having someone from outside the house to advise us."

Mikhail had a catering event that evening, so when the social worker had left for her next appointment, Karina went to the kitchen to warm the soup. Lionel and Patty sat on the sofa, ready to begin their evening meditation.

He took her hand and asked, "Are we talking enough about how we're all doing with this, Patty? I don't want any of us to dwell on it, of course, but I don't want us to pretend everything is fine, either."

She sighed and squeezed his hand. "I've been thinking lately about how it was when my husband died. He was fifteen years older than me. Most of our married life, that didn't matter, but the last five years before he died were hard. Physically, he was an old man and I was still in my prime, or at least I felt like I was. He didn't take very good care of himself, so his infirmities slowed us both down. I'd get so impatient with how long it took him to do simple things, how many little things he forgot and I'd have to repeat two or three times. And I'd watched the same things happening to my parents. Expecting them to relate to each other like they always had when they couldn't anymore—it wasn't physically possible."

She snuggled closer to him. "Now, of course, I'm seeing those signs in myself. If my husband and I had been closer in age and both experiencing aging at the same time, I wonder if I could have been more patient. Maybe not, because underneath it all, I think my annoyance with him was just an unconscious knowing that he was going to be leaving me alone one day, and I was afraid of that. I think that's what was going on, but I didn't know it then." She stopped and smoothed the afghan over her knees.

"So is that what you feel now—that I'm deserting you?" There was tightness in Lionel's voice.

"No, no, Lionel. I feel sad, but not deserted. No, it's different now. I think I've grown up a bit since he died, or become less insecure or something. I'm not so afraid of being alone. I've lived on my own, I know what it's like, and it's OK. I have my children's families, and now I have this new family. But it's more than that—it's that I have a stronger sense of not being separate, that I'm related to other people. We have things in common, we come from the same place, and we're going back there ultimately. My awareness has changed. Not that I'm an enlightened being or anything." She smiled at him and leaned over to kiss his cheek. "It's hard to explain. I just feel more connected to everything than I used to. Does that make sense?"

"Yes," he said. "I think I know what you mean." He paused, looking off across the living room to the dark lines that were bare tree branches outside the windows. "Feeling connected is usually good, but sometimes it's not so good. You're more aware of the anxiety, fear, anguish, and all that bad stuff that's all around us."

"Mmm, that's tough, isn't it?" Patty said. "I experience that too, especially around certain people—people who seem to go from one crisis to the next. I have a friend like that. I love her, and I want to help her and her family, but I feel depressed and helpless around them. They just don't seem to see how they keep making the same mistakes, that how they live is the result of the choices they've made." She sighed. "It's really a stretch for me to empathize, to think about how stressed they are and just love them, rather than judging them. Isn't it strange how our feelings of connectedness come and go? Sometimes the connectedness is just there, you're aware of it, it feels wonderful: like at a play, or when you're singing with people, or everyone is happy watching a child blow out birthday candles. Why does it come and go?"

Lionel continued to rub his thumb across her hand. "I'm glad I can still feel, even though I can't see much anymore," he said, giving her a little smile. "But in answer to your question, maybe that connected feeling has to do with our ability to let go of our 'stuff,' to see it and let go of it." He put quotation marks around "stuff" with his fingers in the air. "The 'stuff' hides the awareness of connectedness. Like your judgments about these people. Where did that come from? Your parents probably, right?"

"Yes, lots of judging from my mom about how I should be, what was right and what was wrong, unacceptable, on and on. But it's so deep, such a part of who I am, that I don't even notice when I'm judging. Those people I feel critical toward, they have a bunch of internal judgments too, I'm sure. So why don't I just recognize that—about myself and them—and ease off?"

"I'll keep reminding you when I hear you doing it," Lionel said. "Maybe that will help."

"Just be nice," she said. "It's hard to hear about my faults."

"It's not hard for me to be nice to you. No problem, my dear," he said, smiling at her fondly.

*****

A week later, Lionel was with Chuck and Anne at the breakfast table, listening to the NPR news and reading the paper.

Abe came in and poured himself a cup of coffee. "I'm finally finished with my unpacking!" he said. "There're still stacks of stuff to be put away, but I took the boxes to the recycle place yesterday." He grinned at the others. "I'm ready for a break."

"Hey, the weather forecast is for sun today," said Chuck. "Let's go somewhere. I know our regular outing is supposed to be next week, but I feel the need for a nature day today."

Anne folded up the newspaper. "I was reading an article in the Sunday paper about the Nisqually Wildlife Refuge near Olympia. It said they have a really good trail for wheelchairs. How about that? What do you think, Lionel?"

"Sounds good to me," Lionel said. "Let's do it. I'll just call Patty and tell her." He pulled his cell phone from his pocket. "What time should we leave?" he asked. "I know it seems ridiculous to call her when she's just upstairs, but these things are really convenient. Bless whoever figured out cell phones for the blind!"

"I'll make sandwiches," said Chuck, getting up from the table.

"I'll make some too," said Anne. I want something besides peanut butter and jelly!"

Ninety minutes later, all of them but Lin, who had to work, were loading the van with Lionel's lightweight wheelchair, a basket of food, two thermoses of coffee, and a container of cookies—all buried under a pile of fleece and down, mittens, and scarves.

Technically, it was past rush hour, but the traffic on I-5 South was heavy, though moving well. The others took turns describing to Lionel the periodic vistas of Mount Rainier in its full winter coat of snow, brilliant against the blue sky. It was so often shrouded by the clouds that even longtime residents couldn't help but feel they'd been given a gift every time it came into view. And it was a much more inspiring sight than the almost constant roadside unattractions of car and RV lots, motels, and strip developments that lined the freeway for most of the hour drive.

"Did anyone hear *Wait Wait . . . Don't Tell Me!* last Saturday?" asked Lionel. "They had Deepak Chopra as a guest, and he was really funny. I wonder if they write the lines for their guests—they're always hilarious. Anyway, they were talking about how often he'd been on Oprah's show, and that they were friends and so on. And Deepak says, 'And if she married me, she'd be Oprah Chopra.'"

They all had a good laugh.

Then Chuck said, "OK, everyone, what's your favorite joke or funny story? My favorite is a Gary Larson cartoon. It's these three cave men standing around in their bearskins, and one is holding something out for the other two to look at. He says, 'Look at my new Swiss Army rock.'" Chuck pounded the steering wheel with laughter. "That always makes me laugh, and it's been years since I first saw it."

"Did anybody hear the first-grade proverbs?" asked Patty.

"I think I saw something like that on the internet a while ago," said Abe. "But go ahead, Patty. I don't remember them."

"Well, apparently this teacher told her students she was going to give them the first part of a well-known saying, and they were supposed to complete the rest of it. The kids' answers were just priceless. One was 'A bird in the hand . . .' And the answer was 'Is going to poop on you.'" There was a burst of laughter from everyone. "Then there was 'It's always darkest before . . .' and the answer was 'Daylight saving time." More giggles and laughter. "Then there was 'Don't bite the hand . . . that looks dirty.'"

"Oh, now I remember some," said Abe. "You're going to love this, Lionel. 'You can't teach an old dog new . . . math.' And 'If at first you don't succeed . . . get new batteries."

"OK, guys, you've got to stop, or I'm gonna have to pull over," said Chuck, tears running down his cheeks. "I'm laughing so hard I can't drive."

They left the freeway and took the frontage road into the wildlife refuge, parking at the interpretive center. Twenty minutes later, padded in down and fleece and loaded with knapsacks containing food and drink, they walked down the boardwalk with their maps and brochures. A light but chilly breeze blew across the delta, ruffling scarves and making eyes and noses water, as they paused to read the interpretive materials along the trail.

"The brochure says there's a pair of nesting barn owls and that this is the month you're most likely to see them with their little ones," said Patty. "Wouldn't that be exciting to see owls!"

"Oh, look!" said Karina, pointing across the river. "That bird with the long legs—what is that?"

"It's a heron. He's waiting for lunch," said Chuck. "I don't see how they can stay motionless for so long—it's amazing!"

They meandered down the boardwalk, Abe pushing Lionel's wheelchair, trying to identify the birds they saw on the water or in the trees. At the end of the boardwalk, a footpath continued on into the open delta.

"I'll stay with Lionel," said Patty. "You all go on and get some more bird-watching in."

"No, Patty. You go too," Lionel said. "I'm content to just sit here in the sunshine by myself for a while. I can always meditate. I'll be fine."

So off they went, promising to return in half an hour. Lionel turned up his collar and shoved his hands into his pockets; he felt the weak sunshine and the breeze on his face, and smelled the salt water and the green plants coming to life in the early spring. The cold air chilled his nostrils as he breathed in big lungfuls. *It's so good to breathe really clean air,* he thought. At least three different birdcalls floated through the trees and up from the river.

The experience was marred only by the noise of the freeway and the thump, thump of artillery practice at nearby Fort Lewis. *Oh well,* he thought. *At least I have the sun and fresh air.*

It wasn't long before he detected the distant sounds of talk and laughter drawing closer as his friends returned. He was suddenly struck by a jolt of grief. Only months left. He tried to be positive: he wasn't alone, and there was still time for love and many of the good things of life. But there was also loss. He mopped his eyes with his handkerchief and hoped they wouldn't notice his tears.

The Trailblazer

Chuck heard a crash in the bathroom between his and Lionel's bedrooms. "Oh hell, what a mess!" he heard Lionel say.

"You OK, Lionel?" he asked from outside the door.

"Yes, dammit, I'm OK. I dropped a bottle of mouthwash. Come in. Just be careful where you step—there's broken glass."

Chuck opened the door, looked at the pool of mouthwash and the shards of glass on the floor, and said, "I can take care of this. I'll just go down and get the dustpan and a sponge, and we'll get this cleaned up. No problem."

"I'm sorry, Chuck," Lionel said with an embarrassed look. "I think I'd be more a nuisance than a help if I tried to clean it up. I'm afraid my left side is . . . is weaker now than it was. I haven't wanted to admit it. They told me this might happen. It's common for one side to fail faster as the tumor grows. So I've got to be more conscious of what I can't do anymore. We'll all have to be. Sorry."

*****

Mikhail was there two days later when Lionel fell in the kitchen while trying to sit on one of the stools at the island.

"Are you all right, Lionel?" Mikhail said as he helped him to sit up. "Is anything broken?"

"Um, let me see. I'll just sit here a moment." He looked around as if he were trying to figure out where he was. "The kitchen looks different from down here," he said. He moved his legs and turned his head from side to side. "I don't think anything's broken. I'll probably have a bruise tomorrow, but that's no big deal." He held on to the stool with his right hand, and Mikhail helped him to stand. "Guess I'm going to have to spend more time in the wheelchair. Thanks, Mikhail. Sorry to trouble you."

"No trouble, Lionel. No trouble. Would you like tea? I have some of your favorite cookies. Something else?"

"Tea would be wonderful, and cookies too. Thanks again, Mikhail."

*****

Lionel could hear the March wind rattling a loose storm window and wildly thrashing through the budding branches during dinner a few days later. "I'll fix that window tomorrow," Chuck said, passing the salad. Lin was there for her weekly visit with her potential housemates. Mikhail returned from the kitchen with a replenished bread basket.

"Well, my friends, I want to bring up the awkward topic of my decline," began Lionel. "I know this isn't ideal dinner conversation, but we're all here and I feel a sense of urgency."

Lin gave him a furtive look and then devoted all her attention to her dinner. Patty paused, knife and fork in hand and regarded him. Abe put down his utensils and leaned back in his chair, waiting for him to speak. The others kept eating but looked at him expectantly.

Glancing around the table, Abe said, "Looks to me like it's fine with everyone, Lionel. Go ahead."

"Please keep eating. I don't want to bring dinner to a stop. Maybe I should have waited till after dinner, but I know Anne's going out with Margot, and Abe has to leave at seven thirty. So I'll just forge ahead, if you don't mind."

Nods told him to proceed.

"The broken bottle in the bathroom, the fall in the kitchen, the increasing weakness on my left side: it's only going to get worse from here on," he said. "You know how much I appreciate your physical and emotional support—and God knows I need it—but I'm feeling much more uncomfortable about what I'm putting you through, you having to watch all this. It was all theoretical when we decided to move in together. We knew in our heads this day would come, but living with it's another matter. My illness is interfering with your lives, and I don't want that."

"But Lionel," said Anne, "isn't that what we're here for? At least partly? As you said, we all knew this would happen sometime. Sooner or later we'll all be experiencing illness or bodily decline. It's going to happen somewhere, so let's have it happen among people we care about, who care about us. Don't you think that's easier than being among strangers in a nursing home?"

"Yes," he said, "it's easier for the . . . declining person, but it's harder on the others. You can't go home at night and forget about me, like the staff in a nursing home can."

"Sure, it's not easy, seeing what's happening to you," said Chuck, pushing his plate back and leaning his elbows on the table. "But it's not all bad. I know it means a lot to you having us around. You see what's going on in our lives—admittedly not a whole lot—but we're doing stuff, talking about what's going on in the world, and you care, you like to hear and participate in the conversations. That's something we can do for you, something that helps you."

"There's another reason you shouldn't desert us," said Patty, with a little catch in her voice. "You're the trailblazer. You're helping us see what's coming for us. It could have been any of us, but you happen to be the first, and we're in this together, trying to figure out how to be … how to find the positive … how to keep appreciating what we can. You can't run out on that, even if you can see it's hard for us to watch you struggle sometimes." She dabbed at her eyes with her napkin.

The big chandelier with its ten little lamp shades cast a warm glow over the polished dining room table, reflecting light off the silver and glassware. Karina's weekly flower arrangement stood cheerfully among the serving dishes, while the brisk spring breeze buffeted the windows.

Lionel gazed at most of the dearest people in his life, now fuzzy shapes sitting around this table, telling him they loved him and that he still had something to offer them. "I'm so lucky to have you," he said, his voice breaking.

"Lionel," said Chuck. "If you weren't here, we wouldn't have the chance to help, to make things a little better for you. We'd just feel bad, and helpless or guilty or something. And we'd probably have to get in the car and drive somewhere and find a place to park to come visit you. What a pain in the ass! Much better for you to be here with us. I'd rather clean up a broken bottle than find a place to park!"

Laughter lightened the tension and sadness.

*****

"Who said, 'Old age isn't for sissies'?" asked Chuck as he scraped plates and put them in the dishwasher. "I saw it on a poster of Richard Farnsworth. He was shirtless, holding his free weights and looking really buff, with his white hair and beard. Was it his quote?"

"I'm pretty sure it was Bette Davis," said Anne, drying the wineglasses and putting them in the cupboard. "She hit the nail on the head, didn't she?"

"Yeah," Chuck said, "I've been thinking about that as I watch what Lionel's going through, and what we're going through watching him. Maybe that's the big job of getting old—having courage."

"But why would that be the job? Why do you need any job when you're old?" challenged Anne. "After you've had courage your whole life, courage to leave your home, to get married or divorced, to try for challenging jobs, get through difficult situations, have kids . . . why should you still have the job of having courage when you're old?" she said, slapping the dish towel down on the island.

Chuck put the last plate in the dishwasher and wiped the countertop. "Remember that poem we read the other night by Robert Frost, where he says the 'reward of daring should be still to dare'? Maybe it's the same with courage—it's a lifelong task. We both know life doesn't end when you've finished with the kids and career and all that. We've talked about that a lot."

Anne wrapped her arms around his waist and leaned her head against his chest. "You're pretty wise, old man. Stick around, OK?"

"My plan is to stick around you as long as possible, darlin'" He smiled down at her. "Is it time for you to pick up Margot?"

Margot's Love Life

Margot wanted to give her own party for her seventeenth birthday at the end of March. Mikhail had told her that the Ukrainian tradition was for the birthday person to throw the party and for the guests to give verbal wishes. Her grandmother helped her decide on a spring theme, and Margot spent many hours making and hand-lettering the invitations, Googling flower-arrangement photos, and talking with Mikhail about the menu.

Since Easter was early this year, Margot decided to use colored eggs in the arrangements. The Saturday night before the party, she and the rest of the housemates were gathered around the kitchen island, dipping eggs in and out of mugs of dye.

"Is much easier making American eggs than Ukrainian eggs," said Mikhail. No hot wax. No special tools. Very fast."

"But not so fancy, either," said Anne. "Those eggs you brought from home are just beautiful, Mikhail. Did you make them?"

"I made them," said Karina. "Many hours of . . . how do you call it . . . waxing, and then dipping and more waxing and dipping. And they are so fragile. I was afraid they would all be smashed when we unpacked them."

"I'm going to put them in a glass bowl on the piano, where everyone can see them," said Margot. "Then I'll put some of ours with each vase of daffodils. Wow, Chuck, that's really neat! How did you get a whole landscape on an egg? Even a sunset!"

"Yeah, this is kind of fun," said Chuck, sketching carefully on a fresh egg with his wax crayon. "Maybe I missed my calling—maybe I should be coloring eggs instead of painting. Or maybe this will improve my painting. You have to reduce your design to the bare minimum, just a few lines to convey something." His expression was intent. "Pretty challenging."

"The smell of vinegar takes me back," said Lionel. "Wish I could see the colors better. I used to love how vivid they were—especially the orange, next to a blue or green. Then the eggs inside were slightly colored when we ate them. All the kids at school had funny-colored eggs in their lunch boxes." He chuckled. "Well, I'm going to the library to work on my birthday-wishes speech. I'm trying to keep it to twenty minutes."

Margot giggled. "Lionel, you'd better not embarrass me—I'll put salt in your coffee!"

"Hey, Margot, tell us about the wedding. We haven't seen you since you got back," said Patty, dipping her egg in a second color. "I thought they were going to live together for a while. To be sure and all that."

"I guess they decided they were sure enough!" Margot said, and everyone laughed. "Mark and Claire and I flew down to San Francisco, and Claire's parents and sister flew in from Saint Paul, and they had the ceremony in Tiburon at Elaina and Mitchell's house—that's my other grandparents. They're really cool. And Mark's brother and sister and their kids were there, of course. The house was full of flowers, and it was sunny, but not really warm enough for an outdoor wedding. The ceremony was pretty short, and after that, we all went out for dinner at a fancy restaurant. I had scallops."

"What was Claire's dress like?" asked Patty.

"Oh, it was so cool—you'll never believe it. She wore a cocktail dress of her mom's! Claire told me it was her favorite of all her mom's dresses when she was a little girl. And her mom still had it! It was champagne-colored silk, really plain, scoop neck, three-quarter sleeves, barely knee-length. And she wore really high heels and this wispy little hat thing made out of some net and feathers. Same color as the dress. It was like something from an old movie. She looked totally awesome! We'll show you the pictures when they're ready."

*****

Sunday afternoon at three o'clock, Mark was among the birthday party guests arriving at the mansion, its gardens showy with purple and yellow crocuses, snowdrops, daffodils, and an early pale-pink rhododendron.

"Did you order this sunshine for Margot's birthday?" Claire asked her new husband as they crossed the sidewalk to the front door.

"Yup, sure did," said Mark, smiling at his wife and clutching at his scarf, which was whipping in the wind. "Great to see some blue sky for a change, isn't it? Man, that wind is something—look at the clouds!" They stood on the front porch, trying futilely to smooth down their windblown hair as they waited for the door to be answered.

Margot's boyfriend chained his bike to the water spigot and walked up the steps.

"Hey, Jeremy!" said Mark.

"Hi, Mark, Claire. Congratulations! What's it been—two weeks now? From what Margot said, it was a really nice wedding."

Margot flung open the door, and there was no time for more wedding talk. "Hi, everybody! Come in—oh, here comes Katy!" She gave her friend from her old school an excited hug and began introductions as she collected coats. "Everyone, this is Katy. Katy, you've met my dad. This is my stepmom—they've only been married two weeks. She's really cool."

Claire beamed, glanced happily at Mark, and extended her hand to Margot's friend. "Hi, Katy, I'm happy to meet you. I'm Claire."

"Oh! I forgot to tell Katy your name—guess I'm a little excited," said Margot, giggling and reaching for Jeremy's hand. "Katy, this is Jeremy."

*****

In the butler's pantry, Chuck was helping Anne make mimosas. He watched her put more juice and less champagne in three of the glasses on a large tray. "I don't want to get in trouble with anyone's parents," she said. "But I don't want to treat the young people like children either. Here, take these around, would you? And make sure the kids get the ones on the end."

"Yes, ma'am. Got my marching orders—kids get the ones on the end." Chuck kissed Anne on the back of the neck, picked up the heavy tray, and walked carefully into the living room, balancing eleven champagne glasses.

*****

"Come on, Katy, I'll introduce you to everyone else and show you the kitchen. That's where I spend most of my time when I'm over here," Margot said, leading the way. She introduced Katy to Chuck as they passed him in the hall, and picked up their mimosas. "One of the guys who lives here is teaching me how to cook, and I get to help him with his catering business." She pointed to a stool for Katy to sit on, introduced Mikhail, Karina, and her grandmother, and began transferring appetizers to a colorful serving platter, chattering all the time.

For the next hour, the guests munched, drank, chatted, and laughed in little groups that formed and reformed. Margot ran back and forth to the kitchen, refilling trays and passing out food, until Mikhail told her to go be the guest of honor.

She took off her apron and went in the living room to find Jeremy laughing on the couch next to pink-cheeked Katy, who was regaling him with a story. Margot had noticed when Katy arrived that she looked a lot more attractive than she used to. Her blond hair had been highlighted, and it hung down over her low-cut sweater. Her long legs, which had always been hidden by baggy jeans, were now covered by black tights underneath a short leatherlike pencil skirt.

Margot sat down on the arm of the couch, next to Jeremy. "Hey," he said, smiling up at her. "Katy was just telling me the funniest story."

"Cool," she said coolly. "Want to help me with the birthday cake?"

"Yeah, totally," he said, standing up. "What do you want me to do?"

Yet another hour later, the living room was cluttered with cake plates, crumpled napkins, and wrapping paper.

Margot sat among her birthday presents: a Nordstrom gift card from her dad and Claire, a small framed watercolor from Chuck, a high-end whisk from the Azerovs (her first piece of professional cooking equipment), a palette of eye makeup from Katy, *Larousse Gastronomique* from Patty and Lionel, and some antique amethyst earrings that had belonged to her great-grandmother.

"Well, I guess it's my turn," said Jeremy, moving to the piano. "This is called 'Margot's Dream.' I wrote it for her. It's kind of an étude." He blushed as he adjusted the piano bench, then placed his hands on the keys and began.

The main theme repeated in variations, followed by an allegro section, then the main theme again andante. When he finished, there was an astonished silence, followed by wild applause.

"Bravo, bravo!" shouted Lionel. "That's my boy!"

Margot slid onto the piano bench beside Jeremy. "Oh, J, that was just beautiful, so beautiful!" She put her arm around his waist and her head on his shoulder, happy tears dropping into her lap. "I wish my mom could have heard it," she whispered.

Everyone gathered around the piano, congratulating Jeremy, telling him how much they enjoyed his composition. "That was amazing, Jeremy!" said Mark. "Your parents must be very proud of you. I'd like to hear about how you did it—how long it took, and stuff like that. I don't even know what kind of questions to ask, but I'd like to know more. Maybe we can talk the next time you're over at our place. Claire and I have to leave early— we have to put in an appearance at a party one of my clients is giving."

"No problem," Jeremy said. "I have to leave soon too—I have a gig tonight. One of Mikhail's clients asked me play background music at a cocktail hour. I'm a little nervous, but it'll be OK. I've done this a couple of times now, and people don't usually listen very much anyway."

"You didn't tell me you had a gig!" said Margot.

"I just found out—she called this morning. She sounds like kind of a last-minute person. I can help with the dishes," he offered, noticing Anne and Patty collecting plates and glasses.

"No, it's OK," said Margot. "You talk to Lionel, and I'll help with the dishes." She began picking up plates and half-empty trays.

When she came back from the kitchen, Jeremy and Katy were standing at the front door talking. Katy pulled her shiny blond hair from beneath her scarf and shook it down around her shoulders. "It's been really great meeting you," she told him. "I hope I'll see you again." She smiled up at him.

"Uh, sure, that would be awesome. Nice to meet you."

Katy waved at Margot and came over to say goodbye. "Thanks for inviting me, Margot. Jeremy's totally cool—I'm so glad I finally got to meet him. Call me." And she was out the door, leaving Jeremy blushing again and Margot wondering how much of a friend her friend was.

"When do you have to leave?" she asked him.

"I should leave right now," he said. "I have to get home and change, and then get to this house down near Lake Washington."

"Wish you didn't have to go," she said, putting her arms around his neck. "But thanks again for the étude. I'm so lucky to be with you."

"I'm the lucky one," he replied, pulling her closer. "Happy birthday, birthday girl." He gave her a lingering kiss.

*****

Home in bed that night, Margot stayed up late finishing a poem for Jeremy that she had been working on for several weeks.

> He's not like the others
> They just wanted me to use
> I've had enough of that stuff
> And from now on, I refuse
> He brings me flowers
> Calms me down
> His hair is fiery
> His eyes are brown
> He wrote me some music
> It's called 'Margot's Dream'
> He appears to be bashful
> But he's not what he seems
> He's not like the others
> We'll be friends forevermore
> Jeremy's my first true love
> We help each other laugh and soar

She hadn't told him about her few disappointing experiences with boys. Not that she wanted him to know the details—that would be horrifying. But she wanted him to know how much his respect for her meant, how much she cared for him.

The next morning, she slipped an envelope containing the poem into his jacket pocket as they parted in the hall for first period. At lunchtime, she was already in the cafeteria when he came in, flanked by the first-chair cellist on one side and one of the flutists on the other, both flirting for all they were worth. The cellist had thick, curly violently red hair and was something of a fashionista. She tugged Jeremy's shirt sleeve as she said something to him. They all three laughed, but at the same time Jeremy looked distracted; he seemed to be searching for Margot.

He left the two girls and came over to sit beside her when he finally found her. "Hey," he said. "How's it going?" He seemed nervous and didn't make eye contact the way he usually did.

"OK. How about you?" *What's wrong?* she wondered. *Is it my poem? Does he wonder about the other guys? Does he think I'm slutty? Or maybe he likes that redhead.*

"I'm OK." He took a sandwich and an apple out of his pack and began eating. "Cecile—you know, the cellist—her mom's giving this fancy party at the tennis club next Saturday, and Cecile asked me to play with her. She wants to learn how to do these kinds of gigs so she can earn money."

Margot was pretty sure that Cecile had more on her mind than making some extra cash.

"Are you going to do it?"

"Yeah, I guess so. The pay is good. No reason not to. I need to make all the money I can for college." He took another bite of sandwich and glanced at her.

"Did you read what I put in your pocket?" she asked.

"No, not yet. I wanted to save it for when I had time, and no distractions."

She smiled at him. "OK. Why don't you come over tonight? We can do homework together."

"Uh, I don't think I should tonight. I've got a ton of stuff due tomorrow, and it takes an hour by the time I bike both ways."

Was it Margot's imagination, or did she get the sense that he wasn't telling her something.

"How about tomorrow night?" he said.

"I've got a test Wednesday," said Margot, "and I have to help Mikhail with a catering job tomorrow night."

"Jeez, life is getting complicated—I can't even get together with my girlfriend!" He gave her a quick smile and bit into his apple. "I'm going over to play for Lionel Friday night. Want to come too?" He leaned over and bumped his shoulder against hers. "I'll meet you there and walk you home afterward."

"Sounds good," she said, bumping him back.

That week, they didn't see each other in the halls as much as they usually did. He was slow answering her texts and didn't call. On Friday between second and third period, Margot was walking down the hall behind the flutist she'd seen Jeremy with on Monday, and the girl was telling her friend, "Yeah, Cecile's going all out. She's really after that guy. He is kinda hot, in a quiet sort of way. Nice eyes. Anyway, she got him to come over to her house every night this week to practice for this thing they're doing Saturday night. She's all, 'Oh, I'm so nervous, Jeremy, but I won't be if we practice enough.' Yeah, right—I've never seen her nervous in my life, and we've been friends for four years."

Margot answered the door when Jeremy arrived that evening. He bent to kiss her, and she turned away, walking into the living room to sit down on the couch. "What's wrong, Margot?" he said, following her.

"How's Cecile? I hear you were over at her house every night this week. I'll bet you've really got those pieces down perfectly after all that practice."

"Well, you heard wrong. I was only over there Monday and Wednesday."

"Why didn't you tell me?"

"I was afraid you'd get the wrong idea. And it looks like you did, didn't you?"

"Why didn't you just tell me? Then I wouldn't have got the wrong idea."

He looked at his shoes and put his hands in his coat pockets. "Well, I guess I should have. Look, Margot—I don't care about Cecile. She's a pretty good cellist, but otherwise, kind of an airhead. Why don't you trust me?"

"Because of the poem," she said. "You never said a thing about it, and I thought you didn't respect me anymore."

A look of confusion crossed his face. "The poem you gave me?" She nodded, looking away from him. "Margot, I loved that poem. I've wanted to talk to you about it since I read it Monday night! But there just hasn't been the right time. It's not the kind of thing where you can say, 'Oh, cool poem. Thanks.' I wanted to talk about it with you. And I'll always respect you—I don't think you did anything wrong." He sat down beside her and took her hand. "Look at me, Margot."

She turned to him and threw her arms around his neck. "Oh, J, I'm so relieved! I was so jealous—and afraid you didn't care about me anymore. I'm sorry I didn't trust you. I won't ever do it again."

He put his forehead again hers. "So we've had our first fight. It's no big deal. And at least we get to make up now, right?"

The Dinner Guest

The weeks and months were flying by, and in the back of Patty's mind was her languishing dinner invitation to Lionel's university colleague Antonio Diaz. She picked some possible dates with her housemates and asked Lionel to call Antonio to see when he could come. Anne had received a call from Lin the previous week, telling them that she had decided against moving in with them. She was vague about her reasons but profuse in her appreciation of their willingness to consider her, and in her desire to remain friends with them.

On a blustery evening in early April, Antonio arrived bearing daffodils and a bottle of amontillado. "Oh, how lovely," said Patty, putting the flowers and the bottle on the foyer table. "Something cheerful for this gray day. And we haven't had sherry for ages. Thank you, Antonio. I'll take your coat. Go on into the living room. They're all waiting for you."

Everyone was introduced, and they settled comfortably around the fire. Patty came in with a tray holding the daffodils and glasses—and the sherry, which she poured and handed around. "It's hard to believe it's been six months since I attended your . . . art gala," Antonio said. "*El tiempo vuela.* It must have been successful—there was such a crowd. I hope you sold many paintings, Chuck."

"Yeah, I did," he said, "and nobody was more surprised than me! I owe it to my housemates. They forced me to be more proactive in promoting my work.

And we made about twenty-five hundred dollars for the preschool. Plus, Jeremy and Mikhail launched their new businesses. So it was a really big deal."

"Have you had any big events in your life in the past six months, Antonio?" asked Anne.

"My life is very quiet . . . Perhaps too quiet. I did a little benefit concert in my hometown in Spain in early December. I practice and read a lot and still teach some, but I'm mostly retired. I have grandchildren, but they're a bit much for me to handle on my own, so I don't see them as much as I did before my wife died. That was a little over two years ago." He took a sip of sherry. "How does it work for you all—does life seem quiet, or does living in a group make things more lively? I would imagine more lively."

"Well," said Lionel, "I think we all do the things we'd do if we were living alone, but we also have other activities because we're living in a group. For example, we have a nature outing at least once a month, we have business meetings, Chuck took us on an art walk, we had our gala. Those things are less likely to happen when you're living alone, I think."

"It's the conversations I love," said Abe. "I haven't had such good conversations since I was in college. The education and life experience and wisdom gathered around the dinner table here is just amazing! Mikhail can tell you how to cook absolutely anything, Chuck can explain modern art. Lionel can talk about pure math in a way you can understand. I could go on and on. So, yeah, I'd say it's pretty lively."

"I've always been curious about how you got this lovely home," said Antonio. "Would I be prying to ask?"

"Not at all," said Lionel. "I inherited a pile of money, and we used it to acquire and remodel the house. Technically, it belongs to me, and my will allows a nonprofit we formed to occupy it The nonprofit's board of directors is composed of the residents." While Lionel was talking, Karina refilled the sherry glasses, and Mikhail left to attend to the dinner. "If, someday, the residents can't maintain it anymore, the house becomes the property of a foundation. They can sell it or whatever. Theoretically, it could go on for years, depending on who chooses to live here."

"Brilliant, absolutely brilliant!" said Antonio.

"Speaking of brilliant, it's time for dinner prepared by our brilliant housemate, Mikhail," announced Patty. "Shall we adjourn to the dining room?"

After dinner, they sat around the table with their coffee. "From what you all said earlier about living here," Antonio said, it sounds like there're lots of positives. Would I be out of line to ask if there are negatives too?"

No one said anything.

"I'm sorry," he said. "I didn't mean to ask an awkward question." He smiled apologetically.

"No, it's a fair question," said Lionel. "I don't think we're unwilling to talk about negatives, or difficulties, or what's hard about group living—we'd be defeating part of the purpose of living together if we didn't talk about what bothers us. If something's bothering me, I try to figure out why it bothers me, if it's my problem, or really is someone else's problem. For example, I always try to put things back where I found them in the fridge or the cupboards. Someone else might just stick the item back in anyplace, but then it's not where I expect to find it and I get annoyed—"

"You didn't tell me that annoyed you!" said Patty. "I know I'm the one who just sticks it in anyplace."

"Well, it's really no big deal, is it?" said Lionel. "I just have to look a bit longer to find it. It's not something to make a fuss about."

"Yes, but if I'd known, I'd have tried harder to put things back right where they came from. It does make sense that you shouldn't have to go on a hunt every time you open a cupboard!"

"As you can imagine, Antonio," said Anne, returning her napkin to its ring, "it's just like marriage or any long-term living arrangement. People do things differently, and we have to either change or give up what bothers us about others. But what I've found is that things don't bother me as much now that I'm older as they did when I was younger. And when they do, I really think much more about *why* they bother me than I used to. And I often find that the reason is pretty insignificant."

Getting Old

"What's it like, getting old, Gramma?" said Margot. Anne and her granddaughter were sitting in the kitchen on an April afternoon.

"Hmm . . . Well, I think it varies a lot, depending on who you ask," Anne said. "If you're 'age-adverse,' or afraid of death, getting old can be annoying and scary. To me, there's a difference between getting older and getting old—at least physically. When you notice your balance isn't quite as good as it always has been, when you just can't do as many things in a day as you used to, when you can't hear as well, and your digestive system doesn't work as well as it used to, then you realize you're old, not just older." She got up and put their dishes in the dishwasher. "More tea?"

Margot nodded.

"It seems to me," said Anne, "that old age is a stage of life that has challenges and rewards, just like the other stages: childhood, adolescence, marriage, parenting. Oh, look at that rain—it's pouring!" They both looked out the window at the curtain of rain between the mansion and the house next door.

"I love being nice and dry and comfy and watching it rain outside," Margot said, "and hearing it on the roof and the windows." She dipped her tea bag in and out of her mug. "So anyway, Gramma, I still don't really get why being old is such a challenge. Don't you just get to retire and not raise kids anymore?"

"There're lots of challenges. For one, what *do* you do when you don't have a job and your kids don't need you? Some people feel as if they don't have a purpose anymore, as if the important stuff is over. So one big challenge is finding meaning and satisfaction and growth in new things. Finding meaningful things to do has never been hard for me." She stirred her tea bag around in her mug and gazed out the window.

"But as I experience the changes in my body and I watch what Lionel's going through, I realize that another big challenge of old age is coping with physical decline and not getting morose or angry or bitter. *That's* a lot of work! You live in a body for seventy years and then it doesn't work the way it did for all those years, but you feel like you're the same person in this body that's acting weird. It's kind of disconcerting." She shifted her tea bag from her mug to a little dish.

"And then there's getting ready to die. That's kind of at the back of all our minds now—I mean all five of us. We want to do whatever we need to do so we don't have a lot of regrets, so we feel good about our lives, and give all the love we can while there's still time."

"Are you afraid of dying, Gramma?" Margot glanced over at Anne, then back at her mug.

"Well, I'm not afraid of being dead. But, yes, I'm afraid of dying, of being in pain, of being alone."

"You won't be alone, Gramma—you'll always have me." Margot gave Anne a quick hug and got a big smile and a hug in return.

"Thank you, sweetie. That means a lot to me." Anne's gaze again focused outside the window, taking in the wind now blowing the trees, and the slackening rain still pattering against the windows. The big clock in the foyer chimed the half hour, and they could hear Patty moving about in the room above. Otherwise, the house was quiet, standing warm and solid, a fixture in their lives.

"You said you were afraid of dying," said Margot, "but not of being dead. Why is that?"

"It's because I think we still exist in some way after our bodies die," Anne said, taking a cookie from the plate between them. "And who knows—maybe it's even a bigger deal than physical life. I think the quality of life after physical death depends on what you did when you were alive on earth. So you can affect it. And I think we get more chances for other *physical* lives, and they're also, um . . . shaped by what we do in this life. But what brought all this up for you, Margot? I'm curious about your interest in getting older, and death."

"Oh, I don't know," she said. "I guess . . . Jeremy and I were talking about Lionel's . . . you know, about Lionel, and I've been thinking about Mom dying, and I just wondered what you thought."

"Well, it makes me feel really good that you wanted to discuss these subjects with me. I feel really complimented. But I don't expect you to agree with everything I've said. Ultimately, you have to come to your own conclusions."

There was a quiet moment while they sipped their tea. "What are you afraid of, Margot?" said Anne. "Everyone has fears, you know."

"Yeah, I guess so. Sometimes I see kids do stuff or say stuff and it's so stupid, and I know it's just because they're afraid. But it's harder to see myself doing it. It's, like, hard to admit you're afraid." She picked up a pencil and doodled on the back of the grocery list that lay on the island. "I guess I'm afraid people won't like me. Not all the time, just sometimes. And I guess I'm afraid of being alone. I never thought about that till Mom died, and now I think about it a lot, even though I've got a dad, and you."

"You know what I think?" Anne said. "I think we're never really alone. We just think we are. But really, we're all connected—everyone, everything. We just have to be aware of the connections."

A buzzing sound came out of Margot's backpack, which she'd dropped in the corner when she came in. Anne smiled and said, "That's one of your connections right now."

"Jeremy said he'd call me after his audition." Margot located her phone in a zippered pocket. She pressed it to her ear as she walked into the dining room. Mikhail came in the back door carrying two bags of groceries, his coat and hair wet from the rain, just as Patty came in, asking if today's paper had been thrown out yet.

Anne sighed, disappointed that her conversation with Margot appeared to be over, but at the same time happy that it had happened at all. She couldn't remember ever having a conversation like that with Giselle. She wandered into the living room and stood in front of the windows, looking out at the dripping trees and thinking, *Why couldn't she have had with her daughter what she had with her granddaughter?*

Confrontation

Jeremy heard an unmistakable sound when he came home from school—the sound of a belt hitting flesh. His little brother, home with a fever, was standing by the front door, crying. "I called nine-one-one, like you told me to, Jeremy."

"Good boy. Wait upstairs while I help Mom," he called to his brother as he rushed to the kitchen.

His father was lifting his arm for another slash at his wife, who was cowering on the floor. Jeremy grabbed his father's shirt, dragged him away from his mother, and slammed him up against the refrigerator. "All right, you drunken bully. I've been wanting to do this for a long time. Let's get this over with." His eyes still on his father, he said, "Mom, wait for the police at the front door."

She crawled out of the kitchen, sobbing, and Jeremy crouched slightly, waiting for the expected attack.

His father lunged at him, shouting, "You're no son of mine—I'll show you who runs this house!" He raised the belt, one end of which was wrapped around his wrist.

Jeremy grabbed the belt and jerked his father off balance, then shoved him as hard as he could against the wall. His forehead hit the corner of a cabinet and began to bleed. Shaken but still standing, his father grabbed a knife from the countertop and staggered toward Jeremy again.

"Drop that knife!" a voice shouted. "Drop it right now, mister. I wouldn't want to have to shoot you." A police officer advanced slowly, gun raised, his partner visible in the door behind him. Jeremy's father dropped the knife. "All right, young man," said the officer, "can you just back out to the other doorway there? That's right. OK, now, mister, turn around slowly and put your hands on the wall."

The officer kicked the knife under the table while his partner got out handcuffs, shackled Jeremy's father, and sat him down on a kitchen chair. "All right, folks," the other officer said. "We're going to be nice and calm, and you're going to tell us what's going on here. I'm Officer Kwan, and this is Officer Jefferson."

"My son attacked me," Jeremy's father said. "I was just trying to defend myself!"

"He was beating my mother," said Jeremy. "He's been doing it for years. He's already been taken to jail once. As far as I'm concerned, they should have locked him up and thrown away the key!"

"Yeah," Officer Kwan said. "The dispatcher told us on the way over that officers have been here before for a similar incident. Since we caught him threatening you with a knife, we're arresting him: it's mandatory. If you folks will wait here, my partner and I will take him to the patrol car. Another unit will be here soon, and we'll take statements."

They took Jeremy's father out to the patrol car and locked him in the back seat. He didn't resist, just looked around furtively, as if to see if the neighbors were watching.

Meanwhile, another pair of officers had arrived and come into the house to take statements. They interviewed Mrs. Freeman, Jeremy, and his little brother with an audio-recording device and explained that their report would be filed with the prosecutor's office, which would be in touch to tell them what would happen next.

After they left, Jeremy sat on the couch with his mom and brother, all three of them shaking. "What happened, Mom?" he said. "I thought he was getting better."

"They say relapses often happen with alcoholics, and I guess that's what this was." She dabbed at her eyes with a shredded tissue. "Let me take Tommy up to bed, and then we can talk some more." She took her younger son by the hand. "Come on sweetheart, let's get you some juice and get you settled. Everything's going to be OK now. You don't have to worry. Your father's going away for a while." She kept trying to reassure her trembling son as she led him up the stairs.

Jeremy was in the kitchen, making her some tea, when she came back. "I've had enough of all this now," she said, sitting down at the kitchen table. "I've been going to a group for abused women and I've learned that . . . that our . . . situation . . . is partly my fault. I've let him get away with this, because of my own issues, and I shouldn't have. It's really complicated." She was wringing her hands as she spoke. "I've learned so much from the other women in the group and from the counselor. But I won't stay with your father any longer. I don't know how we'll survive, but we'll figure something out. I know our church will help us."

"I'm sorry I didn't help you sooner, Mom. I—"

"No, Jeremy, you're not to blame. I don't want you thinking like that. Let's just look ahead, not behind. Anyway, we can't settle everything today. I'll call Pastor Bob and see what we should do next." Now she sat straight-backed in the kitchen chair, her hands around her mug, gazing across the room. "I can hardly believe it.

Something that's been going on for years is over. Just like that! Forty-five minutes ago, he was terrorizing us, and now it's over." She looked up at Jeremy, her face pale and pinched. "I know it's not going to be easy. We have to figure out where the money will come from and all that. But at least we won't have to worry about our safety anymore. I can't believe it's over."

The Purchase

Chuck stopped at the mailbox on his way home from the drugstore. There was a letter for him from the Seattle Office of Arts and Culture. *Probably a rejection letter,* he thought.

He ripped open the envelope and read, *Dear Mr. Ganatt, We are pleased to inform you that we would like to purchase your painting . . .*

"Woo-hoo," he shouted.

He burst into the kitchen and called out, "Hey, anybody home?"

"We're in the library."

He found Anne, Patty, and Abe around a coffee table covered with sheets of numbers and a laptop. "Hi, Chuck," said Anne. "We're working on the household budget for next year."

"Well, I've got exciting news," he said. "The city wants to buy my painting for its Portable Works Collection. And they've invited me and a guest to a party for the exhibit opening."

"Oh, Chuck, that's fantastic!" said Anne, getting up and giving him a hug. "See, we told you that you were good enough."

A big grin on his face, Abe stood up and reached across the table to shake Chuck's hand. "Awesome, Chuck, totally awesome. Congratulations, man."

"To think I'm the housemate of a soon-to-be-famous painter," said Patty. "What wonderful news. This calls for champagne! I'm pretty sure we have a couple of bottles in the wine rack. I'll go put them in to chill. Why don't you tell Lionel, Chuck. He'll be so pleased for you."

*****

Anne called Margot after dinner. "Want to go shopping with me? I need something new for an art opening." She told Margot about Chuck's good news.

"Awesome, Gramma! When shall we go?"

"Why don't you come over after school sometime this week, and we'll go through my closet and see if we can find anything usable. If not, we'll hit the shops."

The closet search yielded nothing Anne wanted to wear. "Everything is so old. I've had it all forever," Anne told Patty and Margot, who were sitting on Anne's bed watching her take outfits out of the closet and hold them up, then return them to the closet. "At my age, it seems silly to spend money on clothes I won't wear more than once or twice. Worse than silly—wasteful."

"I know what you mean," said Patty. "But try to think about it differently. You could take these old things you don't wear anymore to Goodwill. Someone will be glad to have them, and you can get yourself something new. It feels good to wear something different, something stylish, and it's not like you're a clotheshorse or something. I don't think it's a sin to buy something new occasionally. Besides, you'll shop for bargains anyway. Go for it!"

Anne gave herself permission to get a new outfit. Friday after school, she and Margot took the bus downtown to Nordstrom Rack. "We have to start with shoes," Anne told her granddaughter, "because there're so few I can wear. Ballet dancers' feet are not to be seen in public. Sandals and heels are out."

"Maybe ballet flats would work, Gramma, or maybe some of those ankle-length boots. Ooooo, this is going to be fun!"

After thirty minutes of trying on shoes, Anne selected a pair of short pale-gray suede boots with a slight heel. They moved on to the clothes section and found some slim ankle-length pants that would look great on Anne's slender frame. Margot picked out a gray pair and a red pair.

"Now, if we can just find a top that works, I'll be happy," Anne said. They finally found a flowing, silky top in a colorful print. It had gray in it, so they chose the gray pants.

"Perfect, Gramma!" said Margot. "You're going to look so 'in.'"

"Well, that'll be a welcome change," said Anne, smiling at Margot. "How about some dinner?"

On the way out of the store, they passed the men's section, and Anne found a fine white linen collarless shirt for Chuck, which she thought would look very classy with his best jeans.

They ordered dinner at Pacific Place and sat in the three-story atrium, watching the people, as they waited for their food to arrive. "There's something I've been wanting to say to you, Margot," said Anne. "And this seems like a good time to bring it up." She paused to take a sip of water and cross her legs. "I hope you won't take your body for granted. It's hard not to when you're a young person. You hardly even think about it—it's just there. But now that you're a young woman and you'll have relationships with guys, I hope you feel good about your body and appreciate all the good things about it." She stopped to assess how Margot was taking all this. She didn't look too uncomfortable, so Anne took another sip of water and continued.

"Our culture has too much emphasis on physical appearance," she said. "We've talked about that before. But I hope you appreciate your youthful skin and nice shape and lovely face. Not many people, male or female, have all the ideal features, but we all have lots of good features, and it's important to focus on them, not compare yourself with movie stars and women in fashion magazines. Anyway, sorry to go off like this, but it's just something I've been wanting to say. I didn't really mean to give a speech." Her eyes searched her granddaughter's face.

"It's OK, Gramma. Those are good reminders." Margot played with her fork. "You know, it's kind of weird. If Mom had said that to me, I would have totally ignored her. But I don't mind you saying it at all. I feel like you're just trying to be helpful, not trying to control me. I guess Mom was trying to do the same thing."

"Well, it's really hard sometimes between children and parents," Anne said, leaning back in her chair. "Parents want the best for their kids. They don't want them to have to learn the hard way, reinvent the wheel, and so on. But children need to become independent, and sometimes the way they do that is to ignore their parents. It's hard to get it just right—for kids and for parents. Anyway, thanks for letting me say my piece."

"You know, Gramma, just the other day I was thinking about something Mom said, not long before . . . you know. I asked her why she didn't get along with you, and she said you were 'a hard act to follow.' What do you think she meant by that?"

Anne was at a loss. She leaned forward, elbows on the table, hands cradling her chin. "Well, I'm not sure. It kind of surprises me. It sounds like a compliment, like she thought I'd done something well, and maybe she wasn't sure she could do it herself. She always acted like I was a terrible parent, but maybe that's not what she really thought at all. Maybe she just needed to make me look bad to make herself look better. I'm sure she had doubts about herself, just like everyone else does."

On the bus ride home, Anne realized she felt less guilty about her relationship with Giselle. She was sad; she'd always be sad for the loss of Giselle and the chance for them to mend their relationship. But the guilt seemed to be dissipating. *How does that happen?* she wondered. Maybe the growing closeness with Margot had eased the guilt, erased it, or . . . something. Whatever it was, she was grateful.

*****

The appointed evening arrived, and Chuck tapped on Anne's door to see if she was ready.

"Wow, aren't you a knockout!" he said when she opened the door. "People are gonna wonder how an old geezer like me got hooked up with you. You look terrific, Annie."

"Old geezers don't wear white linen shirts, I'll have you know. You look very spiffy, Mr. Painter Man."

When they came down the stairs, Patty snapped a photo of them with her cell phone.

They went out to the car. "My God, you'd think we're going to the prom," said Anne as Karina, Mikhail, and Patty waved from the front steps.

The pleasant young woman at the gallery door gave them name tags and invited them to get a glass of wine and see the show. She congratulated Chuck on having his work selected and said, privately, that his was her favorite piece.

"I'll bet she says that to everyone," he whispered to Anne, as they moved through the crowd to the bar. "These things make me nervous. I always get this pain in my gut."

"Hey, you're the one who told me we have to have courage in our old age. Get with the program, old man!"

"It's not about courage," he muttered. "I don't know what it's about."

She put her hand on his arm and looked him in the eye. "Chuck, it's about your mother's judgment of your first artwork. You can let go of that now. *You* know you're good. This"—she motioned to the gallery—"proves that *professionals* know you're good. So your mother's opinion doesn't matter anymore. She was wrapped up in her own stuff. She didn't have a clue what kind of weight she was hanging around your neck when she made that offhand remark. So let it go. Let yourself have a good time. The judgments here are only going to be good ones." She walked off and left him standing there, wondering how the hell you were supposed to let something go.

And just like that, he felt it. He'd known in the back of his mind for a long time that his mother's dismissive comment decades ago had had a profound effect on him. But now he actually felt it in his body—right across his midsection. He stood in front of a painting, not really seeing it, and felt the tightness. But it gradually lessened and finally disappeared. *Well, I'll be damned,* he thought. He realized he hadn't had that feeling as often in the past year or so as he'd had it for most of his life. *Could it really be going?*

A young woman with spiky blue hair came up beside him. "That your piece?" she asked.

"No, I just happen to be standing in front of it, thinking about something."

"Well, I don't think it's very good." And she proceeded to list all the things that she thought were wrong with it. "I just come to these things to see what's in. My work isn't in, so I never get selected."

"I felt that way for a few decades, but then it occurred to me that my work just wasn't good enough yet," said Chuck. "So I started taking classes, and reading, and going to galleries and museums, and—what do you know—my work got better, and I actually started selling things. Maybe your judgments about other people's work are really judgments about your own. Ever think about that?"

She stalked off, passing Anne, who was returning with two glasses of wine.

They worked their way around the gallery, looking at the art and listening to the conversations. "Isn't that our neighbor Dave over there in the corner?" asked Chuck. Just then Dave spotted them and came over.

"Congratulations, Chuck! I hope it was my encouragement that got you to apply, but whatever it was, good for you." He shook Chuck's hand enthusiastically. "Hi, Anne. Nice to see you again. How's Lionel?"

"As well as can be expected," she said. "But he's in good spirits."

*****

Anne enjoyed listening to Chuck and Dave talk about Chuck's painting and the other works on display. They met a few of the other artists and dignitaries and shook hands with the mayor, who zoomed in and out. Then Chuck said he was starving. "Isn't the Metropolitan Grill around here somewhere?

"Yes," Anne said. "It's about two blocks up."

"I've always wanted to check that place out. Let's go have a steak. I'm feeling flush," he said. "Hey, want to go to Paris with me?"

"Paris!"

"Yeah, I've always wanted to see the Louvre," he said as they walked up the street.

"You're going to have to sell a lot more paintings to take us to the Louvre."

"Maybe only one more. They're paying me five thousand dollars for this painting."

"Five thousand dollars! Good God!" Realizing that he could misinterpret her exclamation, she hastily added, "I'm sure it's worth every penny, but I had no idea it would be so much. And of course I'll go to Paris with you—when do we leave?" She took his arm and smiled at him.

"I was thinking this fall, or whenever things are . . . settled . . . with Lionel."

"You're really serious, aren't you? Goodness, I'll have to think about this."

It was early for dinner, so the Metropolitan had a cozy booth for two with no reservation. They simultaneously pulled out their glasses to peruse the menu. After a moment, Anne set her menu aside, leaned back, and looked out across the restaurant. "Life is good, isn't it?" Chuck looked at her over the top of his menu. "I mean" she said, "I'm just feeling so . . . I don't know . . . Things are so vivid . . . intense . . . present. Like there isn't anything but right now." She looked down, turning her water glass around and around, then looked back at him. "The art was so stimulating, and I'm wearing these beautiful, stylish clothes, and a man likes looking at me, and the street trees are so green and leafy . . . Why do I worry about getting old? Why worry about *anything*? At this moment, even Lionel's death seems OK. A little sad, because we'll miss him, but natural, real. Not superficial. Not like so much of the attention I've given to things that don't really matter. Know what I mean? That sense of intense . . . 'presentness'?"

Chuck took off his glasses. "I think I know what you mean. I've had times like that. When you feel like the past and the future have . . . disappeared or something. There's nothing but what's right now, and it seems to matter a lot, whatever it is: a picnic on a sunny beach . . . making love . . . when I get something just right in a painting. I heard somebody call it a 'peak joy experience.' I think that fits perfectly." He reached over and took her hand. "Are you having a peak joy experience?" He kissed her fingers. "'Cause if you are, I'm sure glad to be part of it."

Acceptance

Lionel was completely blind by the end of May. He had almost no use of his left side, was having increasingly severe headaches, and slept a good deal of the time. "How do you do it, Lionel?" asked Abe, pushing Lionel down the sidewalk in his wheelchair on a sunny spring morning.

"How do I do what, Abe?"

"How do you stay in such good spirits? Given . . . what you're dealing with. I'd be a complete SOB!"

"Well, I really have to work at it, and it's up and down. But imminent death kind of puts things in perspective, you know?"

"No, I don't know. What do you mean?"

"Oh, so many things don't matter anymore," mused Lionel. "I don't care if my pants are sharply creased, like I used to. It's not a big deal that I was chairman of the math department. I'm sorry Greta and I didn't have a better relationship, but I don't feel guilty anymore about having a failed marriage. All that stuff is just dropping away." He looked up at Abe. "I just like to listen to Jeremy play, and hear the interactions between him and Margot. And Mark and Claire. All that young love. And the old love between Chuck and Anne, Karina and Mikhail. I can still hardly believe I've been so lucky to have what Patty and I have." They continued down the street, enjoying the warmth of the sunlight on their faces. "It smells like spring. I think I get a whiff of lilac now and then. Wonderful!" said Lionel, giving a lopsided smile.

"Latte?" Abe asked.

"Absolutely," answered Lionel.

"Hey, Lionel, how ya doin', man?" called a voice from behind the hissing espresso machine at Victrola. "Abe, you dudes want the usual?"

"Yeah, that'd be great, Sammy—thanks." Abe found a table at the back of the café, moved a chair, and parked Lionel across from him. "I wonder where all the laptop people are this morning," he said, looking around.

"Yes," said Lionel, "it doesn't seem as noisy as usual."

Sammy—whom Lionel remembered as mohawked, tattooed, and pierced—arrived with their coffee. "OK, Lionel, it's right in front of you," he said. "Complete with straw."

"Thanks," said Lionel. "Perfect service, as usual. Say, Sammy, do you get feedback on the artwork you hang in here?"

"Yeah, we do. Of course it varies, because people like different stuff, ya know? But I'd say we've got more comments on Chuck's stuff than we do on most people's. He even sold one, which doesn't happen that often." Sammy left to go back to his machine.

"Lionel," Abe said, "can you tell me more about how you all worked out the budget and decided how much each person should pay—all those details?"

"Ah, yes, we need to go over more of this background stuff with you." He brought his attention back from the smell of coffee and the clanking of coffee cups. "It took a lot of meetings and discussion. At first, we just assumed that we'd all pay equal amounts for the monthly upkeep. But that wouldn't have worked, because some of us had less income than others. It took a while, but we all eventually accepted 'from each according to his ability, to each according to his needs.' Right here in this bastion of capitalism!" He laughed. "The budgeting wasn't hard. We made very conservative estimates of operating costs, and it turned out that things weren't as expensive as we had thought. Besides, none of us is really interested in acquiring more stuff or having an impressive house, or anything like that. Though I have to admit, we did end up with a pretty impressive house." Lionel tugged his sweater sleeves down over his cuffs as he talked. "Anyway, part of our monthly payment goes to a major maintenance fund, so there'll be enough money when we have to repaint, or dig up the sewer or something. But we did so much upgrading when we bought the house there shouldn't be any of that for a long time."

"Either of you dudes want a refill?" It was Sammy again.

"No, I'm good," said Lionel.

"Me too. Thanks, Sammy," said Abe.

"Are you settled in now, Abe?" asked Lionel. "You seem very comfortable."

"Yeah, it's great to have a home. I don't think I've had a real home for years. My office was more 'home' than where I slept. I know it'll take some adjusting to, but it's been pretty easy so far. And I wasn't too worried. There were so many times when I was with you all that just felt so right, so comfortable. I'm sorry Lin decided against joining us. I don't think she was completely honest about why, do you?"

"No," said Lionel, pausing to reflect on Lin's decision. "I think candor was hard for her. But I think the real reason was fear. It's a big deal to move in with a bunch of strangers. She didn't know us well enough, and we didn't have enough of a relationship to overcome the fear. *You* didn't seem afraid of moving into a group-living situation, though. How did you get past the fear, or the discomfort, or whatever you call it?"

Lionel could hear the clink of a spoon as Abe stirred his coffee. "Like you said for yourself, it was up and down. Sometimes I got nervous. Other times I thought, 'what the hell—it'll be fine.' You know, I've come to the conclusion that fear is a habit. It's an emotion, of course, but I also think it's a habit. You can break habits if you really work at it, so I work at it. And the prospect of living with all of you was kind of a relief, you know, not to be alone." He spoke with typical masculine understatement, but Lionel knew an understatement when he heard one.

"On another topic," Lionel said, "how are you with numbers? The reason I ask is that I've been thinking about who could take care of the family finances when I'm gone. The others don't want to talk about it, but I'd feel better if I knew how that would be handled. Patty, Chuck, or Anne could do it, but that kind of thing isn't their strong point. It's not a lot of work: four or five hours a month, paying the bills that aren't paid automatically, checking the bank balance, et cetera. I've prepared a little job description." He shifted, and sat up straighter in his chair. "Of course, it's not just my decision. The group will decide. But I'm hoping to make the transition as easy as possible for all of us."

"I'd be happy to help with that," said Abe. "I did some budget work when I was a cop. I can use Excel, and balance a checkbook, and I like working with numbers. They're precise, you know? It's satisfying, making things add up, come out right. As a matter of fact, I've already done some work with Patty and Anne on the house budget. It was pretty straightforward, and kinda fun. I don't think you need to worry about the finances at all."

"Oh, good," said Lionel. "I'll cross that off my list." He finished his latte and wiped a bit of foam off his lips. "We've never talked much about your career. Did you enjoy it? And if so, why did you decide to retire? You're still vigorous and in good health." He caught a whiff of fragrance as someone brushed by him.

"It was a good career," said Abe. "Overall, it was satisfying for most of the time. But it could be pretty trying—stressful at times—and I finally got to the point where, you know, been there, done that. Time to move on." He paused. "What I saw in all those years of law enforcement was pain, so damn much pain. Don't get me wrong. I don't excuse breaking the law, but so much of what I saw boiled down to hurt people inflicting their hurt on others. I think that's what happens when people don't have love in their lives. But they still have the need for it, the capacity for it." He pushed his chair back from the table. "You know, I think criminal behavior is an act of twisted love. It's a way to get attention, to relate to people—even if it's in a negative way. But after years of that kind of life, it's almost impossible for them to . . . what? Recover? How is love going to get into the life of a guy serving fifteen years for aggravated assault? Anyway, I'd had enough of watching that and decided to get out and get involved in something more positive. I'm still looking for what that's going to be."

While Abe went to the restroom before the walk home, Lionel sat listening to the door open and close, the clickety-clack of keyboards, the clink of coffee mugs, the quiet conversation. He drank in the smell of the coffee, and a whiff of hazelnut as someone walked by with a spiked latte. *Will I miss all this?* he wondered. *Will I miss anything, or does missing cease?* He wiped his eyes with a napkin. *I don't want to lose touch!*

When they got back to the mansion, Abe parked Lionel on the patio in the sunshine, and went in to tell Patty they were back. She came out and sat down in the chair beside him.

"Well, my dear," he said, I've decided to discontinue treatments. The tests show things aren't getting any better, and they say there's often an improvement for a little while after you stop the chemicals. Maybe that will last through Jeremy's graduation."

She didn't say anything, but she took his hand in her lap.

"Abe and I were just talking about fear," he said. "I still have some fear about what's coming, and I don't think it will ever go away completely. I just try to have courage. And I just keep reminding myself how lucky I am to have you and the others taking care of me."

The Senior Assembly

Lionel missed Jeremy. As his senior year came to a close, Jeremy had less and less time to come over and play the piano. But in early June, he finally found some time. Lionel could hear him take the stairs two at a time up to his room. "Hi, Mr. B, how's it going?"

"I'm having a good day, Jeremy. Every day's a good day when you don't have many left, but today's better than some." He smiled. "What are you going to play for me today?"

"What would you like?"

"I'd like something with energy, something boisterous. And maybe some songs from musicals. There's a stack of show tunes on the third shelf from the bottom.'

"OK, coming up." These days, Lionel was usually in the hospital bed that had been installed in his room. His hearing was unaffected by the cancer, and he was soon totally immersed in the music filling the house from the grand piano downstairs.

Jeremy came up to chat after playing for about thirty minutes.

"Wonderful, Jeremy! You've really got that polonaise down. And that suite from *Phantom of the Opera* is so poignant. I saw it on Broadway, years ago. Thanks so much for coming over, I know this is a busy time for you."

"No problem, Mr. B. I just wish I could come more often."

"Don't worry about that. How's school . . . life . . . Margot?"

"Oh, it's going OK. There's all the end-of-the-year stuff: special concerts, papers to finish and all that. I've been getting some gigs, so that really helps, money-wise. After graduation's over and things aren't so crazy, I'm taking Margot out to a fancy dinner," he said proudly.

"And you're all set for Western this fall?"

"Yeah, all the paperwork's in—the acceptance, the scholarship. I should hear about my roommate by the end of the month."

"Well, you deserve it all, Jeremy. You've worked so hard, and you've got so much talent. I can't tell you how much it's meant to me to have you as a student and . . . and, really, part of my family."

"I . . ." Jeremy choked up. "I couldn't have done it . . . without you, Mr. B. Not just the lessons. You've been kind of like a grandfather to me . . . and it's meant a lot." He took Lionel's hand and squeezed it awkwardly.

"I'm afraid I won't be able to make it to the graduation," Lionel said, "and I hope you won't be too disappointed. I'm really sorry."

"No problem, Mr. B. Graduations are boring anyway. But I have another idea. We have a senior assembly next week, and it's only an hour. The whole school comes, and the seniors perform and get awards and stuff like that." Lionel could hear the eagerness in Jeremy's voice. "I checked," he said, "and it would be really easy to get your wheelchair into the auditorium. Since it's short, maybe it wouldn't be too much."

"What a good idea! Let me talk to Karina and Patty and see if we can work it out. Just give Patty the details.

I'd really like to do this, and I will if I can. Thanks for the invitation."

*****

Patty met Jeremy at the front door on the way out. She put her hand on his arm and said, "I think you should know it's probably only a matter of weeks now. I know he seems stronger, but that's because he's stopped the chemo. It takes so much out of you that you seem better when you stop it. This improvement won't last long."

"I had a feeling he wasn't as well as he was acting," Jeremy said. He told her about the assembly. "It would mean a lot to me if he could be there. It'll be fun, and I know he'd enjoy it. It's only a week from now. But of course I understand if he's just not well enough."

"We'll talk about it and see if we think it's possible," she said. "I'll give you a call.

Karina was with Lionel when Patty went into his room. They discussed Jeremy's invitation. "I'll call the school tomorrow and find out about parking and wheelchair access and all that," said Patty.

"That sounds good. We can decide on day of assembly," said Karina, "And I'm happy to go along with you to help."

"I want you both to plan on it," Lionel said. "I'm determined to go." And his tone made it clear that he would stand for no resistance.

*****

Mikhail dropped onto the sofa beside his wife that night after dinner and rubbed his eyes. She put down her

321

magazine and patted his leg. "I'm glad you have no jobs for a few days," she said. "You look very tired. And I think you are worried about the dentist."

He leaned over and kissed her cheek. "How do you know *everything?*" he said, smiling at her and covering her hand with his.

She smiled back. "It is wife's job to know everything about her husband, especially after twenty-five years. Just think about how nice your teeth will be when all this work is done. No worry about them getting worse and losing them. I know is expensive, but what better thing to spend our money on?"

"I know, I know," he said. "You are right. But is so much money! We could buy a van for the business for that much money. I can't use our house vehicle all the time, and is expensive to rent one when ours isn't available."

"Oh, stop worrying, Mikhail. It doesn't happen so often that family van is needed in the evening, and everyone is happy to have you use it. Renting van now and then is not so expensive as buying one," she said. "I think you just want to be American and have big vehicle of your own." She looked at him with raised eyebrows.

He laughed. "We will need van for business sometime in future. I dream of one with words painted on side." He waved his arm expansively. "'Mikhail . . . Catering Mediterranean and Balkan Specialties.' Sounds very good, yes? My old friends would be impressed. I will send picture of van when we get it. But I will be patient, Karina. Since Lionel is paying you for nursing, we will save much money. I can wait for van." He smiled at his wife and squeezed her hand. "And I know you will remind me to be patient."

She kissed his cheek and stood up. "I will visit Lionel and make sure everything is all right, then I will come to bed."

"You look tired too, Karina. Or maybe not just tired. I don't know English word. But I think Lionel's death coming is difficult for you. This is not . . . ordinary patient."

She looked thoughtful before replying. "God has given me a blessing that I can be his nurse. He is so brave and . . . he thinks about his death . . . so carefully. Not like so many people I see die: angry, afraid, mean to their families. So is easy to be his nurse in some ways, but I will miss him so much."

*****

Patty was helping Lionel prepare for the assembly. "What should I wear?" Lionel asked her. "Everything feels like it's two sizes too big now."

"Let's pick out something comfortable," she said. "How about slacks and a sweater? You won't need a tie for something like this."

"How about that tan sweater with a blue shirt, and brown slacks? I always liked that outfit. I'll be sitting down, so no one will notice how big on me all my clothes are now."

They got him dressed and into the wheelchair, then down to the street level in the elevator. "This thing was worth every penny we paid for it," Lionel said as the doors opened near where the van was parked.

"My sentiments exactly," agreed Patty fervently. "And this lightweight wheelchair we got at that garage sale was a real find." Karina helped Lionel into the passenger seat and fastened the seat belt, while Patty folded up the chair and put it in the back.

Jeremy was waiting at the disabled parking space right outside the auditorium door, and he helped wheel Lionel into the building. "The seats are really good ones, Mr. B. You'll be able to see—I mean hear—really well."

Margot came to sit with them. As they were getting settled, the auditorium began to fill with students, laughing, roughhousing, flirting, and jostling for good seats. The noise level grew appreciably.

At two o'clock, an MC started the program. "Welcome to the senior class assembly, everyone. We're honoring the seniors as they prepare to leave Garfield High School and make their marks in the world. You're going to see some very talented classmates perform today, and you'll hear about their impressive accomplishments. So let's get started."

The program began with the drama department. The seniors did a scene from *Romeo and Juliet* and another from the musical *42nd Street*. There were twenty kids on the stage, tap-dancing one of the big production numbers. The applause was thunderous. Then the athletic department gave its "most" awards: most valuable player, most improved, most inspirational, etc. Attention was called to the program, which listed where the athletes were going to college and who had received scholarships.

The music department was next, presenting first a solo by a violinist, accompanied by Jeremy. Then the award-winning jazz band played two pieces featuring senior soloists. Jeremy did the last music presentation, playing "Flight of the Bumblebee." It was a stunning performance; even students who didn't know classical music were impressed. Lionel beamed, applauding vigorously.

The MC returned to the stage to tout the scholastic achievements of the seniors. "Once again, Garfield has the highest number of National Merit Scholars in the Seattle Public Schools." Everyone cheered.

After the National Merit finalists had been recognized, those graduating with academic honors were asked to stand. Jeremy was among them. As the principal was making his way to the stage for the closing remarks, Patty leaned over and whispered in Lionel's ear. "The program says that Jeremy is planning to attend Western Washington University, where he has been awarded the Beatrice Hale Scholarship for a Promising Pianist. His GPA was three-point-eight."

Margot whispered in his other ear. "He also got accepted at Juilliard and the UW Music School—but they didn't give him a scholarship."

Jeremy met them at the van. "Jeremy my boy, I'm so proud of you!" said Lionel. "What an amazing performance—and accepted at Juilliard and UW, as well as winning a scholarship to Western! Why didn't you tell me? I knew you were a good student, but those grades are awesome, as you young people say." His thin face wore a wide smile. "Help me up. I want to give you a big hug." Patty and Karina each took an arm and helped Lionel to stand. Jeremy embraced the emaciated body of his mentor, blinking back tears as Lionel whispered, "I'm so proud of you, Jeremy. So proud."

Patty and Karina helped him into the van, and he waved to Jeremy, who stood on the curb watching them leave.

Lionel talked all the way back to the mansion. "What a wonderful program. Restores your faith in today's youth, doesn't it? That violinist was fantastic. Jeremy is an excellent accompanist. He could have a career just doing that! And hearing those tap dancers—I'm so glad we went!"

Farewells

Patty was on the phone to Jeremy the week after the assembly. "He's failing fast, Jeremy. Doesn't want to eat, has very little energy. The pain is a problem, but we're dealing with it as best we can."

"I'd . . . I'd like to be there . . . at the end . . . if that's possible," Jeremy said. "Will you call me? Even if it's late at night? I'd really like to be with him."

"Yes," she said. "To the extent we can tell when the end is near, I'll call you."

*****

It was a typical high school graduation: "Pomp and Circumstance" forever, idealistic speeches, and an endless parade of graduates receiving their diplomas. Jeremy's mother and Margot had just worked their way through the happy post-ceremony crowd when Margot's phone buzzed. When she hung up, tears were spilling down her cheeks. "It's Lionel," she said.

Mrs. Freeman dropped Margot and Jeremy off at the mansion. "I want to be with him if this is the end, Mom," Jeremy said, "so I might not come home tonight."

"I understand," Mrs. Freeman said. "Lionel and all of you will be in my prayers. We'll talk more tomorrow."

Jeremy and Margot tiptoed into Lionel's room. Patty was sitting beside him on the bed, and Karina was in a chair on the other side. Lionel's breathing was very slow and shallow. "Can I just sit by him and tell him some things?" Jeremy said. "Just for a minute?"

Karina got up. "Sit here. Stay as long as you like. I'm going upstairs for few minutes, and then I will come back."

Patty came over to give Margot a hug. "Has everyone else had a chance to . . . say goodbye?" Margot asked.

"Yes," Patty said. "We're taking turns staying with him, but we've all said goodbye. He doesn't speak, but I think he still hears."

Jeremy and Margot said their farewells, but Jeremy wanted to stay, and Margot wanted to stay with him. They squeezed together in a big chair and put their feet up on a hassock, and Patty threw an afghan over them. They talked quietly for a while, Jeremy telling her about the consequences of the altercation with his father, about his worries for his family's future, about his fear that he wouldn't be able to go to college, even with the scholarship. And now his real father figure was about to leave him.

After such an emotional day, the two of them couldn't stay awake. Abe woke them with a hand on their shoulders when he came in later. Karina and Mikhail joined them, followed by Anne and Chuck. Patty sat on the bed, holding Lionel's hand. And then his breathing stopped.

A profound quiet and a sense of togetherness pervaded the room as they sat there with their thoughts, questions, and emotions.

*****

That night, Jeremy dreamed that Lionel was standing beside him, smiling, his hand on Jeremy's shoulder. There were no words, but Lionel had said goodbye.

The Bequest

Jeremy was at the door with his mother when Patty opened it. "Mrs. Freeman, it's a pleasure to meet you. Jeremy's one of our favorite people." She led them into the living room. "We'll miss him now that . . . now that he'll be going off to college." She smiled, gestured for them to sit down, and asked if they'd like coffee or tea. A plate of cookies, mugs, and carafes were arranged on the coffee table.

When they had exchanged a few more pleasantries, Patty said, "I've asked you here because Jeremy was mentioned in Lionel's will."

"Goodness," said Mrs. Freeman. "Jeremy, did you know about this?"

"No—no idea. It's a total surprise," he said. "Well, he told me once I could have all of his music, but that's all."

"Well, it's more than just music," said Patty. "Lionel had a two-hundred-fifty-thousand-dollar life insurance policy, and you're the beneficiary. It's all yours—no taxes—and you can do what you want with it."

Jeremy and his mother sat in stunned silence until he managed to say, "That's unbelievable. I can't even take it in!"

"He hoped that you would spend as much as you needed for college and save the rest for later in your life," Patty said, "but he left the decision as to how to spend it entirely up to you. There're no strings attached."

Jeremy turned to his mom, groping for words as the implications of Lionel's bequest began to sink in. "Mom," he said, "this means I can go to college, and I can still give you some money to help with the family, now that Dad's . . . gone."

"This is beyond comprehension!" said Mrs. Freeman, her face flushed. "What a generous man Mr. Blackburn was."

"It makes me really happy to be the bearer of such good news," Patty said. "But there's more. When you're settled in a place of your own, or whenever you want it, Lionel wanted you to have his grand piano. Until then, we'll keep it here for you, and you can come play it anytime. We love to hear you play, of course. And when you're ready, it's yours."

Jeremy was too overcome to speak.

Patty went on. "There's one more thing. These were his." She handed Jeremy a small black box and an envelope. "You can open it now, or later if you prefer."

He opened the letter and read it out loud. *"Dear Jeremy, you can wear these when you play at Carnegie Hall. Love, Lionel."* He opened the box to find elegant onyx cuff links and studs, set in a thin gold rim.

It was too much. Jeremy couldn't keep the tears from falling. "I don't know what to say . . . I just can't believe it!"

"I understand," Patty said, giving his hand a quick squeeze. "If I may, I'd like to make a suggestion. Our housemate, Abe, is good with numbers and business affairs. He's willing to take you to a financial planner, and he'll take care of the paperwork with the insurance company, if you want him to."

Jeremy wiped his eyes with a tissue that his mom slipped into his hand and said, "Yeah, totally. I'll need all the help I can get. Please tell Abe I'll call him."

"Good! And now let's have some cookies," Patty said. "More coffee?"

The Cemetery

Patty trudged through the snow to Lake View Cemetery, where Lionel's ashes were buried, a camping chair in its carrying bag slung over one shoulder. The evergreen wreath she'd laid on the stone two weeks earlier was festooned with some of Chuck's "whirlpools" and some red berries for color. She removed the chair from the bag, unfolded it, and sat down, pulling up the hood of her down coat. "It's me again," she said. "The sun is brilliant today, there's snow on the ground and the neighborhood kids are sledding. We're all feeling rather subdued, but the tree and decorations and the good smells coming from the kitchen help." She surveyed the grounds, glistening in the sunshine, and the gravestones topped with little hats of snow. "You know, I don't think I need to talk to you like this. I think you know what you need to know, wherever you are, and that you're . . . in touch with us . . . in some way. But it makes me feel better just to chat. So, where to start?

"Abe wanted your room, and he moved in there when Antonio decided to join us. They're both such dears, and we all seem to be adjusting just fine.

"In January, Karina will start a new job in a hospice program. Meanwhile, she's been spending a lot of time with a childhood friend who tracked her down in Seattle and is staying in our guest room for a while. What a hoot! Her name is Natalia, and she's a former ballerina from the Bolshoi. She's filthy rich—she married and divorced one of those Russian plutocrats. She says our little guest room reminds her of her dressing room at the ballet, and she prefers it to the Four Seasons. Karina's having fun being her tour guide." Patty watched the chickadees flitting from bush to bush. "And Natalia's taken a fancy to Abe! Who knows what's going to happen there. He seems smitten with her too.

"Anne likes Natalia too. They're like two teenagers, talking dance and giggling—they have so much in common. I think Chuck's nose is a bit out of joint. But not too much, because Natalia's giving them the use of her apartment in Paris when they go next spring. And she bought us two season tickets to the ballet—box seats! So we're definitely getting our art fix.

"Margot's language-immersion and cooking classes in France this summer went really well. And of course, Mark and Claire had a fabulous honeymoon. Margot's a senior this year, you know—working more with Mikhail and loving every minute. Let's see . . . What else? Oh, there's a possibility Mikhail will take over Ms. Carlisle's catering business. And I'm sure you want to hear about Jeremy. He really likes Western and is doing very well with his studies. He managed to come see us a couple of times this fall. He and Margot are still dating. They keep trying to get together, but with their classes and schedules, it's not working out too well. I don't know how that's going to go in the long term, but Jeremy will always be like family to us.

"And I should tell you about Chuck. He's selling paintings like hotcakes. He's wondering what he's going to do with all the money, since he has no one to leave it to. He and Abe are thinking of doing something for boys in trouble with the law, though. Maybe an art program."

Patty got up, stamped her cold feet, and walked back and forth before Lionel's gravestone.

"That's about it, except for me. So, what to tell you? I'm meditating more these days, on my own and with my group. We're doing dream work, which is just fascinating. There's plenty to 'unpack'—always opportunities to get rid of old emotional junk that gets between us and other people. And I've been reading about aging and dying. We housemates talk about it a fair amount, not in a morbid, fearful way, of course. I want as few regrets as possible on my deathbed, so I'm trying to focus on gratitude every day and not on what's still wrong with me and the world.

"So there you have it, my dear." She brushed the snow from his grave marker and straightened the wreath. "We miss you and think of you and speak of you often. And given the way time flies faster as we get older, it won't be that long before we're all together again. I'm so grateful that we have each other to love."

Acknowledgments

Many thanks to poet Lisel Mueller, even though I didn't use two poems of hers that would have added so much to the text, because the cost of obtaining the permissions was prohibitive. Please Google them—that's free! The poem Chuck refers to in the "Man to Man" chapter is "Monet Refuses the Operation," from *Second Language*, Louisiana State University Press, 1996. The poem Lionel refers to in "Coping" is "Losing My Sight," from *Alive Together: New and Selected Poems*, Louisiana State University Press, 1996.

Copyeditors don't come any better than Elizabeth Johnson. She knows all the dos and don'ts that make a writer's work professional—and much better. She noticed things I didn't think of, caught chronology issues, and had suggestions for possible additions or changes—all made with respect for my writerly sensibilities. I take all the credit for authorial faux pas.

Bob Lanphear designed the covers for my first two books and I'm so pleased he could do this one too. Not only does Bob have great design talent, he is a joy to work with.

Many thanks to those who read early drafts and gave me valuable input, including Patty McKillop, Clarice Redmond, Nan Little, Michael McAuliffe, and Ed Shope. Beverly Hosea not only gave me input on the draft, but came up with the title that I finally decided to use.

Special thanks to Waverly Fitzgerald, a very fine writing teacher whose classes are loaded with helpful information.

About the Author

Diann Shope has lived in Seattle more than fifty years and worked for the city of Seattle for thirty of those years, mostly in finance. Her husband is a retired marine surveyor. Their yard has a vegetable garden, pears, raspberries, blueberries, and grapes, in addition to the usual flora of an urban lot. They feel lucky to have their two sons living in the Seattle area with their families. Meditation, rowing, partner dancing and volunteer work have been a big part of Diann's life. She has traveled in Romania, France, Ireland, Greece, Finland, and Scotland. And she's an active supporter of Waldorf education. She holds degrees in international relations from Lewis and Clark College in Portland, Oregon, and the University of Denver.

Other Books by Diann Shope

The Upper End of In Between was published in late 2015.

Susannah Emory's problem is that she can't be content with an easy life. Widowed, introspective, attractive, witty, living in Seattle at the upper end of middle age, she asks, *Now what?*

She loves to dance, she rows crew, and she's a serious meditator—but there's a blank space in her life that she'd like to fill with a relationship. And filling that space will require dealing with modern dating and sexual mores, ageism, and her own insecurities.

Maybe it will be Peter, a jack-of-all-trades who lives on a houseboat. Maybe it will be Marty, a cardiologist who loves art and music. Maybe it will be Will, a former priest who's a popular professor at the nearby university.

This is a novel about love in later life, about how difficult it is to overcome old ways of thinking and being and to live more fully, and about the rare satisfaction of learning that one has wisdom to share, and that others are helped by having it.

Do What Matters, the story of Susannah's grandsons, was published in 2016.

Paul and Drew Emory, a senior and a junior in high school, have a lot to sort out. They have big questions and tough situations to navigate through, even though their classmates think they've got it all—looks, smarts, talent, and hot girlfriends.

Paul is left with broken limbs and a seriously messed-up face after a car accident that killed his good friend. When he's finally recovered and leading a big outdoor-education program, he finds his dad trying to get a drunken chaperone into her tent.

Drew wants to help a classmate who has been drawn into prostitution, and in trying to rescue her he's assaulted by her would-be pimp, injuring his hand and jeopardizing his jazz career. His girlfriend, Elektra, a fragile dynamo, has a bipolar "meltdown" and breaks up with him.

The brothers are trying to do what matters.